CLAIMED &
SEDUCED

SHELLEY MUNRO

MUNRO PRESS

Claimed & Seduced

Copyright © 2024 by Shelley Munro

Print ISBN: 978-1-99-106373-1
Ebook ISBN: 978-0-473-30357-0

Editor: Mary Moran
Cover: Kim Killion, The Killion Group, Inc.

Munro Press, New Zealand.

First Munro Press electronic publication November 2014
First Munro Press print publication December 2024

DEDICATION

For Paul, my husband, partner in crime, and fellow adventurer.
Every day is a good day. Love always.

INTRODUCTION

One step out of routine changed everything...

Shapeshifter Prince Jarlath Leandros of the planet Viros is a man who understands duty. As heir, he's had his future as leader of the House of the Cat mapped since childhood. Boring! Jarlath yearns for an indefinable more.

Keira Cloud is beautiful and sexy, she's independent and confident, and not only is she an enemy from the House of Cawdor, but her stepchildren accuse her of murder. Not a suitable woman for the prince, but Jarlath aches to claim her.

When the House of the Cat comes under attack, Jarlath is thrust into the middle of danger where life or death is the only option. A war is brewing, one that brands Jarlath and Keira enemies, yet their hearts shout otherwise, and their animal selves—the leopard and the crow—care nothing for conventional barriers. Right or wrong, passion blooms out of control, and with the city under siege soon Jarlath's life is anything but boring. Now all he needs to do is survive...

Chapter One

"Y ou will choose a wife and marry before this cycle ends. You must follow tradition and do your duty."

Prince Jarlath Leandros of the planet Viros scowled, loathing the demand in his memory as much as he'd disliked hearing the command from his parents in person. A blur of activity in his peripheral vision jolted him, and he signaled Black, his cambeest to halt.

"Halt, beest." Impatient with the order, Black danced on the spot, the broad leathery pads of his feet thumping the ground. Jarlath curled the fingers of his left hand into the shaggy fur of the beest's hump, just in front of his padded saddle to calm him. Glad of the distraction from his militant thoughts and memories of his mother's piercing voice, he peered through the maze of black tree trunks and the tangle of green-and-pink undergrowth.

Brigands or something more innocent?

"Prince? Is something wrong?" Ellard Tetsu, his security guard, pulled up beside him, a heap of dried pink leaves from the overhead trees crackling beneath his beest's feet. Dubbed the feline shifter with a face only a mother could love, he possessed steadiness and competence. Others might poke fun at his large nose and the ears that protruded a fraction too much, but Jarlath spent much of his time with this man he called best friend. Ellard's tan cambeest snorted a protest and shook his shaggy head at the delay to their normal routine.

"I thought I saw something." Jarlath scanned the scrubby bushes a second time. Rather than alarm, unusual curiosity poked at him. Him—the man his younger brother insisted was laughably predictable and always, always did the right thing.

I bet you fuck your women in the same position, at the same time of night, on the same mark of the week-cycle.

Lynx's mocking words still stung like a bumble-wasp. Truth—his brother had the right of the situation. He lived in a deep, dark rut. Grata fire! He and Ellard were riding the exact path they followed each day.

Ellard narrowed his bright green eyes and perused the vicinity with his usual stoic confidence. "I don't see anything." He shifted his huge frame to study the path they'd already traversed.

"Where does this track go?" Jarlath demanded, his tone abrupt as he pointed to a fork in the trail.

"No idea, my prince."

"We'll go that way for a change," Jarlath said and urged his cambeest into motion by squeezing his legs against the barrel body of the creature.

"Wait! Jarlath, that's not a good idea—" His friend broke off with a curse, and Jarlath heard Ellard's cambeest crashing after him. "At least let me go first," Ellard called.

He found himself grinning. Ellard had called him Jarlath, and his friend didn't do that often, which told him the departure from norm was overdue. Maybe this was the reason he'd felt dissatisfaction, the reason his resentment of his younger brother had swelled and festered, the reason his temper stirred with little prodding.

"Jarlath! You should let me go first."

He ignored Ellard, examining their surroundings instead. Ah, there *was* someone on the path. The disturbance wasn't his imagination. He signaled his mount to slow but the cambeest increased his speed.

"Halt, beest!" Jarlath shifted his weight and hauled on the harness reins. Black ignored the command and bolted, the cool air whistling against Jarlath's face. His cambeest shot past a tree. Too close! Jarlath gritted his teeth at the friction of leg and coarse trunk. Pain reverberated down his limb. He gripped Black's shaggy hump with pincher fingers to right his balance. "Stop, you cantankerous beest!"

Without warning, Black screeched to a halt. Jarlath shot forward, flipping over his beest's head. His world slowed, lurching back into place when he struck the ground. Packed earth and gravel punched his head, his shoulder, smacked the breath from his lungs. Fire burned along his cheek. He struggled, wheezed to get air. A groan rippled up his throat as he lay there. Then a familiar snort had him attempting to move. Pain streaked along his arm, and he realized he still held the reins.

"Oh, dear," a soft, feminine voice said. "Are you injured?"

A murky shadow obscured his vision. Jarlath squinted, desperate to see the source of the musical accent. Another breath sawed down his throat. The roar in his head subsided to a dull throb that sat behind his right eye. Flowers. He could smell flowers. Something cool stroked his cheek, wiped across one eyelid and the darkness lifted. He blinked. Once. Twice, and his world came into sharper focus. A woman? A third blink brought the shimmer into one unwavering vision.

A beautiful, exotic woman.

Her skin was pale, and bore a tinge of pastel green while her sable-brown hair hung in loose waves around her shoulders. He dragged in a breath, his mouth dropping open. She was no figment of imagination. Not with the soft ends of her hair tickling his cheek. Black trews constructed of synleather covered her legs and a white tunic clung to the swells of her breasts. A black vest and knee-high black boots completed her masculine attire. The scent of berries and sugary sweetness, greenery and female filled his nostrils. An enticing combination.

Fascinated, he continued staring. Rude, of course, yet his mind cataloged the differences between her and the women he interacted with at the castle. This one wore a blaster strapped to her thigh. The hilt of a knife peeked from the top of one boot. No doubt, her means of protection against wild animals or the brigands who sometimes frequented the forest. His rapt gaze returned to her face, her berry-stained lips and higher to stare into green eyes flecked with gold.

"Have you addled your head? Beest, shift out of the way so I can tend to your master. You have blood on your face."

"No," Jarlath cried, panic overtaking the pain hammering his shoulder and eye. Black would hurt her. His cambeest disliked contact with strangers and several stable hands bore the scars from his beest's uncertain temper. He'd raised Black from a youngster, and like all cambeests, Black had bonded with one person and one person only—him.

"Out of the way, beest." To his amazement, the woman scolded Black and shouldered him away so she could crouch on his other side. Black behaved like an inside pet and nuzzled the pockets of her vest. His cambeest rumbled—the equivalent of a feline purr—and Jarlath felt his mouth go slack.

"Jarlath, my prince." Ellard thundered into the clearing and was off his cambeest in secs. His weapon cleared his holster, his homely face set in ferocious lines. "Take your hands off him."

"I'm checking him for wounds," the woman retorted and brushed Jarlath's hair from his forehead. Her fingers were soft and stained from picking berries. "Hush your prattle, man. It's undignified."

Ellard spluttered, and the chuckle that escaped Jarlath would have shocked his brother. Blood and liver pills, even he was a bit stunned at his amusement.

"Ah," the woman said in satisfaction. "You were winded. Let me help you sit up. The cut above your eye is still bleeding. I'll fix it in a thrice."

Her full breasts brushed his shoulder as she slipped an arm around him to lend him aid. Something bright and unexpected flared in him then that stole his breath, something inconvenient since his father was discussing alliances with him as a bargaining chip.

Jarlath dragged in her scent again and his cock saluted her proximity, but even more astonishing, his slumbering feline stretched beneath his skin. He hissed, gawking at her in shock.

"Prince Jarlath, it's my honor to assist you." She pulled a clean handkerchief from her tunic pocket and pressed it to his eye.

Something about her husky voice tickled his memory. "Have we met?"

"Keira Cloud," she said. "I've attended several of the court gatherings with my husband." She lifted the handkerchief. "Ah, I think the bleeding has stopped, although you might get a black eye after a bump like that. Can you stand on your own?"

"Yes. Thanks." She was married. Some of the excitement fizzling in his gut dispersed in a swell of disappointment. Unusual and exotic. Beautiful. A smart man would have snapped her up at the first opportunity.

"Marcus Cloud?" Ellard shoved his blaster back in his holster without taking his gaze off her.

Something in his friend's attitude made Jarlath study her more closely. As he pushed to his feet, he watched every hint of bright expression drain from her features.

"That's right." She drew herself up to her full height and her chin lifted a fraction before she stomped over to a nearby container of berries. The crackle of dried leaves beneath her booted feet signaled her irritation. Black nudged her arm and she absently scratched behind his long, rounded ears before scooping up her container.

Ellard scowled and fingered the onyx cat he always wore around his neck. "We should go, my prince. We have the formal ball to prepare for tonight."

"Everything is in hand," he said with a sharp glare at his friend. "There's no reason for haste."

"I think it would be best," Ellard persisted.

"I apologize for my friend's rudeness." Jarlath plucked several dried leaves off his shirtsleeves and patted the worst of the dirt from his trews. "Do you and your husband live nearby?"

"My husband died several cycles ago," she said. "I run the farm on my own now."

"I'm sorry."

"Thank you," she said.

No tears. No wailing or angling for favors. She plucked several berries off a bush and dropped them into her basket.

"Can I help?" Jarlath wasn't sure who was more surprised. Him, Ellard or Keira.

"The man first in line to the throne wishes to pick berries?" Her expression held suspicion.

Jarlath's lips curled upward, humor and a trace of awe doing a number on his normal serious mien. Most people treated him like a dangerous animal and practically tiptoed around him in case they caused upset. This woman attracted his attention with her refreshing attitude.

"Of course he doesn't," Ellard scoffed. "You dishonor the prince. Apologize."

"Enough," Jarlath said. "It was my idea, not Mrs. Cloud's."

"Call me Keira," she said.

"Are you unwell, my prince?" Ellard asked, his scowl doing nothing to enhance his plain face. "Your manner is odd today. Perhaps we should seek the opinion of a court physician."

Jarlath ignored his friend. "Do you have another receptacle?"

"Have you picked berries before, Prince Jarlath?"

"Today, I am Jarlath," he said. "No. Show me." Even he heard the trace of arrogance in his voice. "Please," he added to soften the demand.

After a searching look, she turned away to retrieve a container made of a thin transparent material, the like of which he'd never seen. "Pick the dark red berries. They are the ripe ones. And watch out for the thorns. The berries are delicious, but the plants fight to keep their fruit intact."

He picked one and popped it in his mouth. The tart juices exploded across his taste buds. The berry was so delicious he ate another two.

"My prince," Ellard said. "I require a private word."

"It can wait until we return to the castle." Jarlath trotted over to the nearest scrubby bramble bush and scanned for dark red berries. Ah! There was one. He plucked it from the bush. "I have one."

"Good," Keira said. "I need to fill all my containers before I return home."

Jarlath glanced at Keira. Black was following her and kept nuzzling and butting her for attention. He caught Keira's low chuckle and saw her hand flash out to pet his cambeest on its shaggy shoulder. The big creature dwarfed her, yet she didn't show fear. Black let out another throaty rumble of contentment, and Jarlath shook his head. Extraordinary.

"Jarlath, will you listen?" Ellard demanded. "This isn't right.

Keira Cloud is not a suitable person to honor with your presence."

Jarlath glared at the berry bushes. His fingers clenched his container harder, and it buckled under the force. The berries ran to one side before he regained control and leveled it. A quick breath later, he trusted himself to speak. "I do my duty. I serve the House of the Cat and never falter from doing what is right. Once, just once, I'd like to do something for fun instead of sticking to my rigid schedule."

His friend's jaw went slack. "Fun?"

"My life is like the marks of a timepiece," Jarlath snapped. "Monotonous and boring. I'm tired of the continuous schedule and wish for a change."

"Fine." Ellard's voice grated like claws against a fibreblack floor. "But not with her."

Jarlath shot a swift glance at Keira then placed his attention squarely on Ellard. "I'm picking berries, experiencing something new. What is your problem?"

"She's a murderess," Ellard said.

"Suspected murderess," Keira called. "I was never charged."

Ellard narrowed his gaze and aimed a fake smile in her direction. "Eavesdroppers never hear well of themselves."

"Gossips are old women with nothing better to fill their day." Keira reached for a berry and added it to her container as if she hadn't insulted the prince's bodyguard, a dangerous and powerful man.

Jarlath laughed, the sound rusty and harsh but amusement nonetheless.

"Prince, you can't afford to associate with her. Marcus Cloud's son and daughter still accuse her of murder. They say she poisoned her husband to gain possession of his estate."

"And again, I was never charged. The judge threw the case from the circuit court. Oh, flying stars," she said. "Believe what you want. Help or not. I don't care."

Jarlath observed her stiff back as she marched to the berry bushes on the far side of the clearing. Black ambled after her, and Jarlath whistled out a breath of amazement. "I am staying to pick berries."

"This is a bad idea. They say she put a spell on Marcus Cloud, that his marriage to her was most irregular. You are behaving oddly."

"You worry overmuch." Jarlath plucked more berries, his mind on the woman as he completed his task. An accused murderess. Interesting. It took a strong woman to stand up for herself. A thorn scratched the back of his hand as he reached for a berry. He winced, freed himself, and let his mind wander back to Keira. So beautiful. Different from the women he met. He tried to imagine one of them picking berries and failed.

Every woman of his acquaintance spent their days socializing and shopping, never once lifting a finger when servants could work for them.

Soon, he'd have one of those women as his wife.

The idea chafed like an ill-fitting formal suit, as did Ellard's hostile attitude. A woman of Keira's station was fine to bed but not to place in his life on a permanent basis.

His feline stirred again, stretching beneath his skin in a lazy yawn. Jarlath froze, stunned by the sensation, excited and yet apprehensive in case he was imagining things. He'd thought he'd lost his feline, thought he'd suffered the same tragedy as many of their subjects.

A sad truth.

The people of the House of the Cat clan were losing the ability to shift. Their scientists were working on the problem, but a cure for the strange malady eluded them. So far, they'd kept this failure a secret from outsiders, but at some point, their problems would become public knowledge. The kingdom would grow more vulnerable since slowly their fighting force was losing an important weapon in their arsenal.

Jarlath held his breath and focused inward. A flicker, like the sleepy stretch of someone awakening, caressed beneath his skin. Another burst of excitement shot through his veins. He hadn't felt his feline stir for three cycles now. Something to experiment with in the privacy of his chamber. He missed running in feline form, the explosion of sensory details that came with a shift. Yes, the sec he reached his bedchamber, he'd attempt a shift.

"Prince, please don't do this." Ellard resorted to begging, and the emotion didn't set well on his craggy countenance. His broad fingers dwarfed his onyx cat pendant as he rubbed back and forth—a sure sign of his agitation. "They say she comes from the planet Gramite."

"Why don't you help? The sooner we fill the containers, the faster we'll return to the castle," Jarlath said.

Ellard glowered. "Even the cambeests like her. Look at them, following her around."

Jarlath grinned, the unfamiliar expression feeling foreign on his lips. It made him realize how tense he'd become with recent discussions of marriage and duty. "Creatures are good judges of character."

"Humph." Ellard snatched up a container and started to pick berries at a rapid pace.

A day of firsts, Jarlath thought. A change in routine. A new acquaintance. His feline awakening, and now he was smiling. A trip to the wild side indeed.

Keira surreptitiously observed the prince and his guard. She'd seen the handsome prince at several castle functions and thought him dull and pompous. This man, with his bright smile, was a different being. His dark hair was ruffled, the pomade no match for the stiff breeze. His tailored clothes—the trews and heavy cream synsilk shirt—were good quality, yet currently bore forest stains that made him appear more approachable. And his proper manner...today he resembled his younger brother, Prince Lynx. Sexy and way too attractive for her liking.

Maybe she'd rethink her coming evening. As Marcus's widow, she'd received an invitation to the ball. She'd decided not to attend. Meeting her stepchildren in public always proved difficult, and doubly so if the encounter occurred during a social situation. She had few friends, but her acquaintances would rally around her if only to appease their inquisitiveness regarding her presence.

Yes, she'd made up her mind.

She'd follow her curiosity to learn if this Prince Jarlath was real or a fraud and relieve a little of her loneliness in a social occasion.

And meanwhile, she'd enjoy his company. She shot a glance at the security guard and suppressed a giggle. How many teeth could she get him to show during his next snarl?

"What are you staring at?" Ellard demanded.

"Nothing." Wow, ten teeth.

Keira turned away and picked berries with the ease of practice, filling her containers as she worked her way back to the prince and his security guard.

"What do you do with the berries?" the prince asked.

"I make some pies but use most of the berries for wine."

"I've never tried berry wine," Jarlath said. "Have you, Ellard?"

"Yes."

Keira smothered her amusement at the security guard's abrupt tone. "What about berry pie? Do you have a sweet tooth?"

Ellard shifted his big body so she couldn't see Prince Jarlath. "That is not appropriate. Cease your chatter."

"Ellard, we're talking about a dessert. There is nothing inappropriate about food." The prince edged from behind his security guard and flashed her a grin full of boyish charm.

The power of the exchange rippled through her like a gossamer wave and left her breathing rapid and choppy. She managed a weak half-smile in return while scolding her traitorous body to behave.

The security guard would have conniptions, and he was right. This...these thoughts were far from suitable.

"We all like to eat." He cocked his head. "And I love pie." He popped a berry into his mouth. "They're delicious."

"I'll bake you one," Keira said.

"That won't be necessary." Ellard's voice emerged as stiff as his stance. "The prince eats food prepared in the castle kitchens."

"Ellard, that is enough," the prince said. "There. All done. How are you going to transport the berries back to your farm? There are too many here to carry."

"I brought a cart with me," she said, indicating the handcart, partially obscured by a scrubby bush.

"We'll escort you home," Jarlath said.

"I'm perfectly capable of taking care of myself."

"Prince, we will be late to the pre-ball dinner."

Disappointment slammed Keira, the sense of loneliness surfacing again. Today had been the first time she'd spoken with anyone apart from Hilda, the Regit gnome who functioned as her cook and home help, Hortese, her maid and friend, and her other employees. It was nice to share a task with someone new.

She sneaked a glance at the prince and found herself the object of his scrutiny. Her breasts tingled from the intensity of his gaze, and she admitted her fascination. Stupid fool that she was.

During this short space of time, she'd developed a crush on the prince. No, she'd changed her mind. No ball for her tonight. It was best she went with her original plan and stayed far, far away from temptation.

Aware of the lengthening silence, she said, "I'm quite capable of transporting the berries home. I wouldn't want to make you late to an important function."

"Jarlath, see! She understands duty."

"Oh, I understand obligation," Jarlath said with a bite to his tone. "I am always responsible."

Keira frowned at the exchange between the two men, the chilly shift in the atmosphere. With no idea of the reason for the tension between the prince and his security guard, she remained mute. She'd experienced her share of conflict and refused to invite more.

Ellard had a look of relief as he strode over to retrieve the two cambeests. He'd saved his prince from committing an act of stupidity, saved his prince from becoming embroiled in unbecoming gossip.

Keira sighed. Her reputation preceded her, propelled along by gossip and Marcus's two nasty, selfish offspring. It was no wonder the security guard wanted the prince to leave. She'd heard the prince was searching for a wife, and the king and the rest of the court would expect him to marry a woman of impeccable lineage and reputation.

A virgin.

Not one of the required labels fit her character or personality.

The cart wheels squeaked when she tugged the conveyance over to the full containers. She started to load the berries.

"Here, let me help." The prince passed her a full receptacle and waited for her to situate the berries before handing her the next one.

"Prince, we must leave now. We have dallied long enough."

"We will escort Keira to her home," Jarlath said.

"I don't think—" Ellard began.

"That's not necessary," Keira said.

"I insist." Jarlath accepted the reins from Ellard. "Which way?"

Aware of his determination, Keira gave in without further battle. She pushed her handcart in the direction of home.

"Let me," Prince Jarlath said, and he placed his hand over hers. A charge of energy rushed up her arm, stealing her breath and putting the prince at the front of her mind. She stared at his tanned fingers, such a contrast to her own green-tinged flesh. Then she cataloged the sensation of his warm skin against hers—not soft and smooth but callused.

"I..." she trailed off, sucked in by his charisma. His dark green eyes. His scent. Up close he smelled of berries and something spicy and peppery.

"Let me," he repeated.

"Thanks." She wanted to press her nose against his chest, but she forced herself to step away.

Prince Jarlath pushed the cart down the track, and she took a second to admire his arse.

"He's not for you," Ellard said in an undertone. "He will marry a woman of quality by the end of this cycle, if not the next."

"Of course he will," Keira said, and she was amazed at the evenness of her reply. "He's heir to the crown."

"As long as you understand," Ellard said. "I wouldn't want you to hamper the prince's progress and cause problems for the House."

"We picked berries. That's hardly interfering. I didn't know you'd ride along this particular trail."

Ellard glowered down his long nose, his visage harsh and uncompromising. "So long as we're clear."

Oh they were clear. The security guard had done his duty and warned her away from the prince. He'd picked up on her fascination and was now doing his best to make sure she knew her place.

Done. Message received.

The trees of the forest thinned, and the outer farm buildings came into view. Keira hurried ahead to open the gate leading to her house, a sense of pride filling her as she studied the surroundings through the eyes of strangers. Freshly white-washed buildings, lush paddocks full of malpacks—a distant cousin of the cambeest—and everything tidy and in good repair. She might be an outcast, but she knew how to run a profitable farm.

"You can leave the cart here. I don't want to make you late for an official function. Thank you for helping me to pick berries." There. She'd said all that was proper. She sketched a curtsey, a nicety she should have thought of earlier.

"I had fun," the prince said. "Maybe we can do it again."

Keira cast a quick glance at Ellard and blanched at his stony expression. "Maybe," she said but knew it unlikely. She was a farmer, and he was a prince.

No, she wouldn't attend the ball tonight. She'd remain home and bake pies and stay far, far from trouble.

That would be best for all concerned.

CHAPTER TWO

T he ball, held in the city assembly rooms, was tedious, and not one woman grabbed Jarlath's attention. An enormous chandelier, made from the finest rose stone, cast delicate pink light over the scene. The perfume from urns of flowers filled the air while an orchestra, famed for their stringed musicians, played the latest songs. According to his mother, the head composer had even written a special score dedicated to him and his search for a wife—the debut to occur right before supper. Single women—those of suitable blood—chattered and tittered and flocked around him, each trying to outdo the other. Their obvious attentions, the avarice glittering in their countenances, made his head ache and his stomach roil.

He was a person, not a commodity.

"Why aren't you dancing?" his mother asked, her almond-shaped eyes burning him with expectation, impatience.

Dressed in a slim-fitting gown the same pale green as her eyes, her chocolate-brown hair swept up and jeweled tiara glittering, she was the epitome of royal. "Lady Asha is over there. Go and ask her to dance and pray your eye doesn't scare her off. She would make an excellent queen if she can get past your clumsiness."

"Mother, it was an accident."

"The beest is dangerous. Stick to your palace duties. Now, ask Lady Asha to dance."

Jarlath sighed, knowing better than to argue with his mother, and made his way to an urn of greenery and white flowers where Lady Asha stood with her chaperone. He forced a stiff smile and made a formal bow. "May I have this dance?"

"It would be my honor, Prince Jarlath." Lady Asha's delicate hand trembled when she placed it in his, and she scanned his eye briefly before averting her gaze to his chest. Her nerves contrasted with Keira's reaction to his presence. His status hadn't bothered her in the slightest. She'd looked at him, and he'd wager, she saw him rather than a status symbol, despite Ellard's opinion to the contrary.

His feet fell into rhythm with the music while his mind settled on Keira. So different with her exotic looks and feisty attitude. The casual way she'd worn her blaster weapon showed her ability to defend herself, and she managed her farm with minimal help, plus she baked pies.

During their interaction, he'd felt alive, and even more miraculously, his feline had awakened. Alone in his chamber, he'd attempted a shift—to no avail. His feline hadn't stirred or uttered a single grunt. The meaning eluded him, although he intended to experiment. Losing his shifting ability...grata, it pushed him off-balance, made him feel half a Virosian.

"Are you attending the traveling circus performance tomorrow night?" Lady Asha asked.

Captive animals and strange aliens of freakish appearance.

Jarlath suppressed a shudder. None of the performers appeared happy to display their skills. "No," he said, hiding his true feelings behind his prince mask. "I'm afraid I have another engagement."

"All my friends are going."

Another reason to avoid the spectacle.

The rest of the evening passed in a similar vein—dancing, the unveiling of the betrothal song. Supper taken with Lady Asha and more dancing, more eligible single women. His feet became increasingly sore. Sheer willpower stopped him from limping across the ballroom during his departure. All the dancing had given him a blister on the heel of his right foot, and the sore spot throbbed in tandem with the ache at his temples.

A short time later, he acknowledged the doorman and entered the official residence of the House of the Cat—the castle.

"Jarlath, a word." His mother's crisp voice drew him to a halt at the base of the stairs that led to his accommodation wing. Her regal and slender figure retreated into a receiving room before he had a chance to respond.

He sighed and changed his direction. On entering the formal receiving room, he discovered his father present as well. Queen Bryna dropped onto the gel-duo seat at her husband's side, presenting united resolve.

King Hazan speared him with a dignified look, his gray-streaked black hair tidy, his black-and-white eveningwear still pristine despite the late hour. "You must decide on a woman to take to wife. It is time for you to marry and produce an heir."

"Past time," his mother added, her will clear in her vivid green gaze. "We've had this discussion before."

Straight to business. Of course. It was their duty, his duty, to ensure their line lived on at the head of the House of the Cat. Jarlath remained standing instead of dropping onto the gel chair opposite his parents. He disliked this stiff, formal room with its blend of modern tech—the silent servant droid in the corner waiting in sleep mode and unable to record private discussion—and the artifacts from various universes purchased and collected by his mother to impress visitors. A jeweled looking glass from Slyvia, an ornately carved bone chair with a gel cushion pad from Mutto and a locked case of antique hair combs. The formal portraits of previous House rulers glared down from the opposite wall. Both he and Lynx had endured lectures and reprimands in this receiving room.

He took his time while trying to formulate an argument as to why he should wait. He didn't want to argue with his parents. Lynx, his younger brother, caused enough tension, but grata, he was tired of duty. He'd tried to put off this moment, sidestepping each of their attempts at matchmaking. But now, with both of his parents approaching the subject as a team, he found himself trapped.

Fighting a wince and the need to limp, he strode to the window and stared out at the huge public square, which lay outside the castle outer walls. Their subjects strolled beneath colored lights and leafy trees. Others browsed the many evening market stalls that would remain open late into the night. One level down the guidance lights from chubby gray flymos cut through the sky as the vehicles zipped and zapped through the sky, jostling for airspace. The snub-nose utility vehicles with their rounded bodies were popular with the locals for shifting cargo and people around the city. Royal decree stated any pilot who took a flight path over the square or castle would receive an invitation to spend time in the dungeons. Not many accepted the offer.

"Jarlath?" his mother prompted. "What do you say?"

Struggling for patience, he inhaled and turned to face his parents. His father bore the straight carriage of a royal, his lined yet handsome face arranged in a serious mien. His light green eyes had darkened to a mossy green, as had those of his subjects who had lost access to their felines. His father was the perfect ruler, always maintained correct protocol and seemed happy with the responsibility, so why did Jarlath's royal duties make him feel as if a chokenoose circled his neck?

His mother cocked her head, her lips firming in disapproval. His father tightened his hand around the metallic head of the cat that topped his walking cane.

They expected an answer.

One particular answer.

The idea of marriage and the boring rounds of social gatherings, plus the pressure of producing an heir, scared him silly. An entire lifespan of obligation and service. Once that was all he'd wanted, but he'd changed. For once, he'd like to do something for himself instead of following the rules. And didn't that make him selfish?

"Do you have a list of suitable candidates?" His words tightened his chest, his throat until he had to tug at his formal cravat to release the tension.

"Yes, of course," his mother said. "You can collect the list from me in the morning."

"Was there anything else?" Jarlath had to force the words past the lump lodged in his gullet.

"I sought an audience with the head of medicine today," his father said.

Alarm surfaced in Jarlath. "Why? Are you ill?"

"I am aging quickly now that my feline has died. My bones pain me," his father said. "I have discussed this with your mother, and we have decided once you announce your betrothal, I shall step aside, and you will take over my role. You are young. Strong. The scientists will find a cure to save our felines, and you will rule for a long time."

"What?" That knot in his throat was growing, growing, growing until he thought his neck might explode with the pressure. He coughed to clear the obstacle. "What did you say?"

"Once your betrothal is announced, I intend to step aside, and you will take over as king of the House of the Cat."

His mother beamed with approval.

Jarlath...he wasn't sure how to react, which emotion to tag. Worry for his father's health, respect for his father who had carried out his duties as leader with a deft hand and...and the weight of responsibility.

Jarlath found himself nodding like a wooden puppet controlled by some outside force. "It would be my honor."

Stars and meteors, had those words come from him? No, no! He didn't want the kingship. He didn't want marriage to a woman who merely desired position and prestige. He didn't want to provide heirs and subject his children to this bloody yoke.

"You do us proud, my son," his father said. "You will make a good king."

Unspoken were the words of Lynx's embarrassing exploits.

"I find myself fatigued," Jarlath said, anxious to escape. He walked around a low table bearing a glittering black cat statue and over to the gel-duo seat where his parents sat. He stooped to press a kiss to his mother's smooth, perfumed cheek. He kissed his father's hand. "Good rest," he said. "I'll see you in the morn."

"Take care of that eye," his father said.

"I will. Villars has given me an ointment to treat the bruising."

Jarlath strode from the room, praying to every goddess for his legs to get him to his private wing before he crumpled under the weight of expectation.

His valet waited for him, even though he'd told the older man not to bother. Jarlath bit back his grumpiness and gave Villars a stiff nod.

"How was the ball, Prince Jarlath?" His pale green eyes glittered with interest from a face mapped with wrinkles. "Let me help you from your jacket."

Jarlath allowed his valet to tug the close-fitting black garment from his shoulders. Churlish to refuse when the man had waited for him. Churlish to ignore his queries when the man had looked after him since his first shift at the age of twelve cycles. Churlish, too, to unleash his temper when the man was blameless.

"I think I danced with every single woman in the kingdom and several from neighboring planets and satellites. My feet hurt." He yanked off his wrinkled cravat.

"Ah, I did suggest you wear your other shoes."

"You did, Villars, and next time I will follow your suggestions." Once free of his jacket, Jarlath kicked off the offending shoes. "Why don't you seek your bed, Villars? Don't you have an early flight tomorrow? I can manage the rest. I thought I'd have a glass of apecot port before I retire."

"I have set out a glass and the decanter in your sitting room, Prince Jarlath."

"Thank you, Villars. Your ability to read my mind is uncanny. I don't know what I'm going to do without you while you're visiting your new grandchild."

Villars smiled, broad and toothy. "You always have a glass of apecot after a night out."

Flaming meteors, was he that predictable? Things were worse than he'd feared. Ellard met him at the stables every afternoon to go for a ride, even though he never called for him. Villars set out his apecot port. He'd even picked out his shoes, and Jarlath had rejected his choice, just to be contrary. The result—a nice fat blister on his heel.

"If that is all, Prince Jarlath, I'll leave you to your apecot. You know, I can still arrange a temporary replacement until my return."

"No, I don't want a replacement. I'll manage until your return. Good rest, Villars, and thank you for the eye ointment. It has helped to ease the throbbing. Enjoy your holiday and give your new grandchild a kiss for me."

Jarlath waited until the door closed behind his valet before he prowled and paced past the room containing his entertainment center. He hesitated, taking in the screen that took up an entire wall and the holo headset he'd discarded on a float table, then shrugged irritably and continued. His restlessness took him through to his sitting room, where he paused to pour a glass of apecot. The pale golden liquid sloshed into a chill-vessel and out the rim on the other side. Jarlath cursed and snatched up the drink. He fingered the excess drops from the vessel and took a large sip. The liquid burned down his throat, melting the lump of tension so his throat began to feel more normal. With apecot in hand, Jarlath stalked the confines of the luxurious room.

King.

His destiny, and as the heir, he needed a wife. Yes, he'd choose her from a list, but in reality, his parents were picking his spouse—the woman who would stand at his side until death parted their union. It was a sobering, scary thought. Another swallow of apecot slid down as he admitted the truth.

He'd thought of marriage one day to someone who respected and loved him in return. But he wanted this when he felt ready, not on his parents' calendar.

Jarlath wasn't even sure he wanted to take over the role. No, of course he wanted to be king. He was born for the position. Jarlath drank more apecot and consciously relaxed his shoulders. The duties, the responsibility—he'd trained for them all his life. His hard sigh lifted his chest.

Tomorrow he'd choose names off his mother's list. Tomorrow, he'd take the first steps toward becoming king. Tomorrow, he'd seal his fate.

Jarlath woke—much earlier than normal—his mind full of the list and his dreams of steamy-hot sex with Keira Cloud. Eventually his busy thoughts drove him to leave his sleep-bed. He ignored the clothes Villars had set out for him and rifled through his replicator for something plainer and unobtrusive. Unable to find anything suitable, he wrinkled his brow. He needed clothing of the like favored by Lynx.

Ah! His brief dejection lifted, and he plugged in his brother's code. A quite different type of garment showed on the replicator menu. Plain black. No insignia. Perfect.

Jarlath plugged in the code and checked his eye in his looking glass. Nice and black but not painful. He'd live. A quiet hum and the metallic tang on the air showed the replicator was doing its job. While he waited, Jarlath dragged a comb through his hair. On automatic, his fingers reached for pomade to settle his rebellious locks. At the last min, he drew back, frowned into the looking glass then nodded.

Routine was boring, boring, boring.

A ding signaled the replicator had finished, and he lifted the lid of the unit to retrieve his new garments. Plain black trews and a black tunic. Soft black boots completed his outfit.

Perfect.

Jarlath donned the garments and grinned at his reflection in the looking glass. The boots molded to his feet, and he could scarcely feel his blister. It was like a glimpse of his brother, and the possibility of freedom, even if it was for a mere few hours, made him want to whistle. He grabbed his sat-com, although he turned it to vibrate rather than summons mode and stuffed it in his pocket. At the last moment, he strapped a blaster to his hip.

That done, he crept from his chamber, not wanting to attract attention. Unusually, he didn't see anyone except a maid wheeling a tea trolley toward his mother's chamber. The queen was a habitual early riser, yet she never appeared until late morn.

Jarlath let himself outside and strode in the direction of the stables.

A sleepy stableboy greeted him, yawning widely in Jarlath's direction. "Can I help you, sir?"

"I'm going for a ride," Jarlath announced. "I will saddle Black."

"Black? But that's Prince Jar—"

The boy's face paled, and he bobbed a quick bow. "I'm sorry, Prince Jarlath. I did not recognize you. I hope I didn't offend."

"Don't trouble yourself." Jarlath waved away the boy's stammered apologies, strode into the stable, and headed for Black's stall. The aroma of polymox hay, nroc straw and saddle soap filled the air, the scents bringing back lazy days of childhood. He nodded to the stableboy mucking out a stall then collected his personal saddle from the harness room and opened the stable door. His cambeest gave a rumble of welcome and nuzzled his chest.

Jarlath didn't normally saddle his beest, although he knew how and kneed Black in the ribs when the creature tried to hold his air-filled belly. Not a trick he intended to fall for this morn.

He swung into his tan malpack saddle and guided Black toward the forest before giving his beest his head and letting him choose their path. The crisp air chilled his cheeks as Black surged forward. Part of him had expected Black to tread his normal trail, but the beest cantered down a new one Jarlath had never noticed. Instead of going through the forest, the path skirted the edge of the trees. Birds sang, sitting so high in the treetops he couldn't see them. The blue-tinged grass grew tall, and if it weren't for his knee-high boots, his trews would have soaked up the excess moisture.

In the distance, he saw farm dwellings, the lazy curl of purple smoke telling him they were burning the wood of the purple puzzle tree. An introduced species, this tree was an aggressive grower and threatened to choke their native forests. It had been his idea for their people to use it for fuel, and he was pleased with the results and the thinning of the puzzle copses.

The path meandered into the forest then exited near a small lake. The pale green waters steamed. Ah, his brother had mentioned this heated lake. He and his friends used to sneak alcoholic drinks and party here with their choice of the opposite sex. Lynx had seduced many a woman here, or at least rumor pointed that way. When it came to his brother, the tales were oft exaggerated. Lynx no longer bothered denying the gossip whenever he deigned to visit home.

Black trotted past the lake and into the forest again. Around twenty mins later, another farm came into sight, this one familiar. Jarlath hesitated, his heart skipping a beat as he struggled with his decision. This wasn't a good idea, not when he should be at the castle whittling down his list to one marriageable woman.

But he didn't give Black the signal to walk on when his beest pulled up outside the gate leading to Keira's dwelling—an attractive cream farmhouse with two levels. Instead, Jarlath dismounted, opened the gate and led Black into the yard. He tethered his cambeest to a hitching post.

Someone was singing, the words in a foreign language. The language of the Cawdor, he thought with a frown. Ellard had said Keira came from Gramite.

He knocked, and the singing ceased. Footsteps signaled someone was coming to answer the door. He stepped back, heart pounding. Was he walking into the parlor of their enemy? Ellard hadn't mentioned anything about the House of Cawdor, and by mutual consent, they'd ignored the subject of Keira after leaving her yesterday.

The door flew open, and the scent of berries and baking flooded his senses.

Keira blinked at him in clear confusion. "Prince Jarlath."

Jarlath hesitated now that this new knowledge battered his brain. Was this a honeycomb trap? Aware of the lengthening silence, he said the first thing that entered his mind. "I've come for pie."

CHAPTER THREE

K eira stared at Prince Jarlath, took in the black eye in the aristocratic face, the ruddy cheeks, the dusting of stubble and the curtain of untidy black hair before his firm lips with the hint of sharp canines distracted her, brought a flash of a warmth. A tingle.

He was real. He was here—standing right in front of her—and he wanted pie.

"I've come at a bad time," he said, a flash of chagrin making him seem less princelike. "I'm sorry for the interruption."

"No!" She seized his arm and tugged before he could retreat. She stared at her pale green-tinged fingers, felt the ripple of muscle from his hard forearm, even through the black sleeve of his tunic. Heat surged to her face, and she snatched her hand away. "Sorry. I...ah...you don't have to leave. How is your eye?"

"It looks worse than it feels. The bruising will heal quickly."

"Ah, that's good." Stupid, stupid fool. She was behaving like a jackass rabbit, drunken and silly from gorging on allyweed. It was that stupid dream, of course.

The hot, naked dream full of her vivid imagination and fantasies.

That cursed hotness in her face. Without fail, the prince would notice her vivid green cheeks. Gah! She thought she'd outgrown broadcasting her emotions long ago, all emotion sucked out of her by a stern father—the leader of the House of Cawdor—who demanded obedience. She sucked in a calming breath and backed away.

"Come in. The pies are cooking. They're not done yet." There, she sounded almost normal. Bolstered by this, she risked a glance in his direction. What she saw almost buckled her knees. Sweet, hot lust blazed from his moss-green eyes. No, not moss green, she decided as she stared, ensnared by his gaze. His irises were a curious color—a dark green in the center while there were bands of light green around the outside. Stunning, even with the decoration of bruises.

"I can wait."

"But what about your duties? And where is your guard dog?"

Prince Jarlath shrugged. "I rose earlier than usual. No one was awake and I saw no reason to disturb anyone."

"But you're the prince."

He grimaced. "I'm a man first."

Keira cocked her head, his expression and tone prompting curiosity. "People don't see you as a man?"

"They see me as an opportunity to exploit."

"Ah," she said. "This, I know something about. My father sought to marry me off to a man who brought wealth and power to his house. We are—were—both tools."

She'd said more than she should have. He'd start asking questions. He must have heard her singing. Yes, already the queries were forming on his lips. To forestall them, she grabbed his hand, heard his sharp intake of breath and squelched a nervous laugh with difficulty.

"Come," she said, tugging him. "I've done my morning chores and was about to sit out on the terrace and break my fast. I'd be honored if you'd share my meal."

"My cambeest is out front."

"You can turn him loose with my herd of malpacks. They should do well together. I will summon one of my employees to show you the way. You take care of your beest while I organize our meal. Hortese!"

Her employee appeared in the kitchen doorway, her bright pink eyes bulging with inquisitiveness since they didn't receive many visitors. "Yes, Keira?"

"Can you call Melvyn and ask him to show Jarlath the way to the grazing paddock? He needs a safe place for his cambeest while he is visiting."

"I will com Melvyn." Hortese pursed berry-colored lips and her pink hair tendrils rippled and writhed about her head. A sure sign of intense curiosity. "Should I ask Hilda to brew some tay?"

"Yes, please. I'll be in to check on the pies in a min." Smothering her amusement, she waited until Hortese departed before turning to the prince. "I apologize for not using your title. I thought it would raise nosy questions."

"I like the sound of my name on your lips."

"You're flirting with me."

"Yes. Am I doing a good job?"

Flying stars, yes. She moistened her lips and forced barriers between them, never taking her gaze off his attractive features. "I have a bad reputation. Your guard dog was correct. It's not safe to socialize with me."

Showering meteors, if he learned the identity of her father, he'd flee in the opposite direction. After Xavier Cronan—her father—had attempted to marry her to one of his Cawdor men, her mother had made contrary plans to get her off the planet, and she'd ended up with an arranged marriage to Marcus. Something she was grateful for since she much preferred the life of a farmer to one married to a Cawdor casino boss.

"No one knows where I am."

"What if they panic?"

He tugged at his collar, some of the animation leaving his beautiful green gaze. "They will because I'm acting out of character. I did leave a message on my apartment statboard. The staff will find it soon enough, but they won't worry, not at first because I attended the ball and didn't seek my bed until late."

"It must have been an enjoyable occasion." Envy chased her words because she would have given anything to dance with the prince. Although she'd considered attending, the upper-class attendees would have pushed her to the outer fringes. No chance for her to dance with eligible males.

"The event was excruciatingly boring, and by the end of the night, my feet ached."

"The women in the kingdom are clumsy?"

"No," he said with a snort. "Every time I sought a respite my mother induced me to ask yet another young lady to dance."

"Your parents wish you to marry?"

"Yesterday."

"Oh." Which didn't explain why he'd come to visit. She was sure the castle chefs would make the prince a pie. All he needed to do was snap his fingers or dial one up in his chefmate. Gossip in the marketplace said the palace had many mod cons not enjoyed by the Viros citizens. "You are the heir. They want to see you settled."

"Yes."

There was a knock on the door, and Melvyn stuck his grizzled head through the doorway, his swarthy complexion wreathed in a broad smile of contentment. He was a tall man with a solid and fit build, despite his advanced age. As usual, he wore the swinging leather kilt made famous by his Scothage race and paired it with a plain gray shirt. "Hortese said you required me."

"Melvyn, this is Jarlath. Can you show him the malpack paddock? He wants to put his cambeest out to graze during his visit."

Keira caught the exact sec Melvyn recognized the prince. A man of few words, her employee didn't do anything to cause her embarrassment.

"Of course. I wanted to check their water trough anyway. There was something wrong with the pump yesterday."

Jarlath followed Melvyn from the room, and with his departure, she could breathe again. She'd liked the prince when she met him yesterday, but seeing him again was enough to make her foolish heart race.

He desired her. The signals were clear, but did she follow her instincts and let the matter go further? There would be no future in it, and worst of all, she'd be treading the same path as her mother by taking a man of power into her life with no hope of a future. A mistake she'd sworn not to repeat.

"What is the prince doing visiting this house?" Hortese demanded, her pink eyes protruding even farther from her face, confirming the full extent of her curiosity. "What happened to his eye? Did someone punch him?"

"I didn't think you recognized him."

"I'd recognize the rear end of Mr. Hotness from fifty feet," Hortese said with toothy smugness.

Used to her outspoken friend, Keira bit back her amusement. "I don't think the prince would enjoy being called Mr. Hotness."

"What he doesn't know won't hurt him," Hortese said, waving her hand in front of her to illustrate her airy tone. "His eye?"

"From what he said he fell off his cambeest." It wouldn't do to tell the entire truth because the questions would be incessant.

"Where would you like to break your fast? Should I set the table in the formal room?"

"No, something informal out on the terrace would be nice. It's a beautiful morn."

"Good idea," Hortese said and her hair tendrils practically danced above her head such was her excitement. "I'll prepare a tray while you change. Hilda is busy with the berry wine."

She sped off before Keira could thank her. Change her clothes? The prince had already seen her in this casual garb. Besides, she didn't want him to think she was primping. No, better to stay as she was and enjoy the novelty of someone pleasant to share her day. Running the farm was a hard and lonely business. If it weren't for Hortese, Hilda and Melvyn, she might have given up long ago.

Footsteps in the hallway told her Jarlath was back, and she pasted on a welcoming smile. "Is your cambeest settled?"

"Once he got over the shock of the nosy malpacks half his size. You have a decent herd, and they're fairly uniform in their gray coloring. Do you breed them for meat or for their fleeces?"

"Their fleeces. Marcus started the herd with two purebreds and the herd grew from those foundation breeders. I sell off yearlings each season and purchase one or two new additions to keep diversity within the herd. Malpack fleece is in high demand and goes into many clothing replicators as a base material. Come out to the terrace. We'll sit out there to enjoy the morn."

Very conscious of the prince at her back, she strode down the hallway, past the stairs leading to the next level and into the large family room with the enormous portrait of Marcus and out the double doors onto the terrace. The scent of flowers hit her straightaway, centering her as it always did. As a child of the Greenmont tribe, she had an affinity with plants and nature. Another reason to reject marriage to a casino boss, gambling in all forms being the main source of income for the House of Cawdor.

"Keira, this is beautiful. Who takes care of the garden?"

Jarlath's warmth distracted her, his fresh scent pulling her body to sensual awareness. Memories of her vivid dreams brought a burst of heat to her cheeks.

"Keira?"

"I take care of the garden," she said, her words almost tripping over each other. "It's in my genes. My mother comes from the Greenmont tribe on Gramite."

"The House of Cawdor are the dominant rulers on Gramite," Jarlath said.

"Yes." Not much more to say. The House of Cawdor and the House of the Cat were often at war. Xavier Cronan and his Cawdor council coveted the natural mineral deposits of Viros and plotted to gain ownership. A cease-fire was in effect, but relations strained to breaking point.

"How did you meet Marcus and undertake a union?"

"Marcus made the arrangement with my mother during a time of relative peace." Blunt words. The facts, yet this truth hid so much.

"Do you miss your home?"

"No."

"But here on Viros, the locals aren't cordial toward you."

"No, they're not, but this is my home. I have my gardens and the farm to occupy myself. Hortese, Hilda and Melvyn for company."

"But you're lonely." Jarlath stared out over the garden, his attention diverted, yet she was ultra-aware of him and the simmering attraction between them.

"You don't know me," Keira said, stung at her transparency. She *was* lonely, yet hearing the prince state the fact made her seem a helpless loser.

"I'm surrounded by family, by friends and servants. I am lonely, so I think I might recognize the trait in others." Jarlath turned his attention on her, his visage ablaze with lust and passion. "Since the first moment I saw you, I've wanted to steal a kiss. Will you allow me?"

He was lonely too? That didn't seem right. He was the prince and heir to the throne.

"Keira? Are you ignoring me, or have I made you speechless?"

Her defensive shell snapped into place. While her upbringing might be humble and low key, she wasn't stupid. He was playing, teasing her. "Is that why you left your bed so early? Because you wanted a kiss? Any woman in the kingdom would kiss you. I'm sure you don't lack for offers."

"You see me as a man rather than an instrument for advancement. I trust you."

Keira barked out a laugh and clapped a hand over her mouth to dam her amusement. When she couldn't stop her grin, she let her fingers fall away, giving up her fight for decorum. "Marcus's son and daughter would say I am most untrustworthy. They'd tell you to flee before I sink my claws into your tender heart."

"You believe in love?"

She sighed, wondering how their conversation had morphed into this morass. "Love isn't a fashionable concept on this planet, but my people—my mother's tribe—believe in having a true mate. This is the belief I was raised with, and I'm afraid the concept stuck."

"My parents married for expediency. I believe they like and respect each other, but I have never seen them act with true affection."

"How did we get on this maudlin subject? Ah, here comes Hortese with our tray. Please take a seat, Prince Jarlath."

"I like it better when you call me Jarlath. It's nice to avoid thoughts of the castle and duty."

Keira stared, caught by the humor glinting in his beautiful green eyes. While she sensed intimacy was a mistake, she agreed to his request. A flutter of internal wings beat against her breastbone, the Cawdor part of her heritage urging her to go ahead, to give in to instinct. Friends, she told herself sternly and the crow settled with a grumpy caw-caw resounding through Keira's mind.

Much to her father's displeasure her half-breed status didn't let her shift to a crow, which meant his ability to use her as a marriage bargaining chip hadn't been as successful as he would've liked. Flying stars, this talk of loneliness was leading her along memory paths she chose to ignore.

"Jarlath, would you like me to serve your meal?"

"Yes, please. Do you sell the produce from your garden?"

Keira handed him a cup of steaming tay. The pale green liquid bore a mint-fresh taste and cleansed the digestive system. "Hortese and Melvyn help me run a market stall once a week in town. Sometimes we attend the night market in the castle square. We sell most of our garden produce at the markets, and I employ several locals to package and process our crops."

"Would I have heard of your stall?"

"The HKM stall." Keira handed him a glass of breakfast parfait. "This contains some of the berries you helped me pick."

"It's bound to taste delicious then," Jarlath said. "From memory, HKM supplies the castle."

"Yes, a man called Saulite runs the operation. I keep to the background because the minute I show my face, conversation falters, and the whispers begin."

"But the charges against you were dropped."

"Doesn't matter. I come from Gramite, and my husband died in mysterious circumstances. I faced the indignity of not one but two public trials. I am a pariah."

"I'm sorry."

"Not your fault. The situation just is, and I must accept the circumstances. I could depart and start over on another planet, but I find myself stubborn. It's too much trouble to leave and begin again."

Jarlath nodded in agreement. "Sometimes it's easier to go with the known quantity." He spooned up a mouthful of the parfait and groaned in appreciation. "It's tasty."

Keira grinned and applied herself to eating. They made short work of the parfaits and the sliced fresh fruits on the tray. Hortese had also included some of Hilda's savory pastries, and Jarlath devoured two.

"That was delicious," he said, reclining back into his ergo chair. The chair adapted to his relaxed posture, and he gave a satisfied sigh of approval. "If I'm not careful, I'll go to sleep."

She had the luxury of open scrutiny since his eyes remained closed. He appeared calmer today as if he'd left the stiff royal part of his personality back at the castle.

"Do you have any specific tasks to carry out today?"

"Yes." His reply was short and didn't encourage questions.

"I'll make sure I send you on your way soon." Keira kept her voice light and cheerful, despite disappointment striking at the idea of him leaving. He'd mentioned a kiss, and although she pondered his motives, she would have enjoyed an embrace with a handsome man.

"Not before I get my kiss." He cracked his lids open to focus on her. "I was serious about that."

A shudder of longing speared through her, along with a punch of heat. It was as if he'd read her mind. Her thoughts skipped on to the meat of his words. Oh to be held again in the arms of a muscular and attractive man. One who desired her as she desired him in return.

"That wouldn't be proper."

"Frukk proper," he muttered. "I suppose it wouldn't be correct to tell you that last night I dreamed about tasting you. Every part of you. Your mouth. Your breasts. Your quim. I dreamed of removing your black trews to reveal your sassy arse. I imagined undressing you until you were naked."

Keira felt her mouth drop open as she stared at him, and the heat in her face intensified. His gaze blazed with such passion and longing. His words weren't a line designed to get her into his sleep-bed.

"I imagined the hot, tight fit of your quim as I pushed my cock inside you." His voice had lowered and taken on a sexy rasp.

She stared, mesmerized by his words, by the pictures they painted. By him. "Then what?"

"I woke up way too early and couldn't get back to sleep, so I decided to visit you instead of following my normal routine."

"I see."

"I doubt it," he said. "How could you when I don't understand it myself?"

His words were low and private, but her hearing was good, a trait from the Cawdor side of her bloodline.

"I was going to pick some herbs to prepare for the market," she said abruptly. "Would you like to help?"

"No one ever asks me to do anything. They always want to do things for me."

"Well, in that case, let me put you to work. I also need to pick some nuts. You're much taller than me, so you can take charge of that duty."

Jarlath rolled to his feet and held out his hand to help her rise. "It would be my pleasure."

Keira nodded, pleased by his acquiescence, although she wished he'd follow through on his desire to kiss her. An informal breaking of their fast was fine, but jumping the prince might take things past right and proper.

Instinct had led him to Keira, and he was glad he'd allowed himself the freedom. The woman was beautiful, so sexy and gorgeous that all he wanted to do was touch her. Kiss her. Hell, why not add even more honesty to the equation? He wanted her full stop. And wasn't that a kick in the gonads. She came from an enemy planet and was an accused murderess. Add the fact she was a widow and not a virgin, she was firmly in the unsuitable associates camp.

Try telling that to his cock, to his feline, to the man.

The sec he'd entered her presence, his feline had stirred, his other form moving even more insistently than the day before. He'd need to attempt a shift again once he reached the privacy of his rooms to test his theory, but it appeared his feline recognized something in Keira and wanted to interact.

"Where do I harvest these nuts? Are they for the market?"

"Yes, later today, Hortese and I will shell and roast them. We'll grind some into a paste. The nut paste goes well with a slice of fleur-bread. The rest we'll sell to market goers to snack on as they wander the square."

Jarlath accepted a basket and followed her out into the colorful garden. Plants of many varieties bloomed in profusion. He had no idea of the names, but the vibrant colors leaped out and demanded visual attention. Red. Orange. Yellow. Green. Purple. Even gold and silver. The scents were just as intoxicating as the colors and textures. Keira had a true gift since the castle gardens were a mere shadow of her plot.

"This is the tree. Pick the bright yellow nuts. They are the mature ones."

"Where will you be?"

"I'll be clipping herbs from the next row over. We'll be close enough to talk if we speak loudly."

And disturb this slice of heaven? Jarlath set to, picking the yellow nuts. As Keira said, the mature nuts were high in the branches, probably because she'd already harvested the lower level. His sat-com vibrated in his pocket. Jarlath paused to check the screen. Ellard. He pushed a button to silence the call and returned the com to his pocket. His conscience almost got the better of him, but he was safe. He deserved some freedom.

But Ellard will worry.

Sighing, Jarlath removed his sat-com and entered a text message. I need time alone to think. Safe. Will return before dusk. That done, he resumed picking nuts.

"Do you work this hard every day?"

"I like to keep busy."

Jarlath found himself frowning. He was happier doing things, too, although most of the duties his father delegated to him were of administrative nature. He had no true purpose except, according to his parents, finding a suitable candidate for wife. Apart from that, all he did was make appearances during formal occasions and charm visitors. Gods, no wonder he was feeling restless.

Not long ago, he'd chided his brother for his careless attitude. His parents disliked Lynx engaging in trade, yet his brother persisted in hauling freight from one planet to the next. For the first time, Jarlath understood. Everyone needed a purpose, a task to complete. Pride came with honest toil.

"How many staff do you employ?"

"Here at the farm there is Hortese, Hilda and Melvyn who work fulltime. We hire locals from the village if we require extra staff. I also employ people at the factory and weavers to turn the malpacks fleece into cloth to sell to the replicator manufacturers."

Not only beautiful but an astute businesswoman. He let his mind drift back to her body. Shorter than him but strong and feminine. He should have kissed her when he first mentioned the subject instead of yakking like a chatter-bird.

A bark of amusement escaped him at the thought. Cristo, he'd never spoken to a woman in that manner before, yet she hadn't balked at his frank language or—frukk dirty—conversation. If anything, she'd appeared intrigued.

Jarlath dropped a nut into his container and glanced over at Keira to find her staring at him in confusion. He winked, the intensified hint of green in her cheeks charming him. His mouth twitched and he found the corners lifting into a smile.

41

"What are you smiling about? You don't normally smile."

"You," he said. "I like the way you treat me like a normal Virosian."

"You don't have to help." Her tone was sharp this time, a tad defensive.

"I like you. I've already admitted I want you. Before I leave, I intend to kiss you, so I can't be any blunter about my intentions."

Her scowl softened, and a flash of green suffused her face again. "I don't understand. You're the prince. I doubt anyone would stop you if you decided you wanted me delivered to your castle chamber." One brow arched. "Isn't that what your ancestors used to do?"

"Now that you mention it, I like the idea of having you at my mercy."

Her snort was loud and unfeminine. "I can imagine the scandal. Thank you, but no. I've suffered enough nasty gossip. You may have your kiss, but that is all. There will be no more discussion of sexual congress. Any such talk will result in you getting tossed off my estate on your sexy princely arse."

"You think my arse is sexy?"

"And that's the message he distills from my words," she muttered. "It seems men are the same, even the royal ones."

"No one has ever told me they find me attractive," he said, giving up the pretense of picking nuts. "They tell me I'm sensible and dutiful and not like my younger brother. They tell me I am responsible and dedicated to the House of the Cat. They tell me I will make a good ruler."

"These are good qualities."

"Yes, but for once I wish..." He shrugged, a trifle irritably because he couldn't find the right words.

"You want to act for your own pleasure instead of everyone else's."

"Yes! That's it."

"I understand." She ducked her gaze and snipped several herb sprigs. "But I refuse to be your experiment. I am not a plaything for your amusement."

Jarlath battled his instinct to argue and returned to his nut harvesting. He didn't know why he was belaboring the point or pursuing Keira because that was exactly what he was doing. She came from the planet of the Gramite. Jarlath sighed with deep regret. His parents would never consider adding her name to their precious list. He'd finish his task as he'd promised and return to his own world, his reality.

He was a prince of the Cats, the heir to the kingdom, and it was his duty to marry well and secure the succession.

Yes, he'd walk away from Keira and continue with his responsibilities. Keira was right. If he drew her into his world, she'd get hurt and she didn't deserve that sort of treatment.

"I'm sorry," he said. "I don't wish to make you uncomfortable."

"Jarlath, you're not a bother. Your company is welcome. I'm merely pointing out we can never be more than friends who meet in private. I would never wish to injure your reputation or drag you to the level of mine."

Nothing he could say to that, no way to comfort or assuage the pain in her voice because she spoke the truth. This was the way of their world.

Keira's mind raced, and her hands worked without conscious thought, plucking herbs and placing them in her basket. Jarlath was a surprise and not the man she'd met briefly and seen from afar during social functions. He bore hidden depths, and he tempted her on so many levels. If he had been anyone else...

Luckily, he didn't understand how he tempted her to say to hell with right and throw herself into his arms.

When her basket overflowed, she took it into the kitchen and returned with another.

"I've picked all the nuts within reach," Jarlath said. "Do you want me to take these to the kitchen before I depart?"

"Yes, please." Disappointment blasted her, even though she'd known he'd leave. "Thanks for your help. It's saved me a lot of toil. Why don't you ask Hortese to pack a pie? It's the least I can do in exchange."

"My pleasure." He bowed and strode away, making her feel as if she were in the wrong. He had sought her out, not the other way.

Jarlath returned and stalked to her side. "Hortese is packing my pie, but there was something else I wanted to say before I left."

"Oh?"

"This," he said, and he took her basket and set it aside. He wrapped his arms around her shoulders and drew her to him. She gasped at his masterful manner and stared at him in surprise.

"What—"

"My kiss," he reminded her. "I'm not leaving without one."

He lowered his head and blocked further speech. Her heart sang. He'd come back because he wanted his kiss. Then her brain switched off, her mind awash with sensations and emotions, taste and texture. His fingers speared through her hair to cup her skull and hold her in place. His green eyes, lighter than usual, glittered with need and heady desire as he stared down at her.

Now. Please kiss me now.

But it seemed Jarlath didn't intend to hurry.

He shifted his grip to trace her bottom lip with his thumb. His touch left a trail of tingles, and she groaned in frustration, wanting, needing more from him.

"You make me want to know you better. I wish things were different." Jarlath didn't give her a chance to respond but settled his lips on hers.

The kiss was gentle and warm and made her heart ventricles pump faster, stronger as if she flew in crow form. Without volition, her fingers curled into his silky hair to pull him close. She sank

44

against his hard chest and submitted.

Jarlath growled against her lips and deepened the contact. Their tongues flirted, shyly at first before she became bolder. A feline growl rumbled up his throat, a masculine sound of satisfaction. He tasted wild and sweet and she wanted more, craved permission to explore his muscular body. Instead she kept her hands in his silky hair and enjoyed the kiss for what it was—a goodbye.

CHAPTER FOUR

T earing himself away from Keira was the hardest thing he'd ever done. Every part of him ached to sweep her into his arms, to whisk her to the nearest sleep-bed. Grata fire, he'd do it—her—on the floor if need be, but she was right in her warnings.

He'd barely met her, so it was ludicrous for him to think of a future.

Their future.

Aware of the futility of his desire, he caught and saddled Black and headed back to the castle and his obligations. Black seemed content to amble the forest trail, and since Jarlath wasn't in a hurry to face Ellard or his mother and her list, he allowed his cambeest to set the pace. When he reached a fork in the trail, he guided Black to the right and soon glimpsed Van Lake.

Ah, perfect. If he followed this path, he'd approach the castle from a different direction. He plucked out his com and tapped a quick text message to Ellard. That way, his friend wouldn't suspect he'd visited Keira.

And he'd hidden the pie in his saddlebag. He'd eat his treat in the privacy of his rooms. With his message sent, he paused to let Black drink from the lake before urging his mount onward.

The sudden thunder of hooves heralded an arrival—probably Ellard. Ah, correct guess.

"Jarlath, where the devil have you been?" Ellard arrowed his cambeest toward them at a reckless pace and screeched to a halt. Dust billowed in a cloud, and Black sneezed, tossing his shaggy head and stomping his big feet in alarm.

Black's long rounded ears went back, and Jarlath rubbed his hand over the cambeest's hump in a soothing motion. "Steady, Black."

"Impressive bruising," his friend said.

"Yes. I have more on my shoulder." Ellard had made excellent time. Jarlath eased in the reins to exert control over his irritated beest. "I went riding. I needed to think. Ellard, I sent you a text. You knew I was safe."

"I can't do my job if we're in different places. Besides, Queen Bryna requires an audience. She has sent three messages, and in the third one, she threatened to dismiss me because she deduced I didn't know your whereabouts."

Guilt flashed in Jarlath. Keira was right—people got hurt when he didn't do the expected. Jarlath reached over and squeezed Ellard's forearm in apology. "I'm sorry. I'll let Mother know this was my fault."

"Won't make much difference," Ellard said. "You're my responsibility. I should know your location."

"I'm sorry," Jarlath repeated.

They clattered into the stableyard and several stableboys trotted out to take care of their cambeests.

Jarlath waved them away, and they backtracked in clear relief, their stolid faces relaxing into teasing and banter. Black wasn't the easiest charge and Ellard's cambeest wasn't much better.

"Let me stable, Black," Ellard said. "I want to keep my job."

"I will stable, Black. He's my responsibility." One of many.

"Jarlath, at last." Queen Bryna spoke sharply, exasperation quivering in every line of her slender body. "I expected you to seek me out early this morn."

"I'm sorry, Mother. I am here now." He entered her private sitting room with trepidation and hovered just inside the doorway. As a child, he'd thought of his mother's rooms as a cave full of treasures. They'd roused his kittenish curiosity and his mother's fury when he'd accidentally broken a model house full of furniture and shifters the size of his paws. Now, he knew to keep clear since touching or breaking brought parental wrath.

"Sit." His mother pointed at a chair.

He hung his head and attempted sincere penitence while skirting a knee-high table and what looked like a puzzle to take the indicated seat.

"This is the type of behavior I expect from your brother, not you, Jarlath. This is a serious matter, and your father and I expect you to announce your betrothal by cycle end." Her red Venet slipper tap-tap-tapped on the tile floor to highlight her irritation.

Jarlath sat stock-still, his attention on his mother. The queen wore a smart navy robe and a tasteful moon-glow necklace and earbobs, her attire quite at odds with her militant mood. He sighed inwardly in defeat. On the plus side, he had breathing space before they expected his announcement, but it still felt like a blaster aimed at his back when his mind kept drifting to Keira.

His father had kept a mistress, as had his father before him.

Perhaps he could...no. He wouldn't place Keira in that position. Judging by the gossip doing the rounds, her life was difficult enough already.

"Jarlath." His mother's foot commenced tap-tap-tapping again. "Are you listening?"

"Yes, Mother."

"Here is my list. I have included twelve names. They are all of impeccable breeding and reputation. Any of them would make a good wife for you and a queen for our kingdom. I have collected dossiers on each woman. Should you require further information, please contact my secretary. He will assist you."

"Thank you, Mother." Jarlath wondered how he forced out the words when panic tightened around his chest like titum bands.

"Don't thank me," his mother snapped. "Peruse the list and come to a decision. That will please me and your father." A frown took possession of her mouth and flattened it to a thin line of distaste. "What on Viros are you wearing? You resemble a commoner who spends his day toiling in the fields. And your face. Do not enter my presence again in such dishabille."

A sharp retort stung the tip of his tongue, but he gritted his teeth and refused to let the disrespectful reply loose. Instead, he nodded and let his mother treat him like a kitten, a puppet.

She scanned his face and what she saw must have reassured her because she gave a curt nod. "You may go."

Jarlath shot to his feet and navigated the safest path through his mother's clutter. Outside and away from her scrutiny, he checked the list, the neatly written names. His gut bucked like Black in a feisty mood and his feline jabbed, clawed, kicked beneath his skin, equally pissed. He ran up the central flight of stairs, his rapid footsteps muted by the thick red floor covering, and turned in the direction of his suite. A sharp pain in his right hand focused him in his agitated flight. He stared, then a genuine grin took hold, stretching his mouth so wide it ached. He held the list in a crumpled ball and four sharp claws protruded from beneath his fingernails. Even better, a dewclaw curled from beneath his thumb.

Increasing to a sprint, he burst into his suite's sitting room. He thumped on a door, which led to a smaller adjoining suite of rooms.

"Ellard!"

The door burst open, Ellard with his weapon drawn, eyes scanning the corners of the room. "What is it? What's wrong?"

Jarlath thrust out his hand with the claws still protruding. "Let's go for a run." He slid his saddlebag off his shoulder and set it on a low table.

"But how?" Ellard stared at Jarlath's hand, slack-jawed and incredulous.

"I don't know." Theories, Jarlath had, but he wasn't about to share them with his friend since he was certain this had something to do with Keira. "I don't care. Let's go."

Jarlath made for the door he'd raced through mins earlier.

"Wait, let me get my other blaster." Ellard darted deeper into his suite, light on his feet despite his size. He reappeared and strapped his weapon to his leg. "Let's go."

Excitement pulsed through Jarlath as they clattered down the stairs and left the castle via a side gate. They nodded to the sentry and strode to the walled garden where the pair of them habitually carried out weapons training, away from the notice of the rest of the staff and more importantly, his parents.

His father and mother believed diplomacy should come before war, and although, the castle had an efficient fighting force, the Virosian royal family shouldn't train to take up arms to defend themselves. Lynx had informed his parents the idea was stupid, and Jarlath had to agree. As a royal, he felt it was important to possess a variety of skills and lead from the front. Luckily, Danion Tetsu had agreed and he'd quietly taught the princes along with his two sons. Jarlath and Ellard continued to train in private to keep up their skill levels.

"Do you want to try a shift here? There's plenty of room to run and no one else uses this garden apart from us."

Jarlath felt his feline shudder, and the beginning of the shift commence. He struggled to free himself of his tunic to no avail. His feline burst from him, out of control. The fabric of his tunic ripped even as a tortured groan rushed up his throat.

Frukk, this hurt worse than his first time. Every twist, every stretch, every pop of muscle and bone seemed louder, more painful than ever before.

He cried out and fell forward onto all fours. Panting, he tried to relax, even as his body fought to reshape. Fur rippled beneath the torn remnants of his tunic, and his trews and boots melted into his new form.

Scents and sounds battered his senses, the enrichment a shock after confinement for so long within his humanoid form. He flicked his tail and stretched, the shredded material inhibiting him. Jarlath gave a grumpy bark and attempted to wriggle free.

A chuckle sounded. "Jarlath, keep still. Let me help you." Competent hands tugged the fabric free until nothing hampered him. "Cristo, I'm so glad we can run together again. I've missed running with you, and I don't mean that in a weird way either."

Jarlath barked, the caterwaul impatient and demanding.

Ellard chuckled again, but set his shoulder holster aside and tugged his tunic over his head, baring a broad and muscular chest and his onyx cat pendant. He stuffed his weapon and clothes out of sight beneath a tree and removed his pendant, placing it carefully in his trews pocket.

His change was quick and efficient, Ellard's black leopard a powerful and beautiful creature.

Jarlath yowled, and Ellard barked in return. In unison, they bolted across the clear ground and burst into a copse of tall, straight trees.

The freedom, the breeze rippling across his fur exhilarated Jarlath, and he savored the pumping of his muscles and the rich world of sensory details. He'd told himself he hadn't missed his feline. He'd told himself many others in the kingdom suffered the same fate. He'd told himself it didn't matter.

He'd lied.

He ran and ran and ran until his sides heaved with exertion.

The scent of a small animal distracted him, and he slowed to stalk the trail. A deer mouse shot from beneath a purple flowering plant. He pounced and missed. Behind him, a hoarse bark of amusement rasped from Ellard. His friend nudged his shoulder, and Jarlath heaved a sigh.

Time to return to his duty and the wretched list.

Sighing again, he retraced his steps back to where Ellard had left his clothes. Jarlath pictured his humanoid form and shifted back, chest pulsating in exhaustion yet invigorated.

"Hey, your bruising has faded. At least on your shoulder. Your eye looks much better too. Do you want to borrow my tunic in case we run into the queen?"

"A benefit of the shifting. *Grata*, I'd missed it so much!"

"The tunic?"

"No, you keep your tunic," Jarlath said, heading in the direction of their rooms. "It will be too big for me anyway. Mother is already angry because I didn't follow orders."

They entered Jarlath's rooms, sighting only a sentry and a cleaning droid on the way.

Ellard closed the door behind him. "Did the run feel good?"

"The best. *Grata*, I've missed this part of me. You're lucky your feline didn't go into slumber."

"Yeah. I wish the scientists could discover the cause. Rumors of the problem will spread soon. Someone will talk and the Cawdor will use the knowledge to their advantage."

"The knowledge is a ticking timepiece," Jarlath said. "Want to have a drink?"

"Sure."

"I have pie." Exhilaration pushed the unguarded words from his mouth. *Grata!* Too late now.

"Pie?" Ellard smacked his lips. "Who did you sweet talk in the kitchen to give you pie? Not the little blonde kitten? The new one?"

Mentally apologizing to Keira, Jarlath nodded. "Ya got me."

"Are you sleeping with her?"

"No, you go ahead if you're interested." Only one woman dominated his thoughts. She'd burrowed under his skin so damn quickly, he was still confused about how she'd managed the feat. He pressed his palm to his door and stepped inside.

"Thanks, but I'll pass. I have a lady in my sights."

How had he missed that? "Yeah? She gonna let you catch her?"

Ellard winked. "Already caught her."

"Well. We should celebrate." Jarlath strode to his chefmate and programmed two hot toddies. He handed a steaming tankard to Ellard. "I'll get the pie." Secs later, he was back, and he grabbed a knife to cut a large wedge. He arched a brow at his friend. "Do you need a plate?"

"Nope," Ellard said. "Gimme. I'm starving." He took a huge bite, chewed, and swallowed. "Damn, that's good. Did the blonde bake it or is there a new cook in the kitchens?"

"Didn't ask," Jarlath said. "I took the pie and ran." Nothing less than the truth. He took a bite and almost echoed his friend's moan of pleasure. The tart flavor of the berries and the crisp rich pastry was better than anything he'd tasted before. With every bite he thought of Keira, the urge to visit her so strong he had to force himself not to stride from his rooms. "You better not let your girl hear you drooling about pies."

"Not likely. What did the queen want?"

"She gave me a list of marriage candidates. Twelve names for me to check out. I'm under orders to choose one and offer marriage." Jarlath shoved the last bite of his slice of pie into his mouth and chewed. He scratched the back of his neck then his arm. "Want more pie?"

"Are you first in line to the king?"

Jarlath pulled a face. "I'll take that as a yes." He handed Ellard a second piece and scratched at his biceps. "Something must have bitten me while I was out in the garden. I might go and clean up."

"Sure, I have to report to Father. As head of security, he knew you were missing—" He held up a hand when Jarlath went to interrupt. "He knew I was worried, but he was in a meeting when I commed him. I sent a text instead, but I'd better speak with him in person."

"I'm sorry," Jarlath said again. The last thing he'd wanted was to get Ellard in trouble.

"You leaving the castle tonight? Schedule says you're staying indoors."

"I might go for a walk out in the square and check out the market."

"Com me," Ellard ordered. "You can't go out alone and risk an incident."

A scoffing sound escaped before Jarlath could censor his response. "The House of Cawdor is quiet at present, and they wouldn't dare try anything with me. Besides, wouldn't you rather hang with your girl? Much better than guarding me."

"There's nothing to stop the Cawdor from hiring a sniper to take you out."

"They could do that anyway," Jarlath shot back. "I refuse to hide behind the castle walls for the rest of my life. Lynx tried to make a move on a Cawdor cutie and stepped on toes. Nothing like that will happen with me because I'm not my brother. Since Lynx's public apology, things have become peaceful."

Jarlath reached a hand behind his back to scratch at the base of his spine.

"I don't care. Com me if you're going out."

After a long pause, Jarlath gave a curt nod. "Very well."

Left alone, Jarlath strode to his sanitizer room and stripped off his remaining clothes. A glance in his looking glass showed the bruising around his eye had faded dramatically and...was the green of his irises lighter? Because he'd shifted again? Delight had him whistling, then once again his thoughts drifted to Keira. She was from...no, he didn't get the traitor vibe from her. She seemed upfront and honest, and grata, he wanted to see her again.

Damn, he would see her again.

Somehow.

He might not manage to socialize with her in public, but surely he could meet her privately? Surely they could be friends?

Keira stared into the pink-and-red flames of the fire she'd lit to ward off the wintery chill in the air. Faint curls of pink smoke drifted up the chimney. Outside, an unexpected storm battered her home and set the forest trees rustling. Something about the savageness of the storm prickled her skin. She jumped to her feet, her jittery nerves urging her to action.

"Keira."

Keira froze, her hand on the back of a chair as the voice from her nightmares whispered through her sitting room. She spun around, her gaze darting past gel-chairs and other furniture to search all four corners. There was no one present except her. This storm had set her on edge, fueling her imagination.

Razvan wasn't here.

The tenseness seeped from her muscles, and her shoulders slumped in relief. No one here.

"Keira." The voice held amusement at her expense.

When she pivoted, her gaze went to the leaping flames of the fire, and she saw him. She froze, her attention riveted on Razvan's gloating amber eyes and the blue flames licking across his high cheekbones, over his goatee beard.

Magic.

Somehow, he'd managed to send a message via his pet wizards.

She fought to control her shock and the shudders zapping her taut muscles. With her mother's help, she'd escaped him once, but it seemed she hadn't run far enough.

She schooled her face to impassive. "Razvan."

"It's been a long time, Keira."

Not long enough as far as she was concerned.

"What do you want?"

"Invite me in, Keira."

"No." *Grata!* Did she look stupid? If she obeyed him, he'd step into her sitting room. "You are not welcome in my home. You are not welcome on this planet. You are not welcome in my life."

His dark caramel-colored features tightened, his displeasure clear even with the flicker of the magical flames licking across his skin. "I will have you, Keira."

"No! That's sick. We share blood."

"I never forget a slight, my lovely Keira. You will pay, and I will have you."

In her peripheral vision, she caught sight of Hortese and gestured her to stay.

"Who's there?" Razvan demanded.

"No one," Keira said quickly. Too quickly.

"No matter. You won't escape me a second time."

Cristo, he meant that. Her heart ventricles thudded extra hard against the wall of her chest. Fear made her want to run to the kitchen for water to douse the flames and her half-brother's mocking face.

Razvan Cronan was the oldest son of Xavier Cronan, the man who was head of the House of Cawdor and also her father. Not that she'd ever had much to do with either while growing up. When Xavier visited her mother, Keira had always been under the charge of her nurse and instructed to keep away.

She hadn't even known she had half-brothers until she reached eighteen cycles and had attended a celebration ball in Cawdor Square. She gritted her teeth, thrust back in memories and none of them good.

"Our father is dead."

"What?"

"I am in charge of the House now." A mocking smile curled across his lips before his face blinked out and the flames reduced to their normal state of pink and purple. Outside, the storm ceased as rapidly as it had started.

It took long moments before she could force her legs to move. Her knees quivered so much they buckled, and she slumped onto the gel-couch.

"Who was that?" Hortese demanded.

"Razvan, my half-brother."

Hortese hissed, and her entire body vibrated. Her pink eyes glowed and her hair tendrils bristled. "Despoiler."

He was all that and more and very, very dangerous.

"Yes. We must take care. Use every precaution. I will speak to Hilda and Melvyn. No matter what promises, what orders or pleas he uses we must refuse his requests to enter this house."

"We're lucky he didn't appear while the prince was present," Hortese said.

A chill sped over her skin, leaving a series of green bumps pebbled on her limbs. Fear left her lightheaded. The idea of Razvan learning of Jarlath's visit and hurting the prince. If he'd witnessed their kiss...

"Can we purchase a spell to keep him away?" Hortese asked.

"Yes, we'll need protection and repulsion spells. The strongest we can buy. I'm sure he's spying on us."

Something else to worry about. If Razvan was able to spy on her, she was in big trouble. Panic unfurled in her belly, spreading with each rapid beat of her heart ventricles. She could leave—no! He would not drive her from her home as he had done in the past.

Hortese touched Keira's arm to gain her attention. "What do you want to do?"

"Now that the storm has passed, we could take the flymo and attend the night market. We might be able to find the spell or at least order the spell from one of the market stalls dealing with magical charms."

"All right, and meantime, we should all wear a sprig of evil-eye herb on our person. Razvan's magic is strong to travel between the planets," Hortese said.

Keira sighed, Hortese's unease a palpable thing, which ran parallel with her own fears. "It's worth a try. Please com Melvyn and ask if he wants to accompany us. He might like to have a drink at the Cat's Arms with his friends."

"We should take Hilda too," Hortese said. "She likes to visit her sister. We don't know if the despot might try to return."

Keira heaved a hard sigh. Razvan was a brute, and he'd never leave her alone.

She'd never be safe until he was dead.

Looking at the list made his head hurt and his heart ache. The women, or at least the names he recognized, were facsimiles of his mother. Jarlath stepped into the sanitizer and turned on a combination of water and steam. The warm mixture pummeled his body from three different directions, and the irritating, itchy sensation on his back faded.

Grata! He didn't want any of the women, but if he didn't make an attempt and meet or spend time courting them, his parents would become pushier. They might even decide to choose his bride for him, and that would be a disaster.

He switched the unit to dry mode and turned his body until the moisture on his skin evaporated.

Once dressed—this time in clothes suitable for a prince—he wandered out to his sitting room and stared at the crumpled list. The first name—Decima Nabil. A petite woman, he recalled. From a good family. Impeccable breeding. A little older than most since she'd had two seasons already. Her dark green eyes hinted at a slumbering feline. He didn't know for sure since this was a touchy subject and seldom discussed in public, but it was a decent indicator. If he chose her as his wife and they had children, there was a chance their offspring wouldn't have the ability to shift. It mightn't be fair, but he couldn't marry her.

Ernestine Aniko—tall and slender but very shy. From memory, she had a stammer, and she blushed each time anyone drew attention to her. No, he couldn't marry a woman who tried to melt into the furniture.

"Grata," he muttered and reached for his com. "Ellard, I'm going to the night market."

"Wait. I'll take Mareeka home and come with you. It's safer."

"No, stay with your girl. You deserve some down time. I'll wear a disguise."

It was an impulse but the decision felt right. Another departure from habit and one Ellard noted—if his silence was anything to go by.

"You weren't happy with me this morn for going off without telling you. I'm correcting my error. I'll have my weapon and my com unit with me. I can shift to feline. Combined with my disguise, I'll be safe enough. No one expects to see Prince Jarlath ambling around the market."

"No, I'll take Mareeka—"

"Stop treating me like an immature cub. Besides, I don't want to take the blame for mucking up your love life. I'm grown and responsible."

"Not recently," Ellard retorted.

"It's the square outside the castle. The castle guards are always alert. I'm going out and you're remaining in and getting lucky. Maybe you can talk your Mareeka into staying the night."

"Jarlath," Ellard muttered in an undertone.

Jarlath grinned at the unspoken warning. "Give Mareeka a kiss for me."

"Not bloody likely."

Jarlath was still laughing as he clicked off and slapped the com on his bed. He opened his wardrobe and scowled at the rows of suits. Time to look like his brother again.

Five mins later, Jarlath strode from his suite of rooms, paused at the main staircase and backtracked to exit the castle via a lesser used doorway at the rear. He nodded to the guard and stalked outside.

Dusk had settled over the land and colored lights illuminated the castle square. Tables sat in haphazard rows and vendors bustled around, unpacking their wares ready for display. The aroma of cooking meat filled the air and the taverna on the corner was doing a brisk trade. He halted at the top of the steps leading to lower levels. The next level down, flymo pilots jostled for spaces to land and disgorge passengers. A spot opened up, and a flymo pilot pounced on the opportunity. He zipped his compact gray craft into the space, a door flipped open, and two adults and two children exited. The children ran past him, their bright green eyes alive with excitement. Their parents followed at a slower pace.

Jarlath pulled his hat lower on his face and ambled into the thick of the market, past vendors. On scanning the vicinity, he saw a few people of his acquaintance. Not one cried out in recognition.

People saw what they expected to see.

A band set up and started playing instruments of the like he hadn't seen before. The band members' striped skin showed them as outsiders, but their music soon had his foot tapping. A huge group gathered and some of the youngsters started dancing, their arms and bodies jerking and waving to the melody.

Jarlath listened for a time before skirting the crowd. A young man, red-skinned and scrawny, his hair styled in dreads, bumped against him and attempted to pick his pocket. Jarlath might be a prince, but Ellard's father, in his position of Head of Security, had taught him well. Jarlath seized the young man's wrist and tightened his grip to the point of pain.

"Ow," the youth howled. "I didn't do nuffin."

"You were trying to pick my pocket."

"No. No, wouldna do that."

Jarlath made a scoffing sound and maintained his grip on the youth. "Lucky for you, I'm in a good mood. I have shopping to do and require someone to carry my purchases. If you're willing, I'll pay you two gold coins. I'll give you one now and one when you help me carry my purchases home."

"How far you live?" the youth demanded, his black gaze glinting with sharpness. Jarlath could practically see his brain ticking over, considering the angles and possibilities.

"I live five mins from here."

"You be a toff." The strident tone wasn't complimentary. "What happened to your eye?"

Jarlath found himself grinning, the expression feeling more natural since he'd formed his lips that way many times during the day. "I fell off my beest. You should have seen it before. Do you want the job or not?"

"Yes."

"What's your name?"

"Cristop."

"You may call me Lath. I find myself hungry," Jarlath said. "Come, we will eat before we start our tasks." He released Cristop, half expecting the youth to flee.

"You promise coin now."

"Indeed." Suppressing a burst of humor, Jarlath pulled a single coin from his pocket and tossed it to Cristop. He snatched it cleanly, surveyed it with close attention then shoved it into the depths of a pocket.

The youth gestured to the right. "The best food stall is this way."

"Perfect," Jarlath said.

The scent of roasting fowls grew stronger.

"I will wait here," Cristop said.

"No, you will eat with me. I don't wish to eat alone." He located a table and sprawled in a seat.

Cristop perched on the other empty seat, prepared for flight.

"Ah, there is a server." Jarlath signaled for service and pretended to study the menu while he waited.

In reality, Cristop drew his attention—the hungry expression on the youth's face.

Lynx had attempted to persuade his father to set up a program to help homeless youngsters, but the king had listened to his council and built a stadium in which to host cage fighting and arena sports. While it was true, the fights brought money to Viros, the currency flow lined the pockets of the rich instead of filtering down to aid those who needed help.

"You!" the chubby server snarled, his shout jerking Jarlath from his musing. "Get out before I summon the guard."

Cristop jumped to his feet and edged back to dodge the man's fist.

"Enough," Jarlath snapped. "The boy is in my hire. We intend to order a meal before we go on our way."

"Payment first." The server planted beefy hands on his hips, his sneer displaying a golden tooth. "Show me your currency."

Jarlath growled under his breath, channeling a grouchy Ellard. The server broke first, dipping his gaze. "We will have two roasted fowls." Jarlath tapped his finger on the menu. "No, two of this set menu with the fowls, the savory and the sweet to finish. Two barley drinks."

"That will be twenty-five dinars," the server snapped.

Jarlath pulled change from his pocket—two gold coins plus several bronze ones and flung them into the server's outstretched hand. "Bring my change. Cristop, sit."

The man tugged his short, pointy beard and sniffed disdainfully but trotted off to deliver their order to the kitchen.

Jarlath focused on Cristop. "Are they all like this?"

The youth's lips quirked. "Might have cause."

"Why?"

"Sometimes I be hungry."

"The soup kitchens?"

"They charge."

They were meant to be free. Jarlath made a mental note to ask Ellard. No, rather than ask his friend he'd go in disguise and investigate himself. Perhaps it was possible to do good instead of blindly following the path his parents had set him.

The server returned with their order and thumped the serving platters on their table. He thrust Jarlath's change at him, paused while waiting for a tip. Jarlath ignored him and the man stomped off to serve another table of diners.

"Is all this for me?" Cristop asked, his tone one of disbelief.

"Yes, eat up now. You'll need your strength to carry my packages."

Jarlath had no need to shop since he owned the latest gadgets and replicators, but shop he would to appease this young man's pride. He picked up a roasted fowl leg and bit into the crispy skin. The meat tasted even more delicious than it smelled.

"Good choice," Jarlath said and crammed more meat into his

mouth. He studied the crowd and did a double take when he recognized Keira and her maid. He blinked, sure he'd imagined Keira's pretty face, but no—it was her. A wide smile took possession of his mouth, so big his lips protested. His pulse jumped, a sensation he recognized as nerves taking grip.

Damn, he wanted her. One kiss hadn't been nearly enough.

CHAPTER FIVE

"Wait here," he said to Cristop. "I see someone I know."
Jarlath jumped to his feet and hoofed it to catch her.
"Keira."

Both Keira and her maid froze, and when Keira whirled fear shone in her green-flecked eyes.

"Keira, it's me," Jarlath said, wanting to allay her distress even as he wondered the cause of this reaction in both women.

"Jarlath, what are you doing here?" Keira whispered.

"I'm having dinner and shopping," Jarlath said. "Would you and Hortese like to join me and my companion? I ordered a lot of food and fear I'll never manage to eat half of it."

"No," Keira said.

"We'd like that," Hortese said and pinched her mistress on the arm when it seemed she would argue.

"This way," Jarlath said and guided the women to his table.

"Cristop, this is Keira and Hortese. They are joining us for dinner. Can you manage to secure two more chairs?"

"Really that's not necess—" Keira began then yelped when Hortese pinched her again. "Will you stop that?"

"Take these seats," Jarlath said. "Ah, my helper is back already. Excellent." If there was one thing Jarlath was good at it was social chitchat. Since birth, his parents and tutors had drilled him in the art of putting people at ease. Normally the duty irritated him and the giggly females gave him headaches. In this case, using his skill was a pleasure, but he could tell something was bothering Keira.

"This fowl is delicious," Hortese said. "Try some, Keira. It's even better than Hilda's."

Keira's mouth pursed. "Sacrilege!"

Cristop tipped his head and his dreads flopped over his nose. He jerked his head the other way, and they resettled. "I told you meal be good."

Amusement simmered inside Jarlath at Cristop's smugness. "You did," he agreed. "Are you ladies shopping tonight or do you have your stall set up?"

The two women exchanged a fleeting look, full of silent communication.

"Shopping," Keira said.

"Good," Jarlath said. "Once we've finished our meal we can shop together." He leaned toward Keira. "You can help cement my disguise. No one would expect to see me shopping in the company of two beautiful women and a youth."

Keira bit her lip. He smelled flowers and woman and closed his eyes to savor her presence.

"I wish we were alone," he whispered.

"I'm not...it's not a good idea for people to see us together. I don't want to drag you into a gossip storm. You don't know my stepchildren. Sitting with me is bad enough."

"All we're doing is sharing a meal and going shopping," he said and dared to reach over to touch her arm. He swore he felt the heat of her skin through her cloak, and again, he wished they were alone instead of chaperoned by a maid and a street urchin.

"Where do you live?" Keira asked Cristop.

"In the lower town," Cristop said through a mouthful of food.

"Don't speak with your mouth full," Hortese scolded and her pink eyes flashed a warning when the youth opened his mouth again. "Don't."

"Is everyone almost finished?" Jarlath asked. "I'm ready to shop."

"The food isn't finished," Cristop said.

Keira gestured for a waiter. "We'd like a go-pack please."

Jarlath watched her pack the excess and hand it to Cristop. "You're a growing youth. You should take this and eat it later."

"Thanks," Cristop said.

"Masterfully done," Jarlath whispered to Keira. "Where are we going first?"

"You don't need to accompany us," Keira protested.

"I have the evening to while away." Jarlath stood. "Besides, I'd enjoy the company and require help with my shopping. How do I know what to buy? I've never been shopping before."

Keira's hand flew to her chest. "Never?"

"My education is sadly lacking." He watched the thoughts chasing over her face and the way she chewed her bottom lip. He wanted to be the one doing that. Grata! The urge to take her in his arms and snatch a kiss had him sidling nearer. He forced himself to back off and instead breathed in her flowery scent and relished her company.

A relationship wasn't possible. He had to remember his parents expected him to adhere to duty and assume bigger responsibilities. He stepped back farther, his feline stirring, his gruff bark of protest echoing in Jarlath's mind for long secs.

Keira stiffened then retreated to Hortese's side, and Jarlath froze.

She'd heard his feline? Curious. Maybe he should've asked more questions about her heritage and her abilities. He strode to her side and ignored her glower of frustration.

"How long have you lived here on Viros?"

"Just over five cycles," she said, and her chin lifted in hauteur. "I am not a spy."

"I don't believe I suggested the possibility."

"But you were thinking it," she snapped. "The courts cleared me of espionage charges too. I am not, nor have I ever acted as a spy for the House of Cawdor."

Jarlath stared, mesmerized. Keira in a high dudgeon was a remarkable sight. Her eyes flashed with golden lights and a surge of delicate green highlighted her cheekbones.

"What do you want to buy first?" Cristop demanded, his loud voice breaking the tension.

"I need a new hat to cut the cold from the coming wintery months and a coat," Jarlath said. "What are you shopping for, Keira?"

"We need some charms from a magical stall—if we can find one," Hortese said.

"You in luck. The ban against magical stalls relaxed recentlike. Soldiers ignore. This way," Cristop said.

Hortese's hair tendrils stirred, and she frowned. "I thought the magical stalls were nearer the exit streets in case of raids."

"Not true now. New one this way." Cristop gestured with a jerk of his head. "Better spells. More expensive but better."

"Do you get a commission for steering customers to this new stall?" Hortese demanded. "We require top-quality spells, not shoddy pretenders."

"You see, then decide," Cristop said.

Jarlath lifted a brow and offered his arm to Keira. "With that sort of endorsement, you need to at least visit the stall."

Keira ignored his proffered arm and marched ahead.

Cristop cast him a sideways glance, merriment making him appear younger. "She pissed at you."

"For now." Jarlath realized happiness filled him, even though, for some reason, Keira didn't appreciate his presence.

"Buy her some pretties," Cristop advised. "Women like presents."

Jarlath grinned. "Do you have experience with the ladies?"

"Don't get pissed with me."

"I'll keep that in mind." Jarlath strode after the women.

Cristop darted around him and pointed. "This is the best clothing stall. The weaver will not cheat. Good quality. I would buy here if—" He trailed off with a careless shrug but Jarlath filled in the gaps. The kid couldn't afford the price of the clothing.

Shame filled Jarlath then. He knew nothing about the people who inhabited the city. He knew nothing of their trials or how they existed on a daily basis. Lynx had known. If he was to become king, he needed to fill the gaps in his education. This disguise might aid him with learning more of the Virosian people.

Keira and Hortese paused at a stall selling colorful hats.

"I like the one with the green," Jarlath said. "It will go with your skin tone."

"I don't require a hat," Keira said and moved on.

Jarlath handed Cristop a coin. "Purchase the green one and pick one for Hortese too. We'll be at the spell stall."

He strode after the women, whistling under his breath. Not only did he find himself curious about his people, but he ached to know more about Keira too.

"I think the prince has a thing for you," Hortese whispered.

"No." He couldn't, they couldn't ever take their fledgling friendship further, no matter how much she willed it, no matter how much she liked him. A relationship was too dangerous with Razvan sniffing in her direction. She'd thought she'd managed to escape his clutches, but her half-brother seemed determined to get her under his control.

Grata! She couldn't let that happen. She needed a spell to protect herself and her friends.

"Marcus was a good man. He wouldn't expect you to remain alone."

"No, he wanted me to find someone else when I was ready," Keira said and it was true. They'd discussed it before—no—best she didn't travel that road again. "This must be the stall Cristop mentioned. It's not very busy."

"It won't hurt to look at their wares." Hortese scanned the contents of the stall. "Keira, the youth is right. I can feel the magic emanating from the spells. Can you?"

Keira focused and her pulse rate jumped, the flare of magic sizzling across her skin. "Let's speak to the owner."

A crack of thunder rent the air, and the people around them froze, their gazes going skyward. Stars glinted in the sky, yet the deafening clap ripped through the hushed atmosphere again.

"Purchase four protection spells right now," Keira ordered. "Hurry."

Hortese spoke to the vendor, and he handed over four small sachets and accepted a handful of coins in exchange.

When a third boom rippled through the sky, the vendor picked up a protection spell and stuffed it inside his own cloak.

Jarlath moved closer and Keira thrust a protection spell at him. "Here, place it in your pocket or hang it around your neck. Cristop."

"What is it?" Cristop didn't sound afraid, but Keira was because she sensed Razvan was making his move, putting the stamp on his dynasty. If she was right, then this was an arrogant declaration of war.

All around them people stood, heads tipped back to scan the night sky. Somewhere to their right, a woman screamed.

Jarlath wrapped his arm around her shoulders and his touch soothed some of her angst. Surely, she was wrong. It wasn't possible for Razvan to accumulate this much power.

A loud explosion drew everyone's attention. Jarlath's arm curled around her waist in a protective manner. Keira found herself leaning into him, despite her reservations, as she stared into the sky.

Flashes of light burst from a central point, separating and joining into a pattern. Slowly, a shape pulled together and fear tugged her stomach tight. A gasp escaped before she could bite her bottom lip to block the sound.

"What is it? Keira?"

She swallowed, her gaze tracking the pattern as it formed in the sky.

"All hail the leader," a male voice shouted from beside them, and he raised his fist into the air.

"All hail the leader," another voice shrieked, also lifting a hand in salute.

One by one, the people around them shouted the words and raised their hands. Keira didn't think everyone yelled the words but most did. Thankfully, the protection spells seemed to work for them and the stallholder. She glanced at Jarlath and saw him staring at her instead of the image of the giant crow spreading across the sky.

"Do you know anything about this?"

"No! This is my home. My home," she repeated and her heart raced as he studied her, weighed her innocence. He had to believe her. Marcus had been good to her—he'd saved her from certain pain and perhaps death at her half-brother's hands. "Viros is my home."

"Shush. It's okay, sweetheart."

"The crow is fading," Cristop said.

The youth was right, and as the lights in the night sky faded, so did the shouts from the surrounding people. One by one, they lowered their hands and went back to whatever business they'd been conducting before the explosion, as if nothing out of the ordinary had occurred.

"They don't even seem to know what's happening," Keira whispered, shocked and a little freaked by their behavior.

"It's as if they were under a spell," Jarlath said. "Keira, you head home. You should be safe enough. I'll return to the castle and discuss this with my father and the defense council."

"What about your shopping?" Cristop asked.

"The castle guards are coming," Keira said. "Let's move. Cristop, come with us." It wasn't a suggestion, and Jarlath sent her a look of approval.

"I don't know you," Cristop said backing up, his gaze darting left and right as if he was deciding which way to flee.

"I promise on my husband's grave that I won't hurt you or sell you into slavery." On occasion, she knew authorities rounded up and sent away the young and the homeless, and she wondered if Jarlath knew this happened in his kingdom.

"Slavery?" Jarlath's eyes danced as if she'd made a joke, but when he saw her expression, his humor slid away, leaving stark shock. "That happens?"

"Yes," Keira said.

"The slavers made sweep last week," Cristop said. "Took my friend."

"Grata!" Jarlath spat. "I need to get out more. Cristop, Keira owns a farm on the outskirts of the city. She has weapons and knows how to use them. If she promises to keep you safe, she will do it."

A loud snarl came from their right and a man shifted to feline. He turned on his neighbor and pounced, strong hindquarters propelling him through the air.

The castle guards came running but not before several others waded into the fight, some shifting into feline form and others remaining humanoid.

"We have to leave. Now," Jarlath ordered. "This is getting out of control. Let me see you to your vehicle, then I'll get back to the castle. Quick." Jarlath ushered them from the square, and Keira didn't argue.

Their protection spells would keep them safe from a magical attack. A physical assault could still kill.

Hortese hurried Cristop along and it seemed the boy had decided to give his trust. She was glad and would happily offer him a position on the farm. Melvyn would take the youth under his wing.

On reaching their flymo, Prince Jarlath hauled her into his arms and kissed her. It happened so quickly she didn't have time to marshal her defenses. Heat rushed over her, sank its claws into her body. Then, she was free.

"Stay safe," he said gruffly and strode away.

"Oh my," Hortese said.

"He's not bad for a toff," Cristop said.

"He's not a toff," Hortese told the boy as she ushered him into their flymo. The rounded door bore elaborate signwriting identifying the chubby round vehicle as belonging to Cloud Farms. They used it for hauling produce to the factory and zipping around the city when necessary. She shot Cristop a triumphant look. "That is Prince Jarlath."

"Nah." The boy plonked his butt on a fold-down seat and secured the shoulder harness. "You think I fell down in the last rain storm?"

Keira raised her fingers to her mouth and rubbed her tingling lips. He'd kissed her in front of Hortese and the boy.

"Tell me truth," Cristop said to Keira. "Who is he?"

"That is Prince Jarlath, first in line to the throne." Keira settled herself in the pilot's seat, and Hortese took the spot in the only other fixed seating before pushing a button to close the entrance hatch.

"What's 'e doin' kissin' you?" the boy demanded. "The prince doesn't go to the market and eat fowl with 'is fingers."

"He did tonight," Keira said.

"Don't believe you."

Keira shrugged and started the flymo before pulling back on the control stick to guide the vehicle into a climb. "Believe me or not. It won't change the truth."

"What was that up in the sky?" Hortese asked. "It looked like a crow."

"You heard Razvan earlier. He's in charge of the House of the Cawdor. Somehow, he has discovered a way to appear from Gramite. I believe tonight was a declaration of his might."

"It's the start of a war," Hortese said, her tone grim. "The men and women who saluted the crow in the sky are under his power. This will turn the House of the Cat inside out and start civil war. Mark my words. We need to prepare."

"Yes." Keira curled her fingers around the manual control in an effort to stop the tremors slipping over her skin. Razvan was ruthless and she feared the outcome of tonight's display of power. None of them were safe. Razvan had made that clear during their last face-to-face meeting, and he didn't make idle threats.

Jarlath pushed through the crowd in the square. Some ran in panic, crashing into others and sending parcels and people toppling. Jarlath scooped up a young girl who was trying to pick up her packages.

"Leave it," he ordered. "The crowd will trample you."

Tears flowed down her pale face, her bright green eyes overflowing. "My master will beat me if I return empty-handed."

Grata! She was a mere child. "Who is your master?"

"Prince Jarlath," she said. "He orders his head of kitchen to beat me."

"Frukk," Jarlath muttered. How the hell had he managed to escape reality for so long? Lynx was right. The kingdom was rotten at the core, yet he'd refused to see the truth. "I promise you Prince Jarlath will not pass the order this time."

She sent him a look of disbelief.

A black leopard slammed into the girl and sent both her and Jarlath to the ground. When the leopard came at them with its maw wide open, sharp teeth glinting in the lamp light, Jarlath scrambled to his feet and thrust the girl behind him. He met the leopard's bright green gaze and held it, a fierce snarl bursting up his throat. The leopard froze in confusion, and Jarlath repeated the challenge.

"Leave," Jarlath ordered. "Go home."

The leopard backed up and slinked away.

Jarlath seized the girl's hand. "Let's go."

A hefty and bosomy woman attempted to halt their progress and threw a punch. Jarlath gaped at her until her fist connected. Pain burst through his jaw in a thunderclap, snapped his head back.

The young girl darted around him and stomped on the woman's foot. When the woman attempted to strike again, Jarlath snarled and mislaid his courteous manners to punch in return. The woman went down and the girl cheered.

Jarlath grinned. "Bloodthirsty wench. Come along. We'll enter the castle this way."

He picked up his pace and tugged the girl to the entrance. She balked.

"What is it?"

"We must use the staff entrance," she said. "Will lose my job if I enter this way." She shot him a suspicious glance. "Are you new?

Why don't you know this?"

Jarlath glanced in the direction she tried to lead him. Three black leopards roamed the space along with a crowd of men who seemed drunk.

"Bugger the rules," he said and dragged her to the entrance.

A guard stepped out to challenge them. "You can't come in this way."

Jarlath drew off his hat and glared at the man. "I am Prince Jarlath, and we will enter."

The guard did a double-take before paling. "Pardon me. I apologize, Prince Jarlath." He stood to attention and offered a salute.

Jarlath ignored the girl's gasp and towed her past the guard. "Which part of the castle do you work in? I'll escort you there and explain what happened. They will not punish you."

Her eyes were big and wide, and she trembled like a forest leaf. "T-the produce kitchen, Prince Jarlath."

His com buzzed. "One moment while I answer this. Yes."

"Where are you?" Ellard sounded breathless, panicked. "I've just heard what happened. Are you safe?"

"I'm inside the castle at the south entrance. I'm on my way to the produce kitchen."

"What? Wait for me. I'll be there in a sec." Ellard abruptly disconnected.

"Which way is the kitchen?" Jarlath felt stupid asking. He hadn't even known there was more than one kitchen. Another thing for him to remedy. He couldn't fulfill his duty to the people if he was woefully ignorant of the most basic facts.

"I do not know." The girl dithered and stepped from one foot to the other, her reddened fingers clasping and unclasping. "I always use servants' entrance."

"Never fear. I'm sure Ellard will know."

The girl squeaked. "Mr. Ellard—t-the man who eats people?"

Jarlath barked out a laugh until he saw she was serious and terrified. "Ellard is my best friend. We grew up together and I have never seen him eat a person. His favorite food is pie." Jarlath's thoughts leaped to Keira. Pie was his favorite now too.

"Grata, thank the gods you are safe," Ellard said. "I commed you as soon as I heard, but the stories were so exaggerated. Hopefully Father can give me a full report."

"Ellard, do you know the way to the produce kitchen?"

"What?" He seemed to notice the girl for the first time.

She let out another squeak and hid behind Jarlath.

"The produce kitchen. I'm escorting this young lady in order to speak to the person in charge. She mustn't receive punishment for losing her shopping. What is your name, sweetheart?"

"Gertrude," she whispered.

Ellard frowned. "I think I can guide us there."

"Good. We'll follow," Jarlath said. "I need to learn the castle floor plan and get out into the city, see what is occurring with the people. I have much to tell you."

"Did you see what happened?" Ellard asked.

"Yes. I'll tell you everything once we escort Gertrude to the kitchen and I speak to her supervisor. Did you know I beat the staff if they don't carry out my orders?"

Ellard chuckled.

"This isn't a joke, Ellard. Gertrude, tell him. Has Prince Jarlath ordered you beaten?"

"Yes," she whispered, her face parchment white.

"Why did you get beaten?" Jarlath asked.

"Because I didn't peel the vegetables fast enough, and I cut my finger and bled all over the pot-carrots."

"Frukk," Ellard muttered, shooting him an appalled look.

"Did you know slavers make regular sweeps of the lower city and carry away anyone they think they can sell?"

"I'd heard rumors, but I didn't think—"

"Why didn't you tell me?"

"You didn't show any interest," Ellard blurted. "You seemed happy to continue in the same way. And whenever Lynx told us about stuff happening in the city, you told him he was drunk and raving."

That would not happen again. Lynx would make a far better king. He wondered where his brother was and what he was doing and made a mental note to make contact.

"Ah, I was right. This way," Ellard said, fingering his onyx pendant.

"No," Gertrude said in a small voice. The girl still shook like the forest treetops during a storm. "That's the way to the pastry kitchen. It's this way." She darted past them to lead the way, but Jarlath could see the act of bravery cost. Small white teeth dug into her bottom lip, and her eyes held a watery sheen.

"She knows the way, Jarlath. We have more important things to do."

"She will not get a beating in my name this night," Jarlath snapped.

Gertrude turned a corner and disappeared from sight. A feminine roar sounded, and they heard a terrified squeak.

Jarlath strode around the corner with Ellard at his side. A skinny female with straight black hair held Gertrude by the upper arm and was shaking her.

"Cease," Jarlath snarled.

The woman froze. "Who be you to—" She caught sight of Jarlath's face and paled, seconds later sketching a curtsey. Her hand shot out and slapped Gertrude. "Show some respect. It be the prince."

"Gertrude, you can go now," Jarlath said. "If anyone beats you tonight or in the future, you are to let me know. I will come to the kitchens and make sure no one is ill-treating you or any others who work here."

"Thank you, Prince Jarlath," Gertrude said, and after bobbing a curtsey, she disappeared into the depths of the kitchen.

Jarlath fixed his ire on the woman. "I do not beat children, and if I hear of you telling your staff I have ordered them to receive a beating, I will make sure you lose your position. Do you understand?"

"Yes. Yes, I understand," the woman said, her shoulders hunched now and an expression of fear dancing across her features. "But this is the way it has always been done."

"Pardon?" Jarlath's tone was icy.

"The...the...the other two kitchens work in the same man-manner."

"You're kiddin' me," Ellard said.

Jarlath took a moment to tighten the leash on his temper. Gertrude wasn't much more than a child, and he'd wager she did her best to please. She hadn't displayed an attitude—not like Cristop.

"Things will change," he said.

"The queen is happy with the way we run things."

"I am not happy and will discuss changes with the queen," Jarlath said. "I will be back to question the staff, so don't think you can ignore my order. Let's go," he said to Ellard.

On the way to their quarters, Jarlath told Ellard what had happened in the square and the resulting riot. "If it wasn't for Keira thrusting protection spells at us, I might have joined the people saluting the crow."

"I owe her a debt," Ellard said in patent unhappiness. "Did you know she would be there? Did you arrange the meeting?"

"No, it was a happy circumstance. Ellard, the kingdom has problems, and I didn't have a clue. What sort of heir apparent doesn't know what is happening in their kingdom? We need to make clandestine visits to public places and gauge the mood of the people."

Ellard grunted—the kind that said way more than displeasure. "I can see you're determined, and I won't dissuade you, but we have to act smart about this. I have a contact on Gramite. I'll get in touch with him and ask him if the attack came from the Cawdor."

"Good idea."

Ellard's com buzzed and he answered it, listening for a time. "Prince Jarlath is with me. We are in the castle and heading to our quarters." He paused. "Yes, sir."

"Your father?"

"Yes, you are in lock down and we are ordered not to leave the castle for the foreseeable future."

"I am going to visit Keira in the morn," Jarlath said.

Ellard scowled. "If we're under attack, it's important to keep you and the rest of the royal family safe. Lynx will need to come home."

"I'm not sheltering behind my rank," Jarlath snapped, suddenly incensed and determined to stand his ground. "I intend to visit Keira. She knows more about those who live in the city than us, and she will tell me what I wish to know without hiding unsavory truths." Cristop would also help in this area—the slavery for one.

"This is a bad plan. Grata, Jarlath. I thought I had the easiest job, looking after you rather than Lynx."

Jarlath barred his teeth in a wolfish grin. "Think again."

CHAPTER SIX

"The castle requires new security measures." Jarlath strode down a dusty passage, clearing cobwebs at face level. Prior to perusing the castle floor plans, he hadn't known this passage existed. "If we can get out without anyone seeing us, others can enter."

"Aye," Ellard said, his demeanor grim as he glanced back at their footprints delineated on the dirty floor. "We require modernization. An alarm system. Maybe guards with dragoncubs to sniff out danger. The council must rescind the order to expel skilled wizards. The symbiotic relationship must be renewed to combat the House of Cawdor."

"Lynx suggested improvements to your father."

"Aye. Hard not to recall the fallout."

Jarlath had stayed out of the argument, thought his brother's stand ludicrous. Guilt and shame stung at the memory. His arrogance. Next time he saw his brother, he'd make a point of apologizing. Lynx would snigger, ask him if he'd hit his head. Inquire who'd yanked the stick from his arse, and he'd deserve each insult.

Jarlath padded at Ellard's side through the scantily lit gardens and exited the castle grounds not far from the stable. No hiding from reality. He was now awake to the problems. It was the solutions that eluded him.

"There's a guard at the stable. We can't take the cambeests."

"Father," Ellard said with a frown.

"A flymo." Jarlath scowled, his mind shuffling through alternatives. "We can hire one. No one will think anything of a nondescript vehicle zipping overhead."

"Let's go."

They backtracked and headed into the city. Despite the early hour, stalls were doing a brisk trade in fruit and vegetables. Ellard muscled through the crowd, parting them like the Lapsang Moon sea and leaving their path clear.

Jarlath's skin sizzled from the inquisitive glances, although Ellard received most of the attention. They recognized him but not their prince.

"We're not blending." Jarlath perused the bags of fruit on the nearest stall. Lychee-apps. The juicy white-fleshed fruits with the sweet nectar flavor rated among his favorites. "How much for one bag?"

"Four credits." The stallholder named a reasonable price.

"Two credits," Ellard barked.

The wrinkled, gap-toothed man pursed his lips and considered. "Three."

"Done," Ellard said and produced coins from his pocket.

Jarlath wandered to the next stall but didn't stop since the scent of cinnamonbark lured him onward. "How much for one dozen cinnamonbark rolls?"

"Two credits."

Ellard handed over coins without bargaining this time.

With their purchases in hand, they ambled down a muddy path, dodging debris, and a man zoned out on some type of drug until they reached the outskirts of the retail area.

"From memory, there is a flymo dealer in the lane to the left," Ellard said.

"I've never shopped in the market before," Jarlath said. "The last days have made me realize how insulated I am at the castle. I have no idea how the city functions or if our people are happy. That's not right." He halted at an out-of-the-way stall with displays of hair bows and scarves, his mind going to Keira. His gaze lit on a silky scarf that shimmered with blue and green. Perfect match for the hat he'd purchased the previous eve. "How much for this one?"

"Very good quality," the young alien said with a crafty smile. Her striped brown-and-white hair marked her as Tigrus. "Your lady like. How much you pay?"

Jarlath glanced at Ellard, hoping for a clue, and his friend didn't disappoint, lifting his fingers in a surreptitious signal. "Five credits," he said, knocking one off the amount Ellard had signaled.

"Seven," the Tigrus woman countered.

His gaze narrowed, and his pulse raced while he made a decision. Yes or no? Who knew shopping held entertainment value. His gaze drifted across the scarves and bows, and he came to a decision. "I'll pay seven if you throw in a matching hair bow."

"Done," she said with a grin.

Jarlath handed over coins. "Can you wrap it for me?"

"I have a decorative box out the back. Won't be a mo."

"Presents aren't a good idea," Ellard said. "You're due to announce your betrothal. Don't complicate your life."

"Don't you think I've told myself that?" Jarlath challenged his friend's gaze. "It's too late. I want her, and if she's agreeable, I'll spend time with her."

"What if she uses your attraction to leverage a position?"

A wave of fury hurled through him at the insult to Keira. His feline echoed his anger with a ferocious roar, and he shoved him back with difficulty, forcing himself to speak with maturity. "Keira isn't like that. She has integrity. Once you get to know her you'll see it too."

"Your mind is made up."

"All my life I've done the right thing." Feelings spewed from him in a gush. "I've listened to my parents, carried out their wishes. I've taken advice from your father, followed his security and weapon instructions. Just once, I'd like to do something for me. I'm not marrying the woman. All I'm doing is enjoying her company."

Ellard shrugged and tucked his pendant beneath his tunic. "Make her your mistress. That would cushion the disadvantages of a marriage of convenience. You do still intend to marry as your parents desire?"

"Of course." He yanked at his collar and unfastened the top button to relieve the surge of heat to his upper torso. He scratched the back of his neck. "It's tradition."

The woman returned with a red box and packed the scarf and ribbon.

"Thank you," Jarlath said.

She winked in return. "Thank you for your custom. Please visit again."

Even hiring the flymo was fun, and Jarlath realized the dull edge of boredom and dissatisfaction from his pre-Keira days had faded.

"Remember, a late return will accrue extra charges," the male dealer said, his head jerking in the direction of the round gray flymo.

"Yes, sir," Jarlath said, his tone gruff, not that anyone they'd spoken with had glanced at him twice. "We will return your vehicle as arranged."

A thunderous explosion, high in the sky, stopped the fussy

dealer's response. Trading in the lane ceased as everyone stared skyward.

"All hail the leader," the flymo dealer shouted.

Around them, other voices shouted the same sentiment.

"All hail the leader." Jarlath kicked Ellard, glaring at his friend's slow reaction as he lifted his right hand in salute.

"All hail the leader." Ellard added his voice to the chant.

A bright yellow shape formed in the sky. Within the yellow, a black dot grew, seeming to grow bigger as the chanting increased in sound and velocity. The black split into three, one large circle and two others. The black circles shaped and reshaped, until the forms of three crows glowed in the sky. The head of the largest cocked, it let out a victorious caw-caw then flew northward. As the giant wings flapped, the bright yellow light emphasizing the three birds dissipated until nothing remained.

The chanting ceased the instant the crows blinked from sight.

"Let's go," Jarlath whispered.

Ellard piloted, guiding the flymo over the market and the city trade center.

"Why did you chant with the others?" he asked once they were clear of the city.

"Because we would've stood out if we hadn't," Jarlath said with a touch of impatience. "Everyone else saluted the crows. Better to blend and collect information rather than stand out as unusual."

"True that. But what does it mean?"

"I think it's a declaration of war—a form of gloating to let us know the House of Cawdor can strike whenever they feel the urge."

"And the chanting?" Ellard asked.

"It's the Cawdor way of giving us the finger."

Ellard shot him a frown. "That was my thinking too, but I have no idea how we should fight the Cawdor when they're launching their attack from afar."

"Any idea where Lynx and Shiloh are at present? I haven't heard from Lynx for ages."

Ellard landed the flymo outside Keira's farmhouse and shot Jarlath a scowl. "Your brother is a troublemaker who leads my younger brother straight into conflict with Father. Because of him, our father refuses to acknowledge Shiloh."

"Both Lynx and Shiloh would be assets. They have experience and knowledge of the city, and if we're lucky, they might have info on the House of Cawdor. We should contact them."

Ellard gave an irritable sigh. "You're right. Best to put petty differences aside and fight the foe together."

Keira and Cristop came to greet them, Cristop continuing on to the storage shed.

"There was another incident this morning," Jarlath said before they could speak. "Did you see anything, hear anything?"

Keira paled and Jarlath had her wrapped in an embrace before the idea cemented, before commonsense kick-started his brain, before Ellard let loose his growl of displeasure. She quivered, resting against his chest for a sec before struggling for release.

Her gaze sliced and diced, concern furrowing her brow. "What happened? Is it the House of Cawdor? Or someone else trying to cast blame?"

"She's right," Ellard said. "We assumed it was the House of Cawdor with a declaration of might, but it could be a third party wanting to stir trouble between us and our old enemy."

"Let's com Lynx and Shiloh. Ask if they've heard any rumors," Jarlath said.

"I'll do that now." Ellard pulled out his communicator and stepped behind the flymo, giving them the illusion of privacy. "I'll make the other call too."

"Did you have trouble getting home last night?" Jarlath asked, keeping part of his attention on his friend. Ellard paced back and forth. He plugged in another number, waited, then grinned, his manner animated as he spoke. "I worried about you."

"No one paid us any mind. Everyone wanted the safety of their homes."

Jarlath studied the dark rings beneath her eyes, which attested to a poor night of sleep. His gaze dropped to her lips, and the temptation to kiss her left him reeling and his feline snarling in demand. He fought briefly and gave up the struggle. This time, when he gathered her in his arms, he placed a finger under her chin to lift her head.

She gasped, her lips parting, her warm breath feathering across his mouth and detonating explosions of hunger. Desire. He wanted, needed her and...and now wasn't the time. Nonetheless, he swooped, covering her lips with his. At the first gossamer contact, his feline started to purr. Lazy rumbles of contentment echoed through Jarlath's mind while he explored the honeyed taste of her mouth.

Her sigh thrilled him, their breaths mingling before he took the exchange deeper. Their tongues stroked together, and sensations—heat and yearning, pleasure and pure desire—tore straight to his shaft.

Keira must have felt him harden against her belly, and he waited for her objection. To his relief, she looped her hands around his neck and pressed nearer.

"Jarlath!" Ellard's sharp tone held anger.

"Get a sex room," Cristop said. "I'm impressionable. Need to poke out eyes." He juggled the box he carried to rub his face then squinted at them. "Nope, not workin'. Hey, you still owe me a coin."

Jarlath grinned and relaxed his hold on Keira. When they lost contact, his feline growled, and Jarlath snared her hand, twining their fingers together. The contact soothed both him and his feline. "Did you get hold of Lynx?"

Ellard frowned. "No. I tried both Shiloh and Lynx. Their

com units aren't acknowledging signals. I managed to contact Mareeka. She's doing okay. Hopefully, I can see her tonight. And my contact said Xavier is dead. He confirmed Razvan is in charge now. Couldn't tell me much else."

Jarlath's gut jittered at both pieces of news. He'd been counting on Lynx's aid. "Must be out of range."

"Maybe, but I don't like it. I've always managed to contact Shiloh," Ellard said. "At least we know about the Cawdor now and can plan accordingly."

"Yes," Jarlath said, not that he wanted to discuss them right now.

Keira tugged Jarlath's hand. "Come inside. I'll make tay and we'll eat. Your eye is looking much better."

"Perks of being a shifter. We shopped in the market," Jarlath said. "Cristop, can you grab the packages in the flymo please? Take the rolls and fruit to the kitchen and bring me the red box. I'll give you your second coin then."

Cristop darted away. Jarlath draped his arm around Keira's shoulders and directed her inside with a sense of contentment, despite the gravity of the circumstances. Spending time with Keira made him happy. A rare event in a life where he went through the motions.

His own fault, but not too late to change.

Nerves stomped and leaped in Keira's belly until nausea swelled like a Caspan sea wave. Jarlath grasped her hand again and her anxiety settled. She didn't know why she'd suggested this threat could be a third party when she knew her half-brother was behind the phenomenon. Some sort of misplaced loyalty to her house.

One thing was for sure. She wouldn't be lighting any fires in the foreseeable future, no matter how cold or stormy the weather.

After settling her guests in the sitting room, she withdrew to organize refreshments. The crow inside her squawked a protest, wings beating against her skin so vigorously she wondered if her skin might burst.

She rubbed her breastbone in a soothing motion but her heart ventricles kept pumping extra fast, apprehension growing with each step away from Jarlath. Pain—no, not quite pain—it was more discomfort that forced her to hunch. She massaged her chest again and wavered on her feet, each of her senses drawn inward in distress. Her heart and soul fastened on one thing—Jarlath. Her mind—the only sane part of her body—objected strongly, yet her crow ignored her orders and let out a soft *caw-caw*.

Keira kept her fingers pressed against her heart ventricles, the weight grounding her, soothing the nip of pain flaying her senses.

"What is it? What's wrong?" Hortese shunted a stool in her direction. "Sit before your legs buckle."

Keira sank down and fought to keep her breathing calm and even.

Cristop burst through the outer door.

"Don't tromp mud on my floor," Hilda screeched in a booming voice that belied her small stature.

Cristop froze one step into the kitchen. With his arms full of parcels, he couldn't remove his boots.

"Cease your hovering," Keira said to Hortese. "Help Cristop with the packages before he drops something."

"Cinnamonbark rolls," Hilda said with approval, and her hooked nose twitched. "I can smell them."

"Could you make a large pot of tay please? We have guests." Keira rubbed her chest again and the discomfort eased.

"Two strapping men." Hilda nodded, the enthusiasm of the action not shifting her close-cropped black hair. Her ruddy complexion shone as she rubbed her hands together. "I'll make extra, never you fear. Go and act the hostess. Hortese and I will bring the tay and food as soon as it's ready. Cristop, boots off. Otherwise you stay outside."

Keira smiled as the youth backed from the kitchen and sat on the steps to unlace his boots without complaint. She'd do almost anything for a cinnamonbark roll too—most days that was. Today, with the way her stomach was swooping and diving, she doubted she'd manage to keep a bite down.

Jarlath and Ellard conversed in low voices and broke off when she entered.

"Have I interrupted?"

"No, of course not." Jarlath stood in a fluid motion and wrapped his arm around her waist, pulling her to his side. Immediately her nausea faded and her crow *caw-cawed* in contentment.

Stupid creature. They ignored each other for the most part, the crow letting her get on with business, since it appeared she wasn't strong enough to make a physical appearance. Now the wretched creature chose to exert a say?

"You brought cinnamonbark rolls." Keira sighed and barely resisted rolling her eyes. So much to discuss and that was her topic of choice.

"I did." Jarlath's deep voice vibrated through her body.

Caw-caw-caw.

Her crow was doing the birdy version of a purr.

"What's that noise?" Ellard's head cocked, his big ears angled to better listen.

Jarlath chuckled, and the faint tensing of his hand at her waist told her he knew.

"It's not funny," she snapped.

Caw-caw-caw.

Ellard's alert gaze narrowed to focus on her. "You're making that sound. It's almost as if you're two-natured, but you're not a cat. You don't smell right."

"I think she smells wonderful."

Ellard persisted. "Gossip says you're from Gramite. That true?"

Keira drew in a sharp breath, and Jarlath drew her protectively against his chest. He knew she was from Gramite.

"Tell me. Where are you from?" The distrust in Ellard's face informed her of his opinion.

"Leave her alone," Jarlath said, his tone an order. "Keira comes from Gramite. You know that because you told me, so don't pretend this is new. She is of the Greenmont tribe."

"You're from the House of Cawdor. The enemy." Ellard drew his blaster and pointed it at her. "Get away from the prince."

Keira attempted to pull free. Jarlath held tight, and she could feel outrage vibrating through his body. She heard the snarl of displeasure that came from his feline and instantly, her crow began her caw-caw-caw, this time a shrill call of alarm.

"Shush," Jarlath said. "Ellard will realize how stupidly he's behaving any sec now."

"She's the enemy," Ellard snapped, the fingers of his free hand busy rubbing his onyx cat. "She's in league with the people responsible for this attack on our people. She suggested someone else is attacking our planet. She's trying to divert us, making us doubt what we see."

Terror that Jarlath would believe him swept through Keira. She groaned as her insides went into revolt, twisting and turning, and not even the hard press of her hand against her belly pushed the pain back. Sharp stabs like those of a knife pricked her skin from the inside, staccato stabs, painful, tear-wrenching stabs.

"Shush. Easy there, sweetheart. When did you last visit Gramite, Keira?" Jarlath asked.

Sweetheart. The pinpricks faded, and she slumped against him. His scent filled each breath, and her crow began its contented sighing again.

"Keira?"

"My mother arranged my marriage with Marcus during a time of peace between our planets. War broke out not long after, and I've never returned. My mother said it would be best not to attempt a visit. This is my home. Viros is my home."

"Why would your mother tell you that? What sort of a parent is she? And what about your father?" Ellard half-lowered his weapon but suspicion still colored his tone.

"My father is dead," Keira said and hoped he couldn't see her unease. "Viros is my home."

Her mother had urged Keira not to visit to keep her from Razvan's clutches. Because her half-brother made no secret of his fascination with her, and he scared her silly with his charming yet dictatorial personality. Xavier, their father, saw nothing wrong with his devious son taking what he wanted, and she'd been young and terrified. Truth told, Razvan still held the power to petrify her, and they were a planet apart. He scared her way more than Ellard.

"Nothing to say?" Ellard demanded.

"Put your weapon down," Hortese snapped. "Keira is no spy. If you don't hurry, you'll wear this tay and the cinnamonbark rolls over your thick head."

"And that would irritate me since I adore cinnamonbark rolls," Jarlath said. "We're guests in Keira's home."

"But she is from the House of Cawdor." Ellard wasn't giving up easily.

"I'm a half-breed," Keira said. "My father came from House of Cawdor, but I didn't have much to do with him. My mother was his mistress, a nobody in the eyes of the clan. I can't shift."

Despite their interested audience, Jarlath kissed her on the cheek. "Shifting isn't important. It doesn't make you a lesser person."

"Jarlath." Ellard's tone held warning, something Keira didn't understand and couldn't decipher.

"Are we gonna jab all day or are we gonna eat cinnamonbark rolls?" Cristop demanded.

"We're gonna eat," Jarlath said. "Just as soon as Ellard puts his weapon away."

Ellard shoved his blaster into his holster with a grumpy snarl. "I hope you know what you're doing."

"I think we have more important things to worry about, and Keira might be able to help," Jarlath said.

"Everyone want tay?" Hortese asked in a bright voice.

Keira forced a smile, despite the tension riding her gut. "Please."

"Relax, sweetheart," Jarlath said. "You look pale. Did you not sleep?" He tugged her to a gel-seat built for two and seated her before parking himself beside her. He brushed his fingers—soft as a feather touch—across her cheek, and unaccountably, she wanted to cry when nothing, not even Marcus's stepchildren, had raised a tear with their shenanigans.

"It was difficult to sleep after the scene in the market."

Hortese gave a nod of approval as she placed two cups of tay and two cinnamonbark rolls on a small float-table. She pushed a button and the table floated over to them, a sturdy set of legs folding down from underneath to keep it in place.

Jarlath handed her one of the cups, and grateful, she swallowed some of the fragrant liquid. After a second mouthful of tay, she set her cup on the float-table and reached for a roll.

"These are delicious," Jarlath said.

Keira had to agree. "What is the king going to do?"

"I haven't spoken to him yet," Jarlath said. "Ellard and I wanted to see how the people are faring. We left the castle in a clandestine manner."

"You shouldn't be telling her this stuff," Ellard snapped. "You trust her, but I haven't decided yet."

"You sound like your father," Jarlath said. "Eat another cinnamonbark roll. That will take your mind off things."

"You sound like Lynx," Ellard snapped, but to Keira's surprise, he shut up and reached for another roll.

"Good," Jarlath purred. "Now where were we with a plan? Is there anything you can tell us that might help?"

Panic beat at Keira and her crow gave an unhappy caw-caw. "I—"

A com-unit buzzed, and Ellard reached for his pocket.

"Yes," Ellard said.

Keira saw Jarlath tense.

"Stash the prince in his quarters and lock him in so he can't leave without your knowledge," a harsh voice said. "We have a meeting in the war room at two sharp. I expect you there."

Jarlath heard the voice at the other end of the communication as well as she did. Ordinarily, this would have shocked her, but this was another jolt of many, and the surprise subsided speedily. She could hear the speaker, as if she were standing in the same city room.

"Yes, sir," Ellard said, his voice so crisp it was a verbal salute. He disconnected and glanced at Jarlath.

"I'm staying here," Jarlath said. "I refuse to get locked away in my suite like a naughty cub. I'm an adult, and it's about time your father and mine started to realize the fact. Hell, they expect me to choose a wife. They're fine with that grown-up activity."

"It's not safe here," Ellard said.

"It's not safe in my castle suite either," Jarlath countered. "Please, just go to the meeting. If we leave the farm, I'll wear my disguise. I promise."

Horror tore through Keira. What if her half-brother appeared again? She didn't want Jarlath to draw his attention. If Razvan discovered Jarlath's identity, his position within the castle, they'd all be in worse danger.

"Maybe it would be safer for you if you returned to the castle with Ellard," she said.

"No. Ellard, I'll see you on your way. If anyone asks, tell them I'm cowering in my room."

"If something happens to you, I—"

"After you've saved my butt, I'll make sure everyone knows it was my fault and I overruled you."

Ellard appeared torn. "This is a bad idea."

"Come," Jarlath said and grabbed Ellard's arm.

The two men left the room, words of heated discussion trailing in their wake. If she tried hard, Keira could pluck the odd word from their conversation.

The weird pinpricks started again, and she lifted her hand to her chest in an attempt to ease the pressure. Her silent crow had come to life and was busy making up for the cycles of peace.

Jarlath strode into the sitting room and sent her a smile—a warm and private one that sent her crow into caws of approval and pleasure. Keira froze at the odd occurrence. Plain weird.

Yes, she was attracted to Jarlath. Who wouldn't be? The man was easy on the eye, bore a charming manner and seemed to like her in return.

But Jarlath drew her crow too, because the instant he settled beside her, the pinpricks of trepidation subsided. Her heart ventricles reduced their speed to normal, and the anxiety that he might leave with Ellard faded. Keira didn't know what this meant, and now, with Razvan creating chaos in their world, it wasn't a good time to explore these odd yearnings for the prince.

Her gaze went to his face, dropped to his mouth, and she fell into daydreams of how those lips would feel exploring her body. She already knew they were soft.

"Keira." His low voice broke her reverie.

"What?"

"Don't look at me like that, not if you want me to keep my hands to myself."

Heat collected in her cheeks, and her crow grew alert, pulsing with eagerness against her breasts. She shuddered, a visible tremor rattling her cup of tay.

"You two need to get a sex room," Cristop said. "You can't do that...that stuff in front of me. It's not right. I'm a child."

"When it suits you," Hortese said, her voice as dry as a Tamborian desert. "Come, I have some chores for you, young man. I believe Hilda is baking cookies. If you do the chores without complaint, I'm sure Hilda will give you some, warm from the heat unit. Wait for me in the kitchen."

"Your coin," Jarlath said.

Cristop snatched it out of the air and clomped out, leaving them alone with Hortese.

"The boy is right," she said. "Why don't the two of you go and pick berries? You should be safe enough. The two of you can bill and coo to your hearts' content then."

"I do not bill," Keira said. "Or coo."

"Huh." Hortese cleared the float table, deactivated it, and stacked the remains of their refreshments on her tray before bustling out to the kitchen.

"I do not bill or coo," Keira repeated.

"No." Jarlath grinned and slid closer. "I want to kiss you, take my time without worrying about interruptions. When we retire tonight, you are going to take me to your bed. I want you, Keira. Bad. I crave a taste of your sweet body."

His words tempted and tantalized as they whispered across the shell of her ear. The wings within her chest flapped in crazy ecstasy. It felt as if talons dug into her flesh at the same time. Stab, stab, stab.

She groaned, because there was a type of pleasure in the pain, and Jarlath caught the sound with his mouth. His tongue swirled over her lips then explored the soft interior of her mouth. This wasn't a tentative, polite kiss. This wasn't a getting-to-know-you kiss. This was a statement of intent.

Breathless, she clung, giving back as good as she received. Her fingers speared through his hair and a tiny moan of complaint escaped when he lifted his head.

His eyes glowed with an inner light and a grin wreathed his lips.

"Hold that thought while we go and pick berries."

"There is a waterhole where I go swimming when the day is hot. We could spend part of our day there."

"Great, let's go." He reached for her hand and wove their fingers together. Her inner crow did a little shimmy while the human part of her dampened the enthusiasm with caution. Her crow squawked, and Keira offered Jarlath a feeble smile. His fingers tightened, tugged, guided, and she offered no resistance. Point to the crow.

In the kitchen, they collected berry containers, and Hilda thrust a heavy picnic basket at them, her wrinkled face wreathed in a sly matchmaking grin. Regit gnomes were known romantics, and Hilda was in full flight.

"Don't hurry," Hortese said with a sly wink at Jarlath. "I have everything under control here."

Jarlath led her outside, their hands clasped again.

Her breath caught at the close contact, her heart ventricles gave a skip, and pleasure frisked her body. She couldn't remember Marcus ever touching her like this. It was an innocent contact, yet held the potential to become so much more. It was inherent with promise, and her blood sang. Her crow let out a melodic caw-caw, and she shot a glance at Jarlath.

Sure, he'd heard the sound, she expected a frown or at least distaste. The House of the Cat and the House of Cawdor had fought their war for centuries with intermittent peace. Even though she no longer had contact with her people, Jarlath might see her as the enemy.

But why would he kiss you?

"You said your father comes from the Cawdor. Is it true you can't shift or did you just tell Ellard that? The reason I ask is because I keep hearing your crow."

He might try to trick her, but she wouldn't lie to him. Not about this. "I've never shifted. My father had no use for me because of the deficit. Most Cawdor youngsters shift for the first time at around ten cycles. The people consider those who can't transform abnormal. They are cast out and left to die." Her voice remained neutral to hide the sting she'd felt—still felt—at the rejection from this side of her family. Although in hindsight, the dismissal had made her stronger and saved her from Cawdor politics.

"I'm sorry. The inability to shift happens on Viros too, but we don't turn our people away. They still have the protection of the House, but I believe they're treated badly by those who come into contact with them."

"Then they are outcasts too."

"Yes. Will we take the cart?"

"No, the waterhole and the berry patches I have in mind are farther away. We'll need to take the flymo."

"Lead the way," Jarlath said.

"Do you want to pilot?"

"Yes, please." He pulled a face. "Ellard never lets me fly."

Amusement burst from her in a chuckle. "You're the prince. Tell him you want a turn."

"He says he's following his father's orders. His father is security chief, so I've never argued. I believe he's finding me disobedient at present and unpredictable."

"Because of me?"

"Partly, but I've been thinking about my younger brother a lot and come to the conclusion he might have known what he was talking about all these cycles."

"Prince Lynx," she said as Jarlath piloted the flymo into the air.

"Just plain Lynx," Jarlath said. "He doesn't like the title."

"Where is he now?"

"I've no idea. I've tried to contact him. Ellard's younger brother is Lynx's best friend and security guard. Our two families have a close association. Lynx and Shiloh are in partnership and run a successful freight haulage business."

"What do your parents think of that?"

"They've practically disowned him. We don't speak much of Lynx. Shiloh's parents also disapprove."

"But you speak with your brother?"

"I thought Lynx was crazy to give up his life of privilege for one of hard work and uncertainty." Jarlath scowled as if the memory pained him, and she had to halt her urge to offer comfort. "He told me life within the castle was nothing but a pretty cage. We argued and he left."

"You've changed your mind."

"He was right. I might have mod technology at my disposal that ordinary citizens don't, all the currency I could want and position, but my life is a cage. My parents tell me what to do, and I follow their orders. No one will think to check my suite to make sure I'm there because I've followed every instruction or duty imposed on me. My parents wish to reward this loyalty by making me king, but only if I do what they say and pick a wife to continue the succession."

A wife? The idea shouldn't have hurt as much as it did. She forced a smile and prayed her tone neared teasing. "Instead, you're gallivanting with me, picking berries and going swimming."

"And ravishing an attractive woman," he said. "Don't forget that part."

"I thought you were going to wait until everyone retired to their beds."

"Lynx would say that was boring and predictable. I happen to agree. We'll do both."

Her brows rose. "Is that right?"

"Yes." He winked at her.

"But it's not proper."

"Proper is overrated."

"See the weird-shaped hills over to our right? The berry patch is in that direction."

A short time later, Jarlath settled the flymo in a flat forest clearing.

"It's a beautiful spot," he said.

"Marcus purchased this land cycles ago because no one wanted it, but the forest provides for us. We pick fungi and dry it to sell in the market, berries during the warm season as well as a variety of herbs."

A bright red bird fluttered from branch to branch above their heads and chattered in a discordant tone as if telling them off for interrupting the peace.

"We'd better pick the berries first," Jarlath said. "Otherwise I might be tempted to forget about pies and focus on you instead."

She smiled again, this one not as ragged around the edges. "You say that like it's a bad thing."

"Berries," he said. "We don't want Hortese to laser her pink eyes at us in temper."

They picked berries and chatted about commonplace things. Farming. Crops. Technology. Clothes. Music. Keira had never enjoyed berry picking so much.

"You didn't tell me what happened after it became known you couldn't shift."

"The other children teased me, and it became impossible to attend the education center. Instead, my mother taught me to run a house and schooled me in herbs and plants. I stayed close to our home, and whenever my father arrived to spend time with my mother, I remained out of sight."

"That can't have been easy."

"It was a lonely existence, but my marriage to Marcus saved me."

Jarlath frowned when she mentioned her husband.

"Even though his son and daughter disapproved and refused to accept me, Marcus treated me like an equal. He was a good man, and I owe him much."

"Why did he seek a wife off-planet?"

"I've no idea." Her crow cawed, liar, liar, and Keira stared at the bushes, the ripe berries, and prayed Jarlath didn't hear her contrary bird. Marcus had been dying and he'd needed her help and knowledge of herbs to counter the pain. He'd wanted this kept quiet and she still held his secret. Her bird finally subsided, the slice of quiet mocking rather than peaceful.

"You never asked him?"

"I was grateful to leave Gramite and grasped the opportunity, even though I knew I wouldn't see my mother again."

"I lost the ability to shift," Jarlath said without warning. "Well, until recently. For some reason, my feline is alert again."

"What?" Shock made her hand jerk, and a berry bounced off her boot before rolling out of sight beneath a bush.

"It's true. We've managed to keep it quiet, but many of our people have lost the ability to shift to feline."

"But I haven't heard rumors in the market. Not a whisper."

"No, most people are ashamed of the lack and don't speak about the problem."

"Razvan will find out. I'm sure he has spies on this planet."

"I'm sure he does, just as we have spies on Gramite."

Why had he told her this? Because he trusts you. "You don't know me well."

"I'm a good judge of character. People seek to use my position. You haven't."

"We haven't known each other long. I haven't had a chance."

His grin was a burst of white teeth, a crinkling of sexy green eyes. "I plan to use you and use you well. I'm thinking we'll both enjoy the mutual exploitation."

"I've heard Prince Lynx is a terrible flirt and has a reputation with the ladies. I think you're made in a similar vein."

"Only with you." He set his container of berries down and stalked her. His gaze connected with hers and held as he moved toward her with sinuous grace. He cupped her face, his fingers gentle while pure naughtiness curved his lips. "I haven't met anyone else who entices me to exert my charm."

"I'm a widow, and my birth makes me the enemy. You shouldn't be with me." One last attempt to stop this folly.

His chin lifted, his expression sliding into lines of arrogance. "I like you. I have from our first meeting. You don't treat me like a prince."

"How do I treat you?"

"Like a man. We've picked enough berries. Let's go swimming."

Keira glanced down at her container. The berries came up to the three-quarter mark and Jarlath had picked about the same amount. "Hortese will grumble."

"Let her," Jarlath said. "She's lucky we picked any berries."

Keira snapped covers over both containers and placed them in the flymo. "Bring the basket. The swimming hole isn't far."

"I can hear the bubble of water," Jarlath said. "Is it cold?"

"Refreshing," Keira countered with a glance back at Jarlath. With his dark hair loose, stubble shading his jaw and his common clothes, he could have passed for a laborer. "Do you shave?"

His mouth tipped up and she noticed a cute indentation to the right side of his lips. "I use stop-beard. Need another application."

"I like the stubble. It looks sexy on you."

Keira led the way into another clearing, bordered by the forest and more berry bushes. A stream cut through, making the fourth boundary. The solar star shone, making the water glisten.

"It's beautiful. Do you come here often?"

"Hortese and I visit on occasion, but the farm work keeps us busy."

"You work too hard."

"I like activity."

"I understand. It's better to keep the mind and the body active. Last one in is a rotten fodo egg." Jarlath unfastened the toggles of his black tunic and tossed it aside to reveal a tanned and muscular chest.

This man might complain about sitting in a cage, but he didn't laze around eating choc-sweets either. Keira's fingers ceased unfastening her tunic and she gaped, her mouth going dry. Marcus hadn't looked like this—all muscles and fluid motion. Like Marcus, Jarlath bore a tattoo of a black cat, etched into his biceps, signifying he was of the feline species. Her fingers itched to touch every part of him, to explore his sexy form.

Jarlath sat on a rock to tug off his boots. His gaze met hers and he paused. "What?"

"You are beautiful."

"Men aren't beautiful."

"Let me rephrase. Your body is very attractive."

"You haven't seen all of me yet." Humor glinted in him as he stood and stripped trews down his muscular legs. When he straightened again, he was naked and sporting a full-out smirk plus an erection.

For her.

While Keira gaped, he coughed, and her attention darted to his face.

His nose lifted and he sniffed. "What is that I smell? Ah, yes. A fodo egg." He sauntered to the water's edge and dove under the water, the volley of splashes rousing Keira from her stupor.

Feeling unaccountably shy, she disrobed and stepped into the swimming hole. She gasped at the chilly water lapping around her toes.

"It's not bad once you're in." Jarlath made no secret of his interest, and her wretched crow started its insistent caw-caw again.

"Come here, sweetheart. I'll warm you."

"This isn't a good idea." While Jarlath made no secret of his desire to have her, she worried about consequences. The realist in her knew they had no future together. How could there be when he was heir to the throne?

"I'm not going to force you. If you don't want this, I'll walk away. We haven't known each other long, but every time we're together, my feline goes crazy. It feels as if my cat is going to burst from my skin."

"You too," she blurted. "I have never felt this before, but since I met you, my crow has woken and caws in temper. She spears her talons into my flesh. It's disconcerting."

"Maybe it's a sign. Sweetheart, admit it. You want me as much as I want you. Your kisses give away your feelings."

She sighed. She did want him. Maybe she should take what she wanted and worry about consequences later. "Yes, you're right."

"Come to me then."

He was making her feel claimed rather than coerced. Without further thought, she waded into the water, her attention fixed on him.

A tiny smile played around his lips, making him seem more normal rather than the untouchable prince.

"I like it when you smile. When I first met you, I didn't think you knew how."

"Oh, I knew." He drew her against his chest. "Until I met you, there wasn't much to smile about."

His mouth covering hers stopped her reply, but pleasure at his words soothed the last of her concerns. They couldn't have a future, and yet she wanted to enjoy this stolen time with Jarlath.

"I love the color of your skin," he said against her lips. "So pretty."

"Inherited from my mother," she said.

"You miss her."

"Yes." Even though she'd never understood her mother's love and loyalty to Xavier Cronan. The man had creeped her out as a child, and his son—her half-brother—even worse. "I thought you intended to seduce me?"

"I wanted you comfortable before I pounced." His hands slid

CLAIMED & SEDUCED

down her naked back to cup her bottom. "The thought of you changing your mind—"

"Won't happen. I've made up my mind."

"Good."

Mischief lurked in his green eyes, and she found herself smiling, willing to accept his pace.

"I think we've played enough," he said without warning and hauled her to the spot where they'd left their picnic basket.

Jarlath took her in his arms again and sensual tension fired to life. His hands ran up and down her arms and hips and back while he pressed a trail of kisses from her mouth to her jawline and down her neck. His teeth played across the flesh at the base of her neck, scraping back and forth.

She shuddered, pleasure at his touch like warm syrup running along her veins. Her heart ventricles pumped overtime while her crow made soft sounds that echoed through her mind and sounded surprisingly catlike.

"Let me look at you," he said and gently pushed her away. "Beautiful breasts. Slim body yet strong muscle definition too. Ah, Keira. So pretty. I have never wanted another woman as much as I want you."

"I want you too."

He spread the blanket Hortese had sent with them on the ground then swept her into his arms with a broad grin. "Let's get to the fucking."

CHAPTER SEVEN

T he blunt language was an attempt to put this situation in perspective. Keep this thing with Keira rooted in truth, because while he hated the idea of marriage, he knew he'd probably obey his parents. But try telling this to his feline. His other self strained against his skin and threatened to burst free.

Jarlath attempted to slow his racing heart, taking deep breaths while he set Keira on the blanket. His feline stretched then subsided, leaving him in full control. Instantly, blood drained downward to settle in his shaft. Oh yeah. Both he and his feline were working in concert now.

He caged Keira between his body and the blanket. His gaze shifted to her mouth, and he plundered that first, taking pleasure in the way she laced her fingers in his hair to hold him close. She writhed beneath him, communicating a hunger as deep as his own.

"Keira," he whispered when the need to breathe made him break their contact. "You have no idea how much I want this. You."

"Too much talking."

"I don't want to scare you."

"Flying stars! I'm made of stern stuff."

Before he could blink, she rolled their bodies, so she ended up on top, straddling his hips and beaming like a bright solar star at her success. "Since you're not in a hurry, I get a chance to explore."

"Have at it." He hoped he managed to restrain his urgency. He'd try because most women were interested in one thing—scoring with a royal. Keira was different and intrigue filled him at what she might do, so he waited.

She scooted back until his cock collided with her backside. "One part of you isn't patient."

"You'd do well to remember that."

Her husky laugh had his feline bursting to action again. Jarlath curled his fingers—claws—into the blanket in an attempt to remain in place.

Instead of replying, she ran her fingers over his chest and strummed his nipples. A growl squeezed past his lips and she chuckled. She set about taunting and teasing with a lick here, a pinch there and a kiss or two to change it up.

"You're killing me, sweetheart."

"No, my touch won't injure you," she cooed as she moved farther down his body.

He quivered when one hand curled around his shaft. Her fingers were cool against his hot flesh, and he arched into her grip, a moan of pure pleasure escaping. "Again," he demanded in a thick voice.

"My pleasure." Her hand went up and down, up and down, up and down until he trembled like a leaf in the wind.

"Grata," he muttered as desire prickled, as distressing as an uncatchable itch. Raw urgency suffused him, and he flipped her off and under him before she had time to blink. She grinned up at him, the delicate green highlighting her cheeks charming. Super sexy, she called to him on every level. "My turn."

He sealed his lips over hers and cupped one breast. His finger and thumb toyed with the nipple until it hardened and swelled. Her sweet taste filled his mouth while her scent enticed him. Flowers and arousal.

Sweet.

Addictive.

Mine.

His hand drifted down her flat belly. Her navel was a miniscule indent, a discovery he found fascinating. He paused to lick a lazy circle. His actions tugged a giggle from her, and he smiled against her satin skin. Moving lower, he parted her toned legs and trailed his fingers down her slit. She was hot and wet when his fingers slid over her smooth flesh.

"Do that again," she said, her voice thick with need.

He repeated the action, then lifted a digit to his mouth to taste. "You taste so sweet."

Patience at an end, he wedged her legs farther apart with his thigh and positioned his cock at her entrance. He kept his gaze on hers as he pushed inside her feminine heat.

Keira's eyes fluttered closed and she rocked her lower body, forcing him deeper. She sucked in a hasty breath and released it in a sexy moan.

Jarlath withdrew a fraction and surged back into her until he was balls deep. His cock throbbed while he paused to luxuriate in her heat.

"Move," she ordered. "Please. No teasing. I need...I want...please."

"Keira." Her name was a loud purr, full of everything he dare not put into words. Instead, he withdrew and set up a fast rhythm of in and out. Hard friction of their bodies. Soft sighs. Hers. Loud grunts. Him.

Her fingers curled around his upper arms, her nails gouging

his flesh. The pinprick of pain shunted through his body and sweetened the pleasure bubbling in his balls. He groaned, and helpless to hold back, he surged into her channel again and again. His teeth pierced the skin at her neck, and he tasted her coppery blood as he licked the wound. Pleasure, so hot he didn't think he'd survive, whooshed through him and up his cock. He thrust again and his seed burst from him in hard pulses, taking everything with it, his thoughts, his heart and soul. His last thought as he exploded into Keira was it had never been like this before.

Never.

It took long mins to come back to himself. Keira's hands pushed against his shoulders.

"Heavy," she muttered. "Move."

"Grata! Sorry, sweetheart." He pulled free and flopped over onto his back, breathless and sated from the experience.

"Is that it?"

Jarlath turned his head to look at her. Her beautiful face was flushed green and the golden flecks in her eyes seemed brighter than ever. "What?"

"When is it my turn for pleasure?"

"What?"

She hit his shoulder, and his brain belatedly interpreted the signs in the correct manner. Not pleasure or happiness but temper. He frowned and sat up.

"I thought you'd be different. Never mind. I'll do it myself."

Jarlath gaped as her hand slid down her body to delve between her legs. For a moment, disbelief kept him frozen.

"No!" The word burst from him. "I'm sorry. Please let me." He moved over her and jerked her hand from her sex. "Let me. I'm not usually this selfish. Please let me prove it to you."

They fought a swift duel by gaze, and finally, she nodded.

This time he noticed the things he'd failed to observe. In arousal her pink nipples took on a tinge of green, as did her lips, currently pursed in a firm, flat line. He kissed her mouth until the frown gave way to acceptance.

While his hands glided over her breasts, shaping and testing their weight, he castigated himself. Something had happened to him. For the first time in his life, he'd lost control. It couldn't happen again, not if he hurt Keira in the process.

He pressed his lips to her neck then licked her skin. The faint taste of salt hit him and it contained an underpinning of something floral. He moved his attentions farther down her body, pausing at the base of her neck to nibble on the fleshy pad of skin where her shoulder began, the spot where his teeth had pierced earlier.

She'd remained silent until that point, and he was heartened to hear her soft cry of pleasure. He bit down a little harder, giving her a hint of pain, and her hands crept around his shoulders, holding him to her.

Relief kicked him in the gut. This was fixable. He'd apologize later, ask her what had happened because he'd missed something in his stupor. For now, he'd focus on her pleasure. His tongue lapped across the skin he'd bitten, and she cried out again, her fingernails digging into his skin.

Next, he paid attention to her breasts, took a moment to taste the pink-green nipples. His hands coasted across her skin, stroking, sometimes pinching while he worshipped her breasts. She mewed—a very catlike sound that grabbed him in the chest. Beating back amusement, he moved his explorations south.

She had a strip of soft black down—almost featherlike—guarding her sex. How had he not noticed earlier? Because his brain had traveled to his cock. She was the same pretty combination of green and pink down here. He lowered his head to taste her again. His feline let out a rumble of satisfaction, and he echoed the sound. His tongue flirted with the hard nub of nerves that would bring her pleasure but he didn't settle in this spot.

Instead he explored and tested her reactions to each of his touches. The flat of his tongue. The soft stroke. The hard.

Her muscles tensed. Her fingers curled in his hair, and she tugged each time he gave her a firm stroke with his tongue.

"Hey," he chided. "Stop trying to snatch me bald."

"Sorry." Her grip eased.

Jarlath slipped one finger into her, his cock jerking as he recalled the tight heat of her. He added another finger and stroked her internally while his tongue circled her nub.

She made another mewing sound and yanked his hair. The sharp pain jerked his fingers inside her and her sharp cry of pleasure told him he'd hit a hot spot. He stroked the same region, and she shrieked, her passage clamping down on his fingers.

He repeated the suck-and-stroke action and her nub pulsed in time with the sensual grip and release on his fingers. He kept up the massage and licking until she pushed at his head instead of gripping him closer. His heart gave an anxious beat until he noted the curve of her lips. That secret smile was the sexiest thing he'd seen in eons.

Jarlath rolled over onto his back and immediately missed the physical contact. He reached out and ran his fingers over her hipbone.

"That was better," she said.

"I'm sorry. I didn't mean to ignore you." Hellfire, he wasn't sure what had happened and damn if he could remember. Pleasure emblazoned his mind, deep and intense and colorful—the best he'd ever experienced.

"Marcus was greedy with his pleasure."

Jarlath's hand froze on her belly, a soft growl emerging. The contrast with her husband irritated him.

"Not that I meant to compare. It's just..." She rolled to face him and propped herself up so she could see his face. "The pleasure was there—intense and ready to explode into more—and then there was nothing. Frustration made my tongue sharp."

"I am glad you said something. More than anything, I want to please you as you please me."

"You did."

"My pleasure," he said.

"Are you hungry?"

"A little. Let me see what Hilda packed for us." Jarlath sat up and opened the basket. "Some wine. Is this the berry wine you make?"

She glanced at the bottle. "Yes, it goes the pretty golden color when it ferments. We make a plumson wine, which is a deep burgundy shade. That's delicious too."

"We have egg and veg pie, I think." He cut a piece and handed it to her. "You want wine?"

"Please."

The rest of the day passed in more berry picking and a swim to refresh. Although they didn't have sex again, Jarlath didn't mind. Instead, he planned his seduction for the coming eve. The second time he'd get everything right and make sure Keira came to completion before him.

His com rang not long after they'd returned to the farm. "Ellard."

"We had an explosion in the lower city," Ellard said in a terse tone. "That's why my father called on me. Looters are out in force and it's chaos. Tell Keira not to come into the city. It's dangerous to travel. You stay put too."

"Has anyone missed me?"

"Not yet," Ellard said. "But if anyone demands your presence, I'll tell them I've stashed you in a safe house."

Ellard's words rubbed him the wrong way. "I'm just as capable as you."

"I'm not heir to the throne."

Not mollified in the slightest, Jarlath said, "Call if you need my aid." He ended the call before Ellard could reply.

"Trouble?" Keira asked.

"An explosion in the city. The looters are out. Ellard said not to leave the farm. Travel is risky at present."

"Hortese, com the factory and make sure everyone is safe. No, wait. I'll do it. I'll give the foreman instructions." Keira hurried off and Jarlath followed her into what was an office. Her husband's office since it still held a masculine air. She pulled out a holo headset and placed it on her head. "This won't take long."

Curiosity had him studying the desk and the piles of paperwork, the awards for farm produce on the wall and the painting of Marcus Cloud. He quashed the tiny sliver of jealousy trying to punch a bigger hole in his mind. The man was dead, and Keira was with him now. "I'll ask Hortese if I can help. I'm sure she'll put me to work."

Keira grinned and the genuine reaction stomped out his residual envy. "Without hesitation. Hortese adores slave labor."

The holo call connected, and Keira began her discussion with her foreman as he left.

Jarlath strode up to Hortese. "I need a task to keep me busy."

"Stack the dishes in the washer cube."

He frowned.

"Job too lowly for you?" A note of teasing at his expense.

"No, but you'll have to show me what to do. I have no idea."

She snorted out a laugh but gave him instructions, and he fell into the mindless task. One washer cube for pots and larger items and another for platters and utensils.

During the next hour, Hortese showed him how to prepare vegetables and to make a berry pie. Jarlath enjoyed every moment, and once again, he realized how much he'd missed while playing the role of prince. Satisfaction came with honest everyday toil. Now, he understood what drove his brother to run his own business.

"Sorry, the call took longer than I thought," Keira said.

Jarlath attempted to rub the maize flour from his hands. "Is everyone all right?"

"Yes, they'd heard about the riots and have taken security precautions. Do you know what caused the explosion?"

"Ellard didn't say."

Keira rubbed her cheek and issued a weary sigh. "I need a glass of berry wine. Would you both like one?"

"Please," Hortese said.

"Where is Cristop?" Keira asked.

Hortese pulled a pie from the cookbox and slid in another. "He's helping Melvyn with the animals. Hilda wanted a break from the kitchen, so she's gone to help too. I believe they intended to shear the yearling malpacks."

"A lucky escape for us," Keira said.

Hortese barked out a laugh. "The yearlings never take well to their first shearing. Should we wager on how many bruises we'll need to doctor on young Cristop?"

"Six bruises," Keira said.

"I say more. I think eight, maybe nine," Hortese said.

Both women turned to him, clearly expecting him to join in their fun. "Three," he said, plucking a number from his head.

Hortese chortled, her eyes bulging and flaming bright pink for long secs. "We should settle this wager now. You lose."

Keira joined in the laughter at his expense.

"Not over until we see the evidence," Jarlath said.

They were on their second glass of wine and making yet more pies when the pungent scent of animal and manure wafted into the kitchen, preceding Hilda and Cristop.

"Bath house," Hortese snapped.

"Hilda has already ordered me to bathe," Cristop said, his words acknowledging he was the source of the stink. "I don't need one."

"You do if you want to eat with us," Keira said.

"I'll supervise," Jarlath said.

"Marcus designed a bath house to ease his aches. It's outside. Follow the path and it's the first building on the left. You'll find everything you need inside." She glanced at him, a smile quirking the corners of her lips upward. "You're wearing more maize flour than the pastry. Put your clothes in the apparel sanitizer before you start the bathing process. They'll be clean and pressed by the time you finish. There is a separate sanitizer for boots."

"Yes, Keira," Jarlath said and winked at Cristop.

"I don't need a bath," Cristop said.

"Me neither," Jarlath said, "but I want pie."

Later that night, Keira led Jarlath up the stairs into her room on the second level. She shut the door behind them, and turned to glower at him.

"How did you know Cristop would have a gift with the malpacks? Did he tell you?"

"As far as I know Cristop has never left the city. I met him at the market and we shared a meal after I caught him trying to pick my pocket."

"Most men of your station would have summoned a soldier and had him incarcerated."

"The kid was hungry. All he was trying to do was survive."

"You're a good man," she whispered, her warm breath wafting across his cheek.

Unable to resist her allure, Jarlath drew her into his arms. His kiss was slow and thorough and said everything he couldn't say aloud. He wanted her more than he had at the swimming hole, because now he knew paradise awaited.

To give himself time to grip his libido, he studied her bedroom. It wasn't masculine like the office, but looked more Keira. Pretty patterns shone on the autowindow shutters, and the colors and pattern repeated on her sleep-bed coverings.

The faint scent of flowers rode the air, the same one he smelled whenever Keira came close. This room said nothing of her husband and that pleased him.

"Let me undress you." He led her to the bed, and she stood while he removed the kidskin slippers she'd donned on her return. He tugged her trews down her legs and stood to unfasten the toggles on her tunic. Last of all, he removed her undergarments and leisurely perused her body. She was feminine with her curves and sexy shape, yet he adored her obvious strength too. No, fainting damsel, but a woman to stand at a man's side.

"You are beautiful."

"Thanks," she whispered.

He shrugged from his own garments and tossed them aside. A glance showed him they lay mixed with Keira's clothes and that, too, pleased him.

"This time I'll show more patience and make sure you're ready for me."

"I was ready before, but you finished too soon."

"Tell me what you want, show me. Teach me," he said. "I want to please you more than I need my next breath."

Her expression softened, and he knew he'd done the right thing, even though most males of his acquaintance would scoff at the idea of pandering to a mere female.

"Kiss me. Stroke me here." She reached for his hand and placed it at the juncture of her thighs. "Once you hit a certain spot deep inside me, I detonated. I believe the males of the House of Cawdor have a kink in their cocks. At least that's what my mother told me. Hitting that spot helps the Cawdor to stimulate eggs. Not that I can lay eggs. My mother carried me in her body."

"You are safe from pregnancy?" His words were sharp. Abrupt. Words he should have spoken earlier.

"I won't bear your child. Hortese insisted I keep up with my sex shots in case I wanted to take a lover, but my mother said I am a rarity—the child of a Cawdor and a Greenmont. Normally this would never happen, and Marcus said it is the same with the

Cat. Our species only breed with like. It is not possible for you to fertilize me. You and I will never bear a child."

"I'm sorry." Jarlath lowered his head and kissed her forehead. "My words hurt you, and I was not panicked on my behalf. I was worried about you should a child result. You face enough gossip. You don't need a child to add to your troubles."

"I can show you my latest health certificate if you want." Her voice was still stiff, despite his apology.

"I don't need to see proof." With any other woman, he'd ask to see the certificate first since a prince didn't need to create gossip in the form of a surprise cub. Lecture 101 from his father and one emphasized by Ellard's father.

"Maybe not, but I'll feel better showing it to you." She tugged at his hands, and he let them fall to his sides.

Keira marched to a drawer and muttered under her breath as she rifled through papers. She pulled out a card and handed it to him.

Because it was what she wanted, he glanced at the card to check the official stamp and the date of her last shot. Without a word, he handed it back, somehow feeling less because he'd followed her instructions.

She walked past him and climbed into her bed. Jarlath sighed and followed suit, mourning the death of the sensual mood between them.

"I'm sorry," he said again when the weight of silence became too much.

"I understand." Her voice remained tight and disciplined. Standoffish. "Believe me, I understand since I've experienced this before. The people of Cawdor look down on me because my mother was a Cawdor whore, and I'm a half-breed, and the people here on Viros whisper about me because Marcus's children insist I tricked him into marriage and stole their inheritance. I am used to everyone thinking the worst of me."

"Keira." Nothing he could say would make this pain go away.

But in time, he'd show her, make her see he valued her. Ignoring her tense muscles, he drew her into his arms and held her until she started to relax. It took a long time, but Jarlath didn't care. All he wanted was her forgiveness.

Keira fell asleep before him, while Jarlath's mind remained busy with all he'd learned. Guilt sliced at him too. Was he any better than those on Gramite or Marcus's children? His duty as heir was to marry well and hold the kingdom together. Offering Keira a position as his mistress put him on the same level, placed her in another circumstance to allow the people of Viros to look down their noses.

Grata! This was an impossible position, and he had no idea of how he should act to keep everyone happy.

CHAPTER EIGHT

"Hey, sleepyhead."

Keira yawned and rubbed her cheek. "What time is it?"

"Still early," Jarlath said. "I should com Ellard."

Keira grunted and rolled out of Jarlath's arms. She massaged her face again, a weird itchy sensation irritating her skin. "Are you going back to the city?"

"It depends on what Ellard says, but I'd like to. I don't feel right hiding out here or in my suite at the castle."

Keira scratched her cheek. "I want to go too. I need to protect my employees." She also needed to visit the magic man to get a stronger protection charm and a spell to repulse and maybe a special spell to destroy her half-brother if the opportunity arose. The idea of Razvan popping into her home whenever it suited made her gut bounce and jump like a yearling malpack full of hijinks. If Razvan learned she was intimate with Jarlath, she wasn't sure how he'd react since he'd never made a secret of his perverted desires.

In Razvan's mind, she belonged to him.

Razvan had arranged an alibi and persuaded two of his friends and a senior House of the Cawdor official to lie for him and tell everyone she had sought him out and offered her body. If her mother hadn't intervened...

Lies! And she knew her half-brother. With no one to rein him in, he was capable of worse behavior.

The spells were the logical way to fight him.

Magic with magic.

Jarlath rolled out of bed and picked up his trews. He retrieved his com and called Ellard. "How are things?"

Keira watched Jarlath while he listened to Ellard. He'd held her throughout the night, even though she'd effectively called a halt on more sex. Not many men would accept her wishes. If she'd had a tantrum like that with Marcus...well, things would have turned out differently. No, the situation wouldn't have happened with her husband because she'd always gone out of the way to acquiesce with Marcus. Part of it was because he'd saved her from a terrible situation and certain death, so she'd tried her hardest to make her husband happy. But with Jarlath—a man of power...

What was it with Jarlath that made her stand up for herself?

Flying stars, something must have bitten her cheek during the night. She rubbed vigorously at the itchy spot and decided she might as well rise. She was dressed by the time Jarlath finished his call.

"What's happening in the city?"

"More unrest. More looting. More violence. The soldiers have control of parts of the city but there are pockets of resistance. Mostly in the lower city."

"Looting? I hope my factory employees are safe."

"If they're sensible, your people will remain in their homes. I'm going into the city. Ellard didn't want me to, but these are my people. I can't cower and ignore trouble in the city."

"I'm going with you."

"No, it's not safe. I don't want you to get hurt."

Obtaining the correct spells was imperative, not that she could confess her reasons to Jarlath without creating a trouble storm. "I can't hide at the farm and do nothing either, not while my employees are in trouble. Some of them have children and I can offer them sanctuary." A good excuse, although she was sure her employees were safer than most since the factory was on the outskirts of the city in the agricultural belt.

"What if the trouble spreads from the city into the country?"

Keira pictured Razvan's head floating on the flames in her fireplace. Trouble had already arrived at her farm, and she needed a spell to keep her half-brother away. Jarlath wouldn't understand, would start to suspect her motives. No, it was best if she kept this information private.

She met his gaze. "I will go with you or by myself once you leave. Either way, I intend to visit the city."

Jarlath cursed. "What if you get hurt or worse?"

"That is my problem."

"Mine too," he muttered and drew her into his arms. He gave her a hard hug before he pushed back a fraction to kiss her. His kiss was hot and hungry and let her know of his desire. The hard press of his erection against her belly reinforced this truth.

Something tight in her chest released at the possessiveness of his kiss. After her temper last eve, she'd thought things might be uncomfortable between them. Her crow stirred, and she welcomed the once foreign sensation because her existence seemed to act as an emotional balance. Her mind was clearer, at least until Jarlath bestowed his kiss. She gripped his shoulders for balance and poured herself into the exchange. Their tongues met, explored, twirled. He nipped her bottom lip and soothed the sting with his tongue. Sensations poured through her—a sense of belonging, the desire to give, and heady, heady pleasure.

When Jarlath ended their kiss, they were both short of breath.

Unable to resist touching him, she smoothed his black hair from his face to reveal his strong jaw. His stubble prickled beneath her fingertips as she met his passion-heavy gaze. "I thought you'd be angry at me."

"No," he said. "We're learning each other, and sometimes we, me in this case, might misstep. It's part of a relationship."

Happiness suffused her but a slash of fear quashed the feeling before she became too euphoric. Razvan...she shook her head in an attempt to loosen the memory of her half-brother's taunts.

You will belong to me. I will have you.

She shook her head again. "Is that what we have? A relationship?"

Jarlath frowned, so swiftly the expression faded before she decoded his body language. "We're friends, and since I don't have many friends, you're very special."

A tactful reply, but they both knew the truth. No matter how much she hated the idea, this was a fleeting friendship. Best she enjoy the perks while she had the chance.

"Do we have time to break our fast before we fly into the city?"

"I don't want you to go." Jarlath scowled. "I can't change your mind?"

"No. Besides, you'll have to use my flymo. Ellard flew back in yours."

He started to speak and stopped, his brow furrowing. A heavy sigh lifted his broad shoulders. He stepped away and stretched before scratching his back. "We might as well have something to eat and wait until the solar star rises. That way we can see the damage."

After eating and issuing Hortese, Hilda and Melvyn instructions, she and Jarlath left for the city. Plumes of smoke rose in the distance, vision becoming murky once they cleared the city walls.

"I thought Ellard told you the soldiers were on patrol. I can't see any. No one stopped us or attempted to search our flymo." Keira peered through the black smoke and scratched her cheek. A few figures, singly or in small groups, darted from building to building. None of them lingered, and they carried bulging bags, which marked them as looters. "There's no security on the ground either."

"You're right. Lots of looters and no soldiers."

"Where are we meeting Ellard?"

"He thinks I intend to follow his orders and cower in safety at your farm."

"I see. You'd better call him. He didn't tell you the truth when he spoke with you earlier. Either that or he doesn't know how dire the situation is out here."

Jarlath reached over to squeeze her hand, before he pulled out his com. A smile curved his lips, his mood appearing buoyant even though the situation was dire. Maybe she made him happy. The idea made her happier.

"What's going on, Ellard? Where are the soldiers? They're not guarding the walls or attempting to quell disorder in the parts of the city we're flying over."

"I told you not to return," Ellard snapped.

"I don't have to follow your orders," Jarlath retorted, a hint of regal arrogance creeping into his voice. "Where are you?"

"Within the castle with the rest of the soldiers," Ellard said. "We can't get out. There's some sort of magical barrier enclosing the castle and none of us can exit. The barrier is impossible to break, and prolonged exposure bites with an electrical shock."

"Damn, we should have brought the protection spells with us," Keira said. "I never thought of it."

Her concern had been for her staff. At least they'd remain safe from Razvan's power since she'd insisted they wear a charm on their person at all times. Hortese had asked probing questions until finally agreeing, and she'd promised Keira she'd make sure the others wore the protection. One less thing to worry about.

"Who's with you?" Ellard demanded.

"Keira. We'll come to the castle. Meet us at the secret exit. Maybe we can break you out."

"I have to find a magic shop. Preferably the one owned by the man who made the protection spells we purchased in the square. Maybe he has a spell that can beat Razvan's wizards." The words burst from Keira along with a sense of relief. She'd been racking her brain for a way to slip the request into their conversation. If Jarlath would let her go off alone...but she doubted he'd accept her need without asking some serious questions.

"What do you know of wizards? How do you know they're Razvan's?" Ellard asked in a sharp tone.

Jarlath's gaze held suspicion too, and her crow beat her wings in agitation.

"I-I assumed it must be m-magic." She squeezed her hands to fists and forced herself to meet Jarlath's gaze with directness. "The spells we purchased in the market made us immune. The barrier around the castle has all the makings of magic. Doesn't it?" A faint note of pleading came into her words. "It was a logical assumption. There were crows in the sky."

Jarlath noted her agitation and his feline picked up on her apprehension, reacting with an uneasy bark. *Do something*. He disconnected the call with Ellard, considered the facts and came up with the sensible conclusion. "You think the House of Cawdor is responsible, not a third party. This use of magic from afar is an innovative means of attack."

"A new leader always wants to make his mark." Keira scratched her cheek so hard she left red marks with her nails. Shards of black swirled within the red.

Peculiar. Jarlath checked the skies in front. Clear. He switched to auto and reached out to catch her chin with his fingers. He turned her face and studied her cheek.

"What?" Her laugh was uneasy.

"What have you done to your face?"

She frowned. "No idea. It's itchy."

Jarlath caught a flash in his peripheral vision. The flymo shuddered, the secondary seats clacking against the walls of the vehicle. He lunged for the auto and took control again, sending the vehicle into a rapid zigzag pattern.

"Flash bombs," Keira shouted. "Watch out. There's another one."

Jarlath zapped into vertical lift but the flymo rose at a sluggish pace. "Grata! The flash bomb has damaged the circuitry." Someone lobbed another flash in their direction and it came fast and strong. "Up, grata! Up."

The flymo shuddered and lifted at the last sec, the bright flare of the bomb coming close enough to sear his retinas. White light filled his sight, blinding him to everything until he flew by instinct alone.

Keira gasped. "Left. Go left. It's okay. They missed. I think we've passed the firing zone. Can we make the castle?"

The flymo vibrated and whined, fighting every manual control he attempted. "I'll try."

Without warning, the engine stuttered, died. Absolute silence filled the cab. Jarlath pushed the starter. Nothing. The flymo dropped, his stomach diving to catch up. Keira cried out. His hands moved frantically over the controls, pushing buttons, pulling levers. Nothing stalled their uncontrolled fall.

"Hold tight," he gritted out. "We're going down."

"The ECL button." Keira gripped a handhold. "Use the emergency controlled landing."

"What?"

"The red button. Push the red button!"

Jarlath stabbed the ECL and their drop slowed. A sharp hiss had him jerking back from the instrument panel.

"Airbags," Keira said. "An old solution but it works in a flymo."

The flymo struck the ground, bounced. Once. Twice. The collision reverberated through his body, pain a dagger in his torso. Metal shrieked against cobblestones. The flymo left the ground, struck again, much harder and rolled.

His harness gave. He lurched forward. His head struck the controls. Black crowded his vision, and the last thing he recalled was another spine-cracking bounce.

The snarl of his feline, an impatient growl, brought him back. He shook his head, winced, and tested his limbs. Grata. His head hurt. He dragged in a deep breath, recoiled at the shot of pain at his temple.

He sniffed.

Blood.

He turned his head. Couldn't see much apart from the safety bags.

Keira.

He sucked in another breath, the tang of blood obtrusive, feeding his panic.

Jarlath fought the puffy airbag, shoving it from his body to free himself.

"Keira."

"I'm here," she croaked. "I'm okay. I can smell...you're bleeding. Your head."

Jarlath brushed off her concern, instinct propelling him to hurry. "I'm all right. Let's get out of here before someone comes to investigate."

Keira pulled a knife from her boot and hacked at the airbag. She soon had them free, and Jarlath hobbled from the wreck. Keira paused to grab her bag and she slung it over her shoulder so both arms were free.

The image of Keira with the knife in her hand kept reverberating through his brain. "I didn't see that coming, but I like your foresight. Do you have other weapons secreted on your person?"

"Of course. There are times when I need to protect myself. Let me look at your wound."

Voices had his head jerking, his pained gaze darting along the road and the narrow lane branching off it. Every feline instinct went on high alert. "We have to move. Now." Jarlath grabbed her hand and started running. His head went *thump, thump, thump* and pushed misery down his neck in jagged shards.

A masculine shout came from behind, and Jarlath lengthened his strides. Dressed as he was, he didn't think anyone would recognize him, but he wasn't about to take a chance with Keira's safety.

She kept up easily and glanced back. "It's all right. They've stopped to ransack the flymo. They're not chasing us. Which way to the castle?"

Cristo. "I don't recognize any of these streets."

"I think we're still in the lower city."

They rounded a corner, dodged a pile of rubble, some of it still glowing with heat. Smoke filled his lungs, obscured his vision. Keira never slowed, skirting the larger obstacles and leaping over others. The road widened and flattened to a zero incline.

"This looks like one of the main roads that lead to the square," she said.

Jarlath squelched the inadequacy filling him and concentrated on Keira's words. A glance either way yielded no clues. "Which way? Do we keep going this direction or risk sneaking back past the flymo?"

"Fifty-fifty decision," Keira said. "If we follow this road, we might be able to see the castle and orientate ourselves." She scratched her cheek. "What do you think?"

"This way then. We can always backtrack. How much is my head bleeding now?"

"Let me have a quick look."

"Keira, your face."

She touched her fingertips to her cheek. "What's wrong with my face?"

"*Grata*." Alarm pummeled his chest, blocked his throat. He swallowed hard. This wasn't good. "You have a tattoo on your cheek." The damn lump swelled to obstruct his words. Another gulp cleared the blockage. "It's similar to the ones some of the women have here."

She frowned. "A cat? But how—"

"It's a crow."

The healthy green fled her cheeks leaving her visage ashen. Her hand flew to her cheek, her fingertips tracing across the spot. "This is going to cause problems."

An understatement. "Yeah."

"One problem at a time. Let me look at your head."

He stepped closer and gentle fingers probed his wound. The scent of blood wasn't as bad now, although the bang, clang, bang continued playing in his head like a band out of tune.

"It's not bleeding much now. A shallow wound. I'll doctor you up once we get to the castle."

"Thanks." Jarlath winced and not because of the pain. They'd have to hide her tattoo because the locals would act first and ask questions later. This put her in danger and him by association. "You'll have to rub some soot over your face. Yeah, that's a bit better."

He'd worry about the reason for the tattoo later, when they weren't in such a hurry. Jarlath seized her hand, unsure of why he needed the contact, yet obeying instinct anyway. His feline purred and the loud rumble joined the musical band in his head. They hurried around a dry-food store, burst ration packs littering the road. Next door, a giant replicator sat half on the road and half in the store. It had been too large for the looters to move. No doubt they'd be back with reinforcements because a replicator like this was valuable.

At the end of the road, they paused to orientate themselves.

"There," Keira said, puffing in fatigue.

Jarlath was relieved to see the castle. This was his city, by grata, and he wouldn't repeat his mistake. Once they'd sorted this mess, he intended to follow through on his plan. He'd acquaint himself with the city and their people. All of his people, no matter what their station.

"This way," he said. "We'll go through the gardens and around the back."

"Wait." Keira tugged on his hand. "Someone is coming."

Jarlath heard them too. They flattened against the wall of the nearest building, and two men ran past, both bearing weapons.

Jarlath caught his breath, tension bleeding through him and forming claws at his fingertips. The men would see them if they looked back. He had to keep Keira safe. Please don't look. *Don't look.*

His breath hissed between his teeth when the men rounded the corner, disappearing into one of the narrow lanes intersecting the main road.

Keira's fingers relaxed in his. "Which way to the gardens you mentioned?"

She was a miracle. Most women of his acquaintance would have run screaming in the opposite direction. He grinned. His woman carried a knife and a blaster.

"This way." He gripped her arm and squeezed. "Try and hide your face from Ellard. I don't want him to see the bird. The soot isn't sticking." Grata, if his parents saw her face, they'd have a fit.

"Once we get to the castle I'll slap a healing plaster over it and tell everyone I hurt it when we crashed. We have more important things to worry about."

Pride filled Jarlath, and he wanted to tell her how great she was, how he'd prefer to face this situation with her rather than anyone else. He didn't. Instead he upped his pace and led the way, only pausing to dodge opportunistic men roaming the streets. Finally, the castle gardens came into sight.

Jarlath slowed, frowned. "There should be guards on all the entrances. I can't see a single one."

"They can't all be trapped inside."

"How the devil could they let that happen?" Jarlath didn't understand. The magical trap imprisoned Ellard too, which didn't make sense. "Why were the guards at the castle instead of out on the streets? Ellard said rioting went throughout the night."

"Something to find out," Keira said.

Jarlath led the way through the gate and into the royal garden. Someone had ripped plants from the beds, tossing them left and right. The fishpond was a weird yellow color. His mother's precious purple fish from the planet Halibut were floating on the surface, baring their bellies in a macabre display of death.

"Ugh," Keira said. "They're gonna honk soon."

"Shush, the culprits might still be skulking in the vicinity." Needing her touch again, he took Keira's hand and tugged her down a side path into the part of the garden where he and Ellard practiced with their weapons. "This way."

"Can you hear that low whine?" Keira whispered.

"Yeah. It seems to come from the castle. That's the entrance now. I'll com Ellard and tell him to meet us." He pushed a button. "We're almost at the entrance."

"Be there in a few." Ellard disconnected the call.

Stress weaved through Ellard's voice, and Jarlath frowned. Ellard was always calm and faced everything lobbed his way without flinching. Fear slithered in Jarlath's belly and his feline snarled, echoing his uneasy instincts.

"If the Cawdor leader is responsible, I don't know how he managed to get such a powerful spell. This is the work of more than one wizard. If he's responsible, he's been planning this attack for some time."

"I know. We should have noticed." Jarlath halted in front of an unobtrusive door. This was magical, and he'd been wrong to suspect Keira of duplicity when she hadn't put a foot wrong. They should have recruited their own wizards instead of running them all off Viros during the magical purges. "Do you know about the magical purges? No? Before I was born, those with magical powers were forced to leave Viros. The ruling felines at the time worried the wizards were becoming too powerful. There was a lot of posturing and speculation. They feared civil unrest and made a preemptive strike. My father has left the law standing, although there are a few businesses that sell charms now. I'm thinking they made a big mistake and should have come up with a different solution. Hindsight." He shrugged. "This is it."

If their attackers didn't come from the House of Cawdor... He couldn't think of anyone else... No. It had to be from Gramite because of the crow shape in the sky.

Jarlath caught Keira's worried expression and winced at the sight of her new crow tattoo.

"The Cawdor leaders have always been sneaky."

"You don't like them." Keira's thoughts shadowed his.

"I told you before. Besides I heard what Ellard said. If Xavier is gone, then Razvan would grasp the opportunity to step into his place. I could see him attacking in this manner. He's sneaky and clever with it. Never trust his word. *Never.*" She frowned at the door and couldn't see a barrier. "There must be some way through."

Jarlath grasped her wrist. "Don't touch it. Not until Ellard is able to tell us more."

"It's calling to me," Keira said, and she stretched out her hand.

"Don't touch," Ellard shouted. "Two of our soldiers have died after contact with the barrier. It stops the heart."

"At least we can hear him." Keira cocked her head. "Really, I need to touch."

"No," Jarlath snapped, but she reached out and made contact before he could snatch her hand away.

The instant her fingers connected the invisible barrier turned solid. The door came into sight and Keira twisted the knob. It opened and she stepped through.

Jarlath jumped through after her, and the door clicked shut and vanished.

"How did you do that? What the frukk?" Ellard's weapon cleared his holster and jabbed her in the chest seconds later. "Move away from the prince."

Jarlath shoved the weapon away and stepped in front of Keira. He snarled at Ellard, his canines bursting into prominence. "Don't pull your weapon on Keira. Step away."

Ellard ignored the order. "She wears the mark of the crow," he spat. "She's part of this plan to take over Viros."

"Keira is a Virosian citizen and has lived here since her marriage. She hasn't done anything wrong," Jarlath said.

"She's dazzled you, put you under a spell."

Jarlath knocked Ellard's weapon out of the way again. "Are you listening to yourself? Keira opened the barrier. You can get out now, plan a counter attack or at least stop the violence in the lower city. Why are the soldiers locked inside the castle? You can't tell me they were all required here. Why weren't they out in the city?"

Ellard stiffened, his expression going hard. "My father ordered the soldiers to protect the king and queen. You too. You're the royal family and must be protected." He didn't take his focus off Keira.

A laugh of disbelief burst from Jarlath. "One or two soldiers would suffice to protect my parents. The entire squad was unnecessary."

"It is not my duty to question—"

Keira darted around him and snapped her fingers in front of Ellard's stubborn face. He blinked at her in shock. "Confess. It was a bad decision and you know it."

Jarlath bit back his laugh and drew her against his side. He kissed her right on top her tattooed cheek.

"You slept with her," Ellard said, his tone accusatory.

"Not that it's any of your business, but I intend to share her bed tonight and every other night in the foreseeable future."

"I wager your parents don't know," Ellard shot back.

Anger unfurled in Jarlath, propelled by his spitting feline. He had his hands at Ellard's throat and was shaking him and baring his teeth in fury before the thought formed.

"Jarlath, release him." Keira's soft voice pierced the red mist fogging his mind. Her touch on his shoulder eased his fury. "Let him go."

Jarlath thrust Ellard away, pushing so hard his friend fell on his butt. Ellard's weapon clattered to the floor. "Apologize."

Ellard scrambled for his weapon, his glare on Keira the entire time.

"Apologize," Jarlath gritted out and took two warning steps toward his friend.

"Sorry." Ellard's tone and expression said the opposite, but Keira grabbed Jarlath and halted his attack.

"Leave it," she said. "We have more important things to deal with right now."

Jarlath forced himself to relax. His teeth clicked into hiding, but his claws remained prominent. He sucked in a deep breath then another. She was right. "We'll see if we can help the soldiers to exit the castle. Do you mind helping, Keira?"

"I'll help if I can."

Jarlath placed his hands on her shoulders and tipped up her chin. "Thank you." He smoothed his thumb over the tattoo of the black crow on her cheek. It was cute, but he knew the Cawdor mark would cause suspicion. "Cover this up before anyone else sees it and jumps to conclusions."

Ellard snorted but wisely remained silent.

"We'll try the main entrance," Jarlath said. "I'd like to keep this exit private in case we need an escape route at a later date. Has anyone missed me?"

"No. They think you've remained in your suite."

"Cowered," Jarlath said in disgust. None of them knew him, and the idea they thought him capable of hiding in safety while others were in danger rankled.

Keira squeezed his arm. "Put a cover on my cheek, and we'll get started."

He and Keira followed Ellard through the narrow passages until they reached the servants' quarters and the two kitchens. Last time he'd walked this way, they'd needed to dodge servants and the clang of pots and voices filled the air, but now the hall echoed with their rapid footsteps. They found a medical box, covered her tattoo and tended the worst of his wounds before hurrying onward. Not a voice sounded as they hurried past the kitchens, but when they neared the main hall, he started to hear evidence of the residents.

"My father suggested everyone stay at a central point for safety," Ellard said. "The servants are in there and the soldiers, the senior officials, those of high-ranking families and your parents are in the main hall."

"Yet they left me in my suite," Jarlath said.

"I told them you were safe there, and it wasn't a good idea for the king and the heir to shelter in the same room."

"Good thinking," Jarlath said, even though the statement irritated him afresh. He wasn't a coward, although it might appear this way to the people of Viros. To them he was the dutiful prince who attended social functions and hid in the castle at the first sign of trouble.

The chatter in the main hall fell silent when they entered. The scent of kafe and breakfast pastries told him his parents were treating this like a summer camp—a mere inconvenience and something to laugh about later once things returned to normal.

He watched his mother, his father until the silence alerted them to his arrival. He bowed stiffly, the gesture one of reflex.

"Jarlath, I thought Ellard said it was safer for you to—what on Viros are you wearing?" his mother demanded. "You look like a commoner. Go and change right now. I won't have you dressed like a low-class male while in my presence."

Jarlath stood his ground. The city was under siege and his parents worried about appearances?

"Who is this woman?" his mother asked.

Jarlath drew Keira against his side, felt the tremor that sped through her limbs, but she didn't recoil. Pride suffused him as she stood tall.

"Keira Cloud, my mother Queen Bryna and my father King Hazan."

"Cloud? The woman accused of murder?" Queen Bryna asked.

Keira's chin lifted, and Jarlath couldn't have been prouder. Neither did she try to defend herself, despite the accusation and the flurry of whispers at the queen's words.

"What are you doing with the prince?" His father's gaze went from him to Keira and back. It was obvious from his expression he came up with a conclusion, and while it was right, his parents' attitude irked him.

Ellard stepped into the fray. "We've found a way out of the castle." He directed his words to his father and studied the mass of soldiers. "We need soldiers out on the street to stop the rioting and looting. We'll need all of you. Meet me at the front entrance."

"Wait!" Danion Tetsu, Ellard's father and security head, shouted. "We require top security here in the castle. The soldiers must remain in case our enemy decides to strike against us here.

The most important thing is to keep the king, the queen and the heir safe. Stay."

Jarlath cursed under his breath. In other words, they wanted to save their own skins. He'd noticed several of the upper class, cups of kafe in hand. Most of the women on his prospective wife list stood with their parents.

Disgust swirled in his gut as he returned his attention to Ellard. "I'm not staying here and neither is Keira. You do what you want, but we're going into the lower city."

Keira studied him with approval—a balm to his mental unrest and confirmation he was making the right decision.

"Why?" Ellard demanded.

"I need to check on the people, find some way to stop this attack. We can't do that without knowledge, and we won't find it here."

Ellard's shoulders slumped for a sec before he nodded in acceptance. "Let me talk to Father, persuade him we need a force outside the castle."

"Five mins," Keira said. "I want to find a magic shop and purchase some protection spells."

"You let her speak for you, Jarlath?" his mother scoffed. "I taught you better. Return to your suite and spend time perusing the list of potential wives I gave you. Several are here." She gestured at the nearest woman, a beauty with a leopard tattoo defined on her cheek and marking her as unmated. "You can speak with them, learn if you will suit. And change your clothes. The next time I see you present yourself in proper attire."

"Prince Jarlath," Ellard said. "Perhaps you will wait for me in your suite. I will report to you there momentarily."

"All right," Jarlath said while he struggled to stuff down his words of protest. He caught Keira's arm and tugged her with him.

"She can stay with the servants in the other room," his mother ordered. "There's no need to give a woman of her reputation ideas above her station."

"I heard she killed her husband and slept with the judge to get off the charges," a haughty voice called out.

"It's true," another woman said. "I heard it from the prosecutor's wife."

"She's stolen the Cloud inheritance," a male voice added his opinion.

"Ran them off the farm at blaster point," someone else said.

"That's enough," Jarlath thundered. "There will be no more dispersions against Keira's character in my hearing." Militant silence fell, and he urged Keira to the door. "We'll grab a few things from my suite and wait for you at the front entrance," he told Ellard. "I don't want to spend more time here than necessary."

The sec they stepped from the great hall, voices burst into a discordant chatter. Insults grew louder and more disturbing, and Jarlath knew Keira heard each word dagger thrust her way.

"Don't let them get to you," he murmured and rubbed her back. He wasn't sure if the action was more for him or her, but the physical contact seemed to soothe them both.

"But it's all true," Keira said.

"You slept with a judge?"

"No! Not that. The other things. I fired a blaster at Marcus's children."

"Why?"

"Because I was angry. Marcus was sick for a long time. He wanted to see his children before he died but they refused his summons. They didn't visit the farm until after his death when they thought they'd receive everything Marcus owned. They showed little concern while he was alive yet professed their love and outrage once he died. I understood they didn't approve of me, but surely they could have put their ire aside for one visit? Marcus died thinking his family didn't care about him and that angered me."

"I know, sweetheart. You know the truth. Don't let them get to you. Come to my rooms with me, and we'll grab more weapons and supplies."

In his suite, Jarlath packed a bag and used Lynx's code to replicate another set of clothes. "Grab some snacks from the chillbox. We might have need of them if we can't get back to the farm."

Keira opened the chillbox. "What are we going to do for transport?"

"We'll find another flymo or something faster in the castle garage or as a last resort we can take my cambeest from the stables."

Ellard clattered into his rooms, interrupting their packing. "You're really going out there?"

Jarlath closed his bag and straightened. "I can't stay here and do nothing while someone threatens our city."

"You might as well admit what we all sense," Keira said in her usual straightforward manner. "That was a crow projected up in the sky. The House of Cawdor is declaring war."

CHAPTER NINE

Keira noticed neither of the men argued and her gut twisted. Jarlath hadn't mentioned anything but now that the crow tattoo had formed on her cheek, he must wonder if she had a part in the attacks. Ellard certainly did, if his glowers were any indication.

She spoke before Ellard could spit poisonous suppositions. "I have nothing to do with this. I hate Razvan."

"What do you know of Razvan?" Ellard asked.

Fodo crap. She sucked in a swift breath and prepared to lie through her teeth. "Not much. Just that he's unpredictable." Keira couldn't look at Jarlath. Maybe she should tell them about Razvan appearing in the flames. She hesitated. No, it would only increase their distrust. She'd make damn sure she didn't stand near a fire in the future. Razvan wouldn't surprise her a second time.

"How?" Ellard persisted. "How do you know he's

unpredictable? Have you met him?"

"Before my marriage. I haven't seen him since."

"This is wasting time," Jarlath said. "We should start restoring order. Find a way to stop this attack. Information is the key to beating our enemy."

"I haven't managed to contact the lower guard station," Ellard said. "We have fifty men stationed down there, and they'll be a big help in restoring order." He trailed off, anxiety taking over. "Mareeka is there. I want...need to make sure she's okay."

"You didn't tell me your girl is a soldier," Jarlath said.

"I've told you now," Ellard said. "Move. Don't stand here gossiping."

Ellard clomped down the stairs and Jarlath followed. Keira trailed the two males, and tried not to let her impressions of the beautiful surroundings overwhelm her. She'd never visited the House of Cawdor's aerie fortress, but her mother had told her of the balls she'd attended and raved about the sky views. Their house—the one provided by Xavier Cronan was big and roomy, full of valuable carpets and paintings and other gifts, but this—the House of the Cat castle rated a dozen levels above her mother's abode.

The paintings and sculptures came from foreign planets. She wasn't sure how she knew this, but they exuded an exotic air. She paused in the middle of the staircase and gawked. Flying stars, was that a dragon's egg? The mother must have died otherwise she'd have torn up the castle searching for her egg. Dragons never gave up when it came to protecting their young.

"How many soldiers are leaving the castle with us?" Jarlath asked.

Ellard's mouth twisted. "Six."

Keira hurried to catch up. "But there are dozens of soldiers in the main hall."

"I'll be coming with you." Ellard's gaze settled on her, his expression one of warning.

She understood he was worried about Jarlath's safety, so she kept her fury to herself and struggled to keep her inner crow calm. He means nothing. He doesn't understand.

Caw-caw. Her crow's grumpy reply didn't lend reassurance, and she clenched her hands to fists.

"I am coming with you," Ellard repeated. "It's my job to protect the prince."

"Your father will discipline you for leaving the castle and for letting me loose." Jarlath didn't hold back with his assessment. He slipped his arm around her waist, the calming effect on her crow immediate. "My parents expect me to obey them and for you to make me follow orders. They will demand punishment or demotion, even if your father doesn't. You don't have to come with us. Stay. Tell them I crept out without your knowledge."

Ellard threw up his hands, his agitation clear. "No, how can I stay when my father is making a mistake? What happens if they manage to bomb the castle? They'll take out everybody."

Jarlath scowled. "You speak the truth."

"We might be stuck in the castle too, if I can't get us back out," Keira said. "I have no idea what I'm doing or how I'm doing it."

"So you say," Ellard said in a voice pitched for her hearing. "I'm coming with you. I want to check on Mareeka."

"Fair enough," Jarlath said, and some of the tension in Keira dispersed. Ellard wasn't a bad man. He was merely attempting to do his job.

Six soldiers waited at the front entrance, and their presence started her thoughts on another trail.

"They're going to know it's something I'm doing," she murmured. "That's if I manage to pass through the barrier again."

"Stand in the doorway, right where the barrier is," Ellard ordered. "Maybe if you break the barrier they'll be able to exit and not realize how they managed the feat."

As they neared the doorway, Keira heard the low hum of the barrier. She kept walking, the magic friendly and welcoming. Once she stood in the doorway, the vibrations thrummed through her body. Her crow started to chatter, loud and excited, also feeling the greeting, and Ellard gave her another of those suspicious glances. The longer she stood breaking the barrier, the more the vibration ached and throbbed in her bones. Welcome turned to punishment as if the magic sensed her other half—the foreigner—and wanted to eject the interloper.

"Move," she gasped, a sharp pain in her stomach buckling her knees.

Jarlath took a step and propelled a soldier with him. They smacked into the transparent barrier. It fizzed and sparked and Keira cried out at the sharp pain that shot through her body.

Ellard wrenched Jarlath and the soldier free.

"Grab, Keira," Jarlath said. "Jerk her free."

Ellard hesitated and gingerly grasped her arm. "Walk through," she said through gritted teeth. "Hurry."

When he hesitated, she yanked on his arm. He shot through the barrier and turned to face them.

"The soldiers," she said to Jarlath.

Thankfully, Jarlath understood the urgency in her voice. "Quick. One at a time. Hold her hand and walk through the barrier like Ellard did."

With each soldier who passed through the barrier, the spurts of pain became more agonizing. Her crow shrieked, the alarmed caw-caw almost deafening her. She slapped one hand over an ear and fought the urge to cover her other ear too.

"Keira, are you okay?" Jarlath cupped her cheek, and some of the discomfort receded. Jarlath anchored her and soothed her crow.

"Go faster. Can't. Hold. On. Longer."

The two remaining soldiers observed her with speculation, especially when Jarlath touched her with such tenderness.

"Only two more left, Keira. You can do this," he said.

She helped a soldier pass through the barrier and reached out to grasp the hand of the last man. Her heart ventricles raced, and she groaned as he released her hand.

"Just me left, sweetheart," Jarlath whispered. "Walk through the barrier with me."

Her hand trembled as she reached for him, and it felt as if a heavy weight sat on her chest, constricting her breathing, costing her effort to carry out the order her brain issued. Her vision started to go dark, the color seeping from her world. She blinked to clear her sight but the black grew larger and larger until but a pinprick remained.

"Jarlath." Even forming the words and getting them out proved difficult, and panic began to run in tandem with the excruciating pain.

Jarlath seized her hand, then the black crowded out the last of the color, and she felt herself crumpling, falling, falling, falling.

Jarlath caught Keira before she hit the ground.

"What's wrong with her?" Ellard demanded. "Is she dead?"

"You'd like that. She didn't have to help us." Bitterness coated his tongue at his friend's attitude when Keira had aided them of her free will. "Keira's death would make everyone happy."

"Jarlath, your recent behavior has been—"

"Leave us." Jarlath checked for her pulse rate and found it, fast and choppy but still alive. Her face was pale with not a sign of her usual healthy green tinge.

"You didn't let me finish," Ellard said and squatted beside them to test her pulse rate himself. He grunted. "I might not approve of Keira Cloud, but I like the way she has shaken you from your lethargy. You're acting more like the Jarlath I remember from our childhood. I thought your spirit had been crushed beneath duty and responsibility."

"I'm heir to the throne."

"I know, but that doesn't mean you shouldn't have fun. Our parents think they know everything. They want the status quo. They think sticking to tradition is best. They're wrong. We must modernize, embrace new technology, so we're not left lagging behind our enemies. One day you'll be the king, and you must forge your own path. The right one for our people."

Jarlath stared at his friend. This was practically treason coming from his friend's lips. "What if I don't want to be king?"

"It's your duty," Ellard said with a careless shrug. "Keira seems to be coming around."

Jarlath stared down at her pretty face. He'd noticed the golden flecks in her eyes, but now there was more gold than green. What was happening to her? Had they done this by needing her help to pass the barrier?

"What happened?" she croaked, more crow than humanoid.

"You passed out. You need to rest."

"I'm all right," she croaked again. "Tired."

She didn't look as if she'd manage to crawl on her knees let alone walk.

"Ellard, can we get transport from the royal garage?"

"No, I need to find the owner of the magic stall," Keira said, her reply stronger this time.

"Why?" Ellard demanded.

"We're under attack. Securing a protection spell makes sense. I need to protect my people." Fear flashed across her face, fleeting yet recognizable, and it made Jarlath wonder about her insistence on seeking out the charms.

"I've sent the soldiers off in pairs to gather information," Ellard said. "They'll meet us at the castle. If you're determined to go to the lower city, we should stick together. We won't appear threatening if we have a woman with us."

"No, it's dangerous. Keira is hurt."

"Jarlath, help me up. I'm made of stronger stuff. We should leave before we attract more scrutiny."

Jarlath and Ellard glanced in the direction she indicated. A cloaked man stood in the square, his attention on them. When he noticed their interest, he reached into his red cloak.

Ellard pulled out his weapon. "You! Move along. No loitering outside the castle."

When Jarlath trained his blaster on him too, the man hurried away and disappeared around the corner.

"He wasn't there when I first passed through the barrier," Ellard said. "Let's go before he brings back friends." He waited, his weapon at the ready, while Jarlath lifted Keira to her feet. "Question anyone we see and persuade the able-bodied men to assist in our fight."

"Are you sure you're up to this?" Jarlath whispered. "I can take you back to the farm."

"Not before I purchase the charms." She took a step and staggered, pressing a hand to her head as if it ached.

Jarlath curled his arm around her waist to hold her upright. "You're not well. I'll take you home then return to help Ellard."

"Enough with the lovers' sweet nothings," Ellard snapped. "We need to collect information. Organize the soldiers from the lower city base."

Jarlath was surprised Ellard didn't insist he stay at the castle. Maybe he'd decided to save his breath and battles for the important things. This was war and objectives changed.

"No more sweet nothings," Jarlath murmured to Keira. "This is serious."

A chortle emerged from her, and the small sound heartened him. His Keira was strong and courageous. A true warrior.

House of Cawdor, Planet Gramite

"How is the attack progressing?" Razvan Cronan demanded of the six wizards who stood before a huge scrying bowl. All young, all ambitious, the magic men had volunteered for this job, despite knowledge of his uncertain temper and insistence on results.

Razvan didn't tell them, but their progress pleased him, made him proud. This was innovative and the scope of his plan unique, a scheme he'd conceived two cycles ago and his father had rejected as impossible. A pity the old man wasn't around to see his success.

"Most of the security force is trapped in the castle with the royal family," a man wearing fake cat ears and whiskers said. He was in charge of the wizards' wellbeing.

"Mareeka and Marjo have reported this also," Razvan said, speaking of the women in his life—the other members of his triad—who currently acted as his team on the ground on Viros. "Excellent job."

An unstoppable force and his secret weapon in the war against the House of the Cat.

Razvan studied the magic men. Their bare chests gleamed with sweat and strain showed in their faces. They'd trained for this attack, practiced for the last cycle, but he could see they'd need a break soon. He couldn't afford to lose any of these men because they didn't have replacements strong enough to help.

"Thank you, sir," their spokesman said.

Razvan gave a curt nod and withdrew from the war room, closing the door on his magic men so they remained undisturbed.

"How goes the attack, Razvan? How goes the attack?" His mother, a tall, spare woman with a sharp blade of a nose and golden eyes stared at him in clear expectation of a report. She wore a black mourning suit—a thin tube of fabric that covered her from shoulders to just below her knees—in deference to her husband's demise.

Razvan bit back his impatience but not fast enough.

"I helped you gained the position of leader," she spat. "I helped speed your father on the way to the crow sanctuary. I helped. I helped." Her eyes glowed with inner fervor while her mouth was a thin slash of determination. "The least you can do is to keep me appraised of our progress. Keep me appraised. Keep me appraised."

Not quite true. Officially, his father had died from the fever that had killed many others on Gramite, a mystery illness, which had flared up during the last cycle around the same time as the increase of mossie bugs. The head scientist had tried to tell him he was at fault with his magical trials and the excess rain they'd caused. The rain, he'd said, had created stagnant ponds, which encouraged the breeding of the bugs. Razvan smiled. He'd soon put the scientist right.

"Razvan, I'm talking to you. Talking to you. Talking to you."

Razvan bit back his irritation and answered so she'd go away. "The castle and most of the security force is sealed off. No one can enter or escape. The people in the city are frightened. They are rioting and I understand there has been looting. I intend to contact Mareeka and Marjo soon to make sure they are in position. The bombing will resume as soon as I give the word."

"And his fledgling spawn? His spawn? His spawn?"

"I have located her once and will again." The fledgling was proving more difficult to find. She'd been clever enough to keep her hearths devoid of fire, but he would find another way. She would be his again. Of course, she was no longer virgin, but he could use her as a plaything for as long as she held his interest. Once he'd rid himself of this compulsion to have her, he'd pass her on to his men. They'd appreciate the gift.

But first, he'd teach her who was boss. He'd teach her she couldn't escape his might. He'd teach her the true meaning of fear.

"I'll check in with my women." Razvan halted when his mother's hand shot out to grasp his upper arm. Her bony fingers pierced his skin—a sure sign of her agitation if she couldn't control her crow from bleeding into an appearance. The woman was mad. Useful, but crazy. His gaze went from her hand curled around his forearm to her face. "Yes?"

"Don't let that woman get between you and success, my son. Your father failed because of the mongrel bitch. I wouldn't want you to make the same mistake with the mongrel bitch's fledgling. Same mistake. Same mistake."

Razvan fought to keep his irritation banked behind a bland smile. "I know what I'm doing, Mother. My planning has been meticulous and nothing will get in the way of my success."

Becoming one with Mareeka and Marjo had made him stronger and confident. He would not fail.

They would not fail.

She scrutinized his features with a beady gaze, and he barely repressed his shudder of distaste. He didn't trust his mother, not after the way she'd taken the opportunity to dispatch his fever-weakened father. He might not manage to prove her a murderess but he knew in his gut and that was enough to make him wary.

"Don't make a mistake. You have the Virosians in a vulnerable state. Don't ease up and take your boot from their throats. Boot on throat. Boot on throat."

"Of course not, Mother. We need their resources and workers to man the mines we will seize."

She gave a stiff nod and hopped from the room, the fabric of her black suit rustling with each bounce.

Razvan didn't show a flicker of expression until she disappeared from sight.

"Mother isn't sane," Carrick, his younger brother, said from behind him.

"How long have you been there?" Razvan didn't like to think his brother could sneak up on him without his knowledge. Sneaky and unpredictable, Carrick bore some of the same characteristics as their mother. Razvan didn't trust him either, but he wasn't stupid enough to upset him with hasty words.

"Long enough," Carrick said. "Mother is retreating into her other self more and more. I haven't seen her walk anywhere for ages. She hops."

"I know," Razvan said. "Do you have time to help me plan a bombing?"

"Bombing?" Carrick's wide grin bore a trace of madness. "You've just said the magic word."

"Grata! I didn't think the damage would be this bad," Ellard said. "The soldiers who reported in before the barrier went down spoke of small disturbances."

"We have to stop the fighting," Jarlath said.

"We need more soldiers," Ellard said. "And Father isn't about to release them, even if we could get them through the barrier. Keira blacked out after getting us plus the six soldiers through. No, stick to the plan and get to the lower base."

"Start recruiting men and women to serve as we go through the city," Keira said, seemingly recovered from her blackout. "Offer to pay them if they will help restore order."

Ellard shook his head. "I don't know about payment. Father—"

"The head of security isn't here," Keira said. "You can't expect people to risk their lives for the few who live the high life because that is who you're protecting. None of you care about the people who inhabit the lower city."

"I will authorize wages for a civilian army," Jarlath said.

The upper city streets were empty, and most of the shops had their windows and doors barred. Shouts drifted from farther down the hill and they saw more people on the streets. Some were fighting and others...

Jarlath watched in disbelief as a woman and a child smashed a window and seized the goods they could reach. The woman lifted the child and shoved him through the window. Once through, the child disappeared then reappeared to thrust stolen goods back to his parent.

"Who is that?" Keira asked.

Jarlath looked in the direction she pointed and frowned at the man. He wore a scarlet red cloak, the hood raised to screen his face. He stood motionless, his attention on a fixed point in the distance.

"There's another man at the other end of the street," Ellard said. "I should question them. They're dressed the same manner as the man we saw when we left the castle."

"There's something odd about them. They're standing like statues carved from red onyx. I think we should go," Keira said. "I'd feel happier if we wore protection spells."

"Which way?" Jarlath asked. "I'm not familiar with this part of the city."

"You're right. Best to get to my soldiers first. This way," Ellard said. "The main steps will be quicker. Jarlath, you lead. I'll watch our backs."

"There are more men in red on this level," Keira said a few mins later. "Weird. They're all standing stock still."

Ellard frowned. "Move it, Jarlath. I don't like the feel of this. My gut is lurching."

Jarlath hurried down the steps and paused on each level to scan the shop signs. "Lynx is right. The lack of technology down here is making us weak and vulnerable."

If they modernized the city and welcomed innovation, then maybe they'd attract more merchants and traders and inventors instead of losing them to other planets. Something to ponder and plan for the future.

"There," Keira said. "Over there. I think that's the shop. The sign looks new." She marched along the street, glancing swiftly at the men in red positioned on the street. She increased her speed, and Jarlath didn't blame her. The men stood so still he wondered if they were alive, yet their appearance made the hairs at the back of his neck rise in foreboding.

"They smell wrong," Ellard said.

Keira stopped at the door and pounded her fist on the wood.

Jarlath scented the air, his nostrils flaring. His feline barked out an unhappy sound. Ellard was right. A metallic aroma filled the air. A hint of crow. He thought of the crow tattoo on Keira's cheek.

No, her scent was different.

Keira thumped on the door again and attempted to turn the handle.

"There is a number. I'll com it," Jarlath said.

"No, I hear footsteps," Keira said. "Someone's coming."

A burst of thunder rippled through the air, and Jarlath frowned up at the sky. Earlier, when they left the castle, the day had been clear and fine with reasonable visibility. Now darkness shrouded the solar star and the scent of rain added to the wrongness of the atmosphere.

"I've never seen a storm like this," Ellard said. "Look at the color of the sky. It's scarlet in places."

Rain began to fall, large drops full of ice. They sizzled on hitting the ground.

"I don't like this. This weather smacks of magic," Keira said with urgency. "We need shelter."

The men in red didn't move and their scarlet cloaks began to steam.

Keira banged her fists on the wooden door and shrieked, "Let us in. Please let us enter."

The door flew open and Keira pushed past the tall, scrawny man standing in the doorway. She ignored his angry bellow to glance around at the shelves of bottles and jars. Jarlath stepped over the threshold and sneezed.

"I'm going to talk to one of those men in red," Ellard said. "The one at the end of the street looks familiar. The name will come to me once I speak with him."

"Wait until the rain ceases," Keira said.

"I don't have to take orders from you," Ellard muttered and stomped away.

"She's right," Jarlath said. "I don't like the way this feels."

"Magic." The skinny man attempted to slam the door and lock Ellard out.

"No, wait." Jarlath yanked at the man's arm. He finally forced his way past and sprinted after Ellard.

"No, Jarlath. Come back," Keira shouted. "It—"

An explosion cut off her words.

Ellard flew through the air and hit the ground. Jarlath found himself sprawled on his back. Ears ringing, he picked himself up and scuttled toward his friend. The wind battered his body, tearing his hair and making his black cloak swirl as he tried to reach Ellard.

Ellard didn't move.

Keira appeared beside him. Her mouth was moving but he couldn't understand what she was saying. She grasped Ellard's shoulder and glared at him, her lips moving again. Okay. She wanted him to drag Ellard to safety. Jarlath hoisted Ellard up and grunted at his dead weight.

A second explosion went off down the other end of the road, the blast knocking Jarlath down. His knees hit the cobblestones with a painful whack.

"Jarlath, we must get inside." Keira spoke right next to his ear.

Her panic and determination gave Jarlath a mental push. His gut told him she knew more than she was letting on. Either she knew what was coming or her knowledge was enough to give her a healthy fear. Her terror stirred his feline, and he gritted his teeth and half-dragged, half-heaved Ellard through the open doorway.

A metallic stench filled the air, and when he scanned the street, the men in red had vanished. Smoke obscured his vision, but many of the buildings had turned to rubble and shop signs littered the ground or hung drunkenly off their braces. In the distance, a boom, then a second, signaled more explosions. Secs later plumes of black smoke, tinged with scarlet rose upward.

"Quick, shut the door," the man ordered. "Hurry. You're breaking my protection spell."

At least he hadn't locked them outside. Jarlath shut the door and turned to Ellard. Keira was already on her knees at his side, her hands gentle on his large frame as she checked for injuries.

"Is he breathing?" he asked.

"Yes. I can't find anything seriously wrong with him."

"He hit his head," the man said. "I saw it connect with the cobblestones."

"Did you know this was going to happen?" Jarlath asked in a sharp voice.

"No," the man said.

"No! Of course not, but my instincts told me something was coming," Keira said at the same time. "The men in red were eerie and not of this place." She turned to the magic man. "Did you make the charms you sold at the market stall? I wish to speak to the man or woman who made them."

"I am Zarbo. What do you want with me?"

Keira didn't answer, instead leveling her gaze at him in quiet insistence.

Zarbo dragged a hand through his wiry black-and-white hair, his gaze wary. "Yes, it was me. I made the charms, although I am starting to wish I had not decided to go into business here on Viros."

"Good," Keira said. "I wish to purchase more protection spells, and I'd like to order a protection spell for my house." She shot a glance at Jarlath. "I have received unwelcome visitors and do not want them to return."

"Who?" Jarlath asked. "Not me?"

"Jarlath?" Ellard's weak voice grabbed his attention.

"You're awake."

"Head hurts like a motherbitch. What happened? I remember arguing with you and wanting to question the man in red." Ellard's brow scrunched, as if he was digging through his memories and not getting the answers he wanted. "I think...there was an explosion. The men in red had something to do with the explosions."

"They're all gone," Jarlath said.

Ellard tried to sit up and fell back with a groan. "Gone? They escaped?"

"No, they detonated," Keira said. "The red men were the bombs."

"Grata," Ellard muttered.

"Stay there while we check you for injuries," Jarlath said.

"I'm fine," Ellard said, but when he attempted to stand again, his knees buckled like a piece of parchment. His butt hit the ground with a thud. "Frukk."

"There were a lot of explosions," Keira said. "How many protection spells do you have? We'd like to purchase as many as you can make."

"We don't know if they'll work against the magic warfare," Jarlath said.

"It worked on the night of the market, when the first visitation occurred."

"I am skilled with protection spells. These are some of my best work," Zarbo said with an air of pride.

Given the man's confidence and Keira's insistence they have the charms, Jarlath acquiesced. "All right. What are you thinking?"

"We muster an army and issue a charm to each volunteer. Once they are no longer needed they can hand in their protection spell to receive payment for their services," Keira said and focused on the magic man. "How many do you have? Can you make more if we need them?"

Zarbo's bushy brows squeezed together in tight concentration as if he was mentally tallying his charms. "I have some in stock, but these spells are powerful. They take time to make."

"Round up the soldiers from the lower base and arrange volunteers," Ellard said.

Jarlath stomped the confined space, trying to think what to do for the best. "You think the House of Cawdor is battering our defenses before they attempt to land soldiers."

"From what I know of the Cawdor. You don't want his troops landing on Viros. They are well-trained and armed with the latest technology."

"He seems to have eyes on the city. Where will we hide our volunteers? Organize and arm them?" Jarlath resumed his pacing, aware of the enormity of their problem.

"We could use my factory. I already have a workforce there. It might work since the House of Cawdor has focused its attacks in the city," Keira said. "Or if that won't work, maybe one of the outer squares."

Ellard probed his head with careful fingers. "It's a good plan, and if the protection spells work as you say, it will give us an added edge, but why would you help the House of the Cat?"

"This is my home," Keira said in an icy tone Jarlath had never heard her use before. In contrast, her glare was hot enough to sear at fifty paces. "Why wouldn't I offer my assistance?"

"I have other magical spells that might aid your soldiers," Zarbo said.

Jarlath appreciated the magic man's impeccable timing with his interruption, but Keira never stopped glaring at Ellard. His friend glowered right back.

"I'll see you're given remuneration in exchange," Jarlath said. "You have my promise."

"You will sign a chit, which I shall present for payment." Zarbo glided away and disappeared into a storage room, his robe rustling. His mutters drifted back out to them, a low rumble of unintelligible sound.

"We don't know him," Ellard said. "He could put anything in those spells and make us cluck like damn chicklets. How do we know we can trust him?"

"We don't," Jarlath said. "But we have to do something. Returning to the castle and hiding isn't an option. Sooner or later our attackers will strike."

"Would you rather have Razvan taking over the leadership of Viros?" Keira stared down her pert nose at Ellard. "That is the alternative."

"How do we know you're not siding with the Cawdor already? You bear the mark of the crow." Ellard heaved a mighty sigh, and Jarlath helped him struggle to his feet. "I bet you know more than you're letting on."

"I don't have to listen to you assassinating my character," Keira said. "I'll go and talk to Zarbo." She stomped to the storeroom.

"Wait, Keira." There had been a certain something in her expression, a flicker of thought he didn't want to grasp. In her face, he'd seen guilt. Yes, he'd seen regret and shame at Ellard's accusation.

She ignored him and slammed the storeroom door, closing herself inside with Zarbo. She was in an enclosed space with another man. Jarlath's feline let out a snarl of protest, and he had to fight the urge to wrench open the door and grab her. He let out a chuff, a tiny bit of him amused at his possessive reaction. He ripped his gaze from the door and forced himself to concentrate on his friend.

"Jarlath, you can't trust her. You haven't known her for long. She comes from Gramite. She's a plant, put there by the House of Cawdor to spy on us and gather information."

Ellard had a point—Jarlath admitted it, but in his heart, he didn't believe she was the enemy. A snarl erupted up his throat, his feline agitated and restless, stretching under his skin and objecting to their separation from Keira.

"Put your teeth away," Ellard snapped. "I'm your friend."

Jarlath sucked in a breath and another to settle his feline. "Keira helped us to enter and exit the castle. She didn't need to do that. She didn't need to come into the city today either." But Ellard's harping had started him thinking. Why was she so insistent about the magical charms when she'd grabbed a handful on the night of the first appearance? "No, we met Keira because I decided to take a different route through the forest."

"Keep telling yourself that, Jarlath. She knows about magic, actively seeks out spells for personal use."

"You're saying she cast a spell to make me choose that path?" No. No, he didn't think she was capable of that sort of deception.

Keira stomped from the room with a bag hung over her shoulder. "I'm going to check on my factory then go home. This isn't my fight."

Ellard snorted.

Keira whirled on him with a screech. "What?"

"Walking away makes you look guilty."

"Enough," Jarlath snapped. "Leave her alone. We have more important things to worry about."

"I don't think you should go off with Kiera without me," Ellard said.

"I said enough," Jarlath said. "Are you all right? Can you walk under your own steam? You lost consciousness for a while."

Keira muttered something under her breath, and her scowl grew wider, her ire concentrated on Ellard.

"I have a hard head. I'm fine."

Keira mumbled something else, which Jarlath decided to ignore.

Zarbo shuffled from the storeroom with several charms in his big, bony hands. "Here you go. I found more protection spells. This one here in the baggie is stronger. That should do what you need it to, Miss."

"Thank you," Keira said.

"Anything else before we go?" Jarlath asked.

Ellard managed to walk a few steps and his balance wasn't quite as precarious as earlier. "Yeah, I have a question for Keira. Exactly what spell did you purchase from the magic man? Why was it so important for you to come here and place yourself in danger?"

CHAPTER TEN

The man was strumming her last nerve. She had enough in her worry box without Ellard poking holes in her character. Razvan was ready to make his move. It was like someone rubbing her feathers—no, skin—the wrong way. She'd never had real feathers, never would because of her half-breed status.

"Cat got ya tongue?" Ellard asked in a soft voice, which straddled taunting.

Jarlath crossed the distance between them in two giant steps, and to her surprise, aligned himself with her by slipping an arm around her waist. "We're all going. Ellard, we'll make sure you get to the lower guard station and help you check out the situation."

"Thanks, Zarbo. Stay safe," Keira said and allowed Jarlath to guide her from the magic man's abode.

"Don't let Ellard get to you," Jarlath murmured.

"I'm not."

There were more people on the streets now. Some wandered, white-faced and in a daze and picked their way through the rubble. Others lay on the ground, limbs torn asunder and bleeding. Men and women comforted each other. Some cried. A few prowled in feline form and roared their displeasure.

Their pain was a living thing. It gripped and twisted her insides. Their fear communicated with her crow, became one with her.

"They're broken," she whispered.

"We have to help. Set up a treatment base," Jarlath said.

Behind them, Ellard groaned. "Defense more important. More injured if we...can't stop the attacks." He staggered, his hand held to his head as if it was paining him.

"You need to shift," Jarlath said.

"The injured need to shift too," Keira said. "Why aren't they shifting?"

"Jarlath, need you to carry my shirt and jacket." Ellard said, and there was warning along with the pain in his voice.

They paused while Ellard partially disrobed and handed Jarlath his pendant. He shifted and trotted beside her, so close his hot breath pierced the syncotton of her trews.

Telling them about Razvan's appearance at her house wouldn't help. Yet guilt trickled through her veins, pounded in her head. They couldn't let him win because the idea of her half-brother in charge, the idea of being at his mercy was untenable.

On the next level down in the city, the scene appeared much the same. Traumatized citizens with dozens injured beyond the help of a medic. Twining with the scent of dust and burning dwellings was the metallic odor of blood. Beneath her skin the crow flapped and scratched and clawed and pecked and protested until Keira wanted to scream. Instead, she sucked up her inner torment and marched at Jarlath's side. She scanned their surroundings, any bright colors sending new waves of anxiety swirling across her skin.

At least Ellard seemed to be doing better in his leopard form. He was a big beast, powerful and stocky, and he kept pace beside her, his hot breath on her leg reminding her he could leap at any sec. A bite from his powerful jaw, a twist of her neck and she'd be gone.

On the next level down, the street was devoid of rubble and fallen citizens.

"Why did they leave this street?" Her whisper sounded loud in the oppressive silence, and she flinched.

"I don't know," Jarlath said.

She scanned the street, her crow chirping with uneasiness. "The atmosphere is wrong."

Ellard let out an unhappy bark of agreement, and they resumed walking, although at a slower pace, their gazes taking in every possible hiding place. Before they reached the end of the street, four figures appeared. They wore robes the color of fresh blood. The figures spread out and paused, as if waiting for their approach. Keira's hand slid down to her weapon, the hard grip of the butt reassuring.

The figures didn't communicate, but sprang in concert. Their red cloaks swirled. Large bodies twisted, faces shifted.

Flying stars, they were felines.

Beside her Jarlath cursed.

Ellard sprang at a leopard in mid-shift.

Keira pulled her weapon, squeezed the trigger. Missed.

A large paw swiped at her arm, connected with her blaster. She cried out, tried to maintain her grip. The weapon flew through the air, clattered to the ground.

Instinct told her to jump. She jumped and the charging feline missed her. She found her knife in her hand, slashed and slashed again. Blood spurted from the leopard's chest. A wound she had inflicted. The creature gathered itself to leap, faltered.

Another leopard leaped on it and twisted the injured animal's neck.

It flopped to the ground. Dead.

161

Sorrow filled her, short-lived because an enormous black leopard stalked closer, its eyes a golden glow of hatred. Fear punched, told her legs to run. She stood firm, waited, saw the instant the creature decided to attack.

Keira dodged, spun to the side and brandished her weapon. Her knife slid along the cat's shoulder, sliced a shallow wound down its side.

The cat roared. It whirled, big paws slicing, snagging her cloak. She yanked, panic a hoarse sob as she struggled free. Another leopard roared and charged.

With the first animal distracted, she darted closer and drove her knife into its chest. She watched the life seep from the creature before jerking her knife free. The bloody blade had her swallowing rapidly. Once. Twice.

Something hit her from behind, sent her flying.

She hit the cobblestones hard, cried out. Her knife skittered away.

She pushed to hands and knees, crawled but a big paw knocked her flat. Keira sobbed, scrambled for her knife.

Hot breath heated her neck. She bucked, struggled, tried to throw off the cat. Too big. Too strong.

She was going to die.

The leopard roared, the raspy scream of victory shooting terror to her mind. Her crow screamed, urging her to fight. She wanted to live, to live, to live.

Another roar sounded. The feline holding her down screamed in return then his weight disappeared.

Keira sucked in a breath, stunned, then the desire for life had her scuttling for safety. She rose on shaky legs, took a faltering step and hunched over, agony rippling across her skin. Her breaths came harsh, deafening to sensitive ears. A roaring sound grew louder, louder, louder until a shriek burst up her throat. Her skin rippled, her muscles bunched, released, bunched, released in torturous rhythm.

Her eyesight went wonky. The world filmed over. She blinked and everything magnified. She cocked her head, lifted her arms and croaked in dismay.

A change in the air boosted her warning signals. Jump, her mind screamed. So she jumped and a leopard shot beneath her feet. A second cat charged after it and both sped around a corner, disappearing from sight.

Keira settled to the ground with a relieved sigh and spread her clawed feet—

Fear.

Shock.

Confusion.

Disbelief.

The emotions pelted her like enemy blaster fire as she stared down at the ground.

She...she...

She had big, ugly black feet.

A hoarse grunt came from behind. She jumped, large black wings shooting out to lift her higher off the ground.

She...she was flying.

The instant the thought coalesced, her wings stopped, instincts screeched to a halt and she dropped like a heavy stone. She hit the ground hard, the air smacking from her lung sacs. Stunned, she lay on the cobblestones, the blood and gore of wounded felines spread around her.

The grunt sounded again, and she tensed, ready for the killing bite.

It didn't come.

Instead the grunt repeated. Insistent. Bossy.

Keira managed to lift her feathery body off the ground and she turned to face the feline. Bright green eyes stared at her—not golden like the other cats.

Jarlath?

She cawed, the unattractive croak emerging with a trace of a question.

The leopard sighed and rubbed its furry head against hers.

Jarlath.

Relief replaced some of her trepidation and the tightness faded from her chest. She glanced around and got a better look at the four feline bodies on the ground.

Razvan had worked magic indeed, to turn felines against their own. But how to fix this, and more importantly, how the frig did she turn back to humanoid?

Another feline trotted into sight.

A caw escaped her, one of alarm.

Jarlath angled in front of her. Although she was large in her crow form, many times bigger than the birds that flew through the forest, Jarlath's feline made her feel dainty.

The new arrival halted in front of them. The air swirled around him and he shifted, the transformation fast and pain-free because he didn't show any sign of discomfort.

"What the frukk, Jarlath? She's the enemy."

Jarlath stepped away and shifted. In humanoid form, he sidled nearer. He crossed his arms over his chest and glared at his friend. "Leave Keira alone. She fought with us."

When Ellard continued to scowl, Jarlath stroked her feathers.

A shudder went through her, one of pleasure, and a coo escaped her beak.

Ellard grunted. "She can't stay like that. Shift. The guard station isn't far from here." He frowned and bent to study the face of a dead feline. "Grata."

"What?"

"This leopard looks familiar. He resembles one of the charge soldiers."

"Their eyes were golden. All our people have green."

"I know," Ellard said, and Keira heard the worry in his voice. "I hope they're all right at the station. Hurry, you need to shift before we attract more attention."

"Ellard's right," Jarlath said. "You need to shift. People will shoot first if they see you and not bother with questions."

Keira cawed, the sound grumpy and frustrated.

Ellard pulled on his tunic and cloak, refastened his pendant. "What's the hold up?"

"She hasn't shifted before. She's half Cawdor and didn't know she could shift."

"*Frukk*," Ellard cursed. "Talk her through. The process can't be any different from when we shift."

Keira's escalating panic eased at Ellard's suggestion. Yes. That might work. Her mother had spoken about her crow half but had told her the Greenmont genes were dominant. According to her mother, she'd bear more Cawdor characteristics if she'd inherited the ability to shift. She glanced down and mentally frowned at her feet.

They were so big, so ugly, so *black*.

Jarlath's fingers moved over her feathers again and she pressed against his side, drawn to entice him to repeat the caress. He chuckled and stroked her head.

"Cristo, grata and frukkity frukk," Ellard swore. "This isn't the time for petting. Tell her how to shift so we can get moving."

"Go ahead if you're so worried," Jarlath said. "I'll help Keira and we'll follow."

Ellard shook his head. "We don't know what we might find. It's better if we stick together. Besides, the protection spells didn't help a bit."

Keira didn't want Ellard glaring at her and tapping his foot while she attempted to shift, but she got his point. They were stronger as a team. Not that Ellard trusted her. He'd made that very clear.

Jarlath crouched and ran his fingers over one feathered wing. A shudder sped through her and fierce hunger thrummed along her veins, made her heart ventricles pump double-time. She wanted to jump him, shower affection and rain down lust.

"I want you to picture your humanoid form, sweetheart. The form you see in the looking-glass each morn." His voice was a husky rumble and the sexy sound upped the sensations swelling within her feathery body. "Keira, are you listening? Draw a picture of your human self in your mind. Don't think of anything else except how it feels to be you when you stand on two legs."

Focus, stupid. Keira glanced at her feet because looking at Jarlath wasn't helping. She recalled her reflection and clung to the memory. Long brown hair, green eyes with gold flecks. A green tinge to her skin. Her mouth. The rest of her body.

"Once you have the form cemented in your mind, focus on how it feels when you're walking around the farm, picking berries, helping Melvyn shift the malpacks. Working with Hilda and Hortese in the kitchen."

Keira let his descriptions flood her mind.

"That's it, Keira. Think how much you want to walk on two legs instead of hop."

Shooting stars, she didn't want to hop for the rest of her life. She wanted hands again. Normal feet. She concentrated hard, felt a tingle sweep through her body. The tingle morphed to pain. Hurts. She struggled against the hard press of agony.

"Don't fight it."

"H-hurts." The word came out in a garble of bird talk.

"Breathe. Deep breaths."

The torture grew worse, her muscles convulsing, twisting and cramping. She cried out, desperate to stop the torment. The pain peaked then receded as her humanoid form took precedence. She panted, her skin coated with sweat. Her heart ventricles raced and blood roared in her ears.

"Well done. Hand me my cloak, Ellard," Jarlath said.

Keira lifted her head to see Jarlath frown. She didn't know what caused it. All she knew was she needed him to hold her right now. She threw herself into his arms, sighed when they wrapped around her, drawing her tight to his muscular chest. His naked chest. Every one of her female hormones stood and saluted.

"You're fully clothed," he said.

Oh good. He'd noticed too. They needed to ditch Ellard and get to the good stuff.

"How did you do that?" Ellard said. "Even your bag shifted with you and that was over your shoulders."

"What?"

"When we shift we have to remove our upper garments. If we don't, our shift shreds them. I can't tell you how many shirts I wrecked when I first learned to shift," Jarlath said.

"I've never seen the Cawdor people shift. I've seen them in crow form, but none of them ever shifted in front of me. Most stayed away from Greenmont valley."

"Doesn't matter," Jarlath said. "We'll find someone to answer our questions once things calm down. Maybe your mother will know."

"She won't take my call. She said it's safer for both of us." Keira bit her lip and prayed neither of the men asked questions.

"Although this is fascinating, we should leave," Ellard said.

Jarlath cupped her chin and directed her gaze to his. "Okay?"

"I will be," she said. "We'd better hurry or Ellard will get even grumpier."

"He's concerned."

"The enemy has amassed strong magic if they can turn your people against each other. We should worry."

Keira increased her speed to a trot and Jarlath kept pace.

"How do you feel?"

"Scared. Confused. I don't understand why I shifted. Thank you for helping me shift back."

"My pleasure," he purred, and her hormones did another of those snappy salutes.

Up ahead, Ellard ran to a sturdy building and pounded on the door. It opened and he disappeared inside.

By common consent, Jarlath and Keira put on a spurt of speed. When they burst through the door, they found Ellard with a woman in his arms, her body crushed against his chest because he held her so tight.

Finally, he released her, but he kept her hand clasped in his. Tall and slender, the woman had long black hair, tied back in a braid.

"I've never met his girl before. She's pretty," Jarlath murmured.

"He doesn't talk about her?"

"I knew he was seeing someone but I had no idea—frukk. Look at her eyes."

Keira froze as the woman turned golden orbs on her. Her crow stirred, sending urgent messages of warning through her and the desire to flee. Keira stood firm as she stared at the stunningly beautiful woman. The contrast between her and Ellard startled her because this woman could have any man. Keira was sure Ellard possessed many good qualities but handsome features weren't one of them.

"I need a sit-rep to take to my father," Ellard said. "How many soldiers remain? Where are the others? Mareeka, I'm so glad you're safe."

"He hasn't noticed her eyes," Keira whispered. "How? She's staring straight at him."

"She's shifter. I sense that much, but she reeks in the same way as the men in red."

"Who are they?" the woman asked, her crisp voice full of compulsion.

"We're friends," Jarlath said before Ellard could answer.

"Ellard hasn't mentioned you." No missing her suspicion.

"Mareeka, these are my friends. We've come to help," Ellard said, his voice softer, gentler than Keira had ever heard it before.

"We work with Ellard," Keira said. "Where are the other soldiers?"

"I sent them to reconnoiter," Mareeka said.

Lie. Keira didn't know how she knew, but the woman was lying. She separated from Jarlath in an attempt to split the woman's attention. She couldn't watch them both.

The woman pulled out a blaster and pointed it at Jarlath. "Don't move."

"What are you doing?" Ellard moved to block her aim.

The woman shifted her stance to focus on Keira. "What are you? You don't smell right."

Jarlath sidled farther away. Distract, Keira thought. "I am Cawdor." The acknowledgment almost choked her but the woman brightened.

"Razvan said he would send reinforcements. Seize their weapons. He is bodyguard to the prince."

"Really?" Keira said and pulled her knife from her boot. "Should I gut him where he stands?"

Her harsh words seemed to jolt Ellard from his frozen shock. "You're a spy for the Cawdor? I don't understand. I thought you...we..." he trailed off in confusion.

Keira felt sorry for him, felt his pain and bewilderment.

The woman barked out a brittle sound of amusement. "I'm beautiful. Why would I hook up with an ugly man like you when I could choose anyone? You were convenient and quite stupid. We duped you good."

Keira glared at Mareeka. No, Ellard wasn't attractive like Jarlath, but he was a good man who did his duty and protected others to his best ability.

"You lied?" Ellard sagged, his confidence oozing from his face to leave pale shock.

"Of course I did," the woman scoffed. "We did. So much you

don't know."

Ellard's broad shoulders tensed, and Keira witnessed his pain and embarrassment before he shut his emotions away. It was obvious he'd cared for her, and she'd just stomped on his heart. *We?* Did she mean Razvan or someone else?

"Why?" Jarlath demanded from the other side of the room.

"To serve my lover and master," she said.

"Which master?" Keira asked, although she feared she knew.

"The ruler of the House of Cawdor," the woman said. "Razvan is the true ruler, and he will rule over the cats and crow."

Not if Keira had her way.

"Where are the other soldiers?" Jarlath asked.

"I told you. They're out taking care of their duties," the woman said, her eyes blazing bright gold now with the fervor of a fanatic. "Stop moving. I know what you're doing. I'll shoot."

Jarlath froze. On the opposite side of the office room, Keira did too. She didn't like the way the woman was waving her weapon.

Ellard took half a step toward the woman.

"Stop." She lifted her blaster. "Stop or I'll shoot."

"Put your weapon down," Ellard commanded and took a step closer.

The woman squeezed the trigger, and Ellard dropped like a rock.

Keira threw her knife at the same time as Jarlath fired his weapon. The woman fell, her blaster clattering onto the floor.

Keira kicked the woman's weapon away before she crouched to check her status and retrieve her knife. "She's dead. How's Ellard?"

"His arm is bleeding like a stuck boar-pig," Jarlath said with urgency. "Can you see if there is a medical kit around here?"

Ellard moaned and thrashed.

"Steady." Jarlath kept pressure on Ellard's arm and placed his other hand on his friend's chest. His touch seeming to soothe Ellard.

Keira scanned the room, and when she didn't see a medi-kit, she checked the cupboards. Nothing. She spied a doorway and found a small kitchenette with a chillbox and cookbox—both ancient models—plus a basic replicator, another early version with known bugs. Ah, a medical kit. She grabbed it and hurried to Jarlath while praying it held the requisite items, given the other old technology available at the guard station.

"Is there a blood stopper?"

She rifled through the contents and pulled out a syringe plus coagulant spray. Her first real glance at Ellard's arm deepened her alarm. "That doesn't look good."

Jarlath cast a concerned glance at Ellard. "He's gonna lose his arm. I doubt even shifting will fix this."

"We'll try," Keira said.

Ellard groaned, his cry one of severe pain.

"Steady, my friend. Steady. Is there a knock-out drug or at least some type of painkiller?"

"It's a basic kit. We'll have to take him to the medical center. I'll find transport." She shot to her feet and was halfway to the door when Jarlath spoke.

"Keira."

"Yes?"

"Be careful. I'd hate for something to happen to you."

Warmth filled her as their gazes met and held. So much said with one look. Everything inside her went soft and feminine. "I'll be back as soon as I can."

She raced into the street, pulled out her blaster, ready to fire if the need arose. The street was deserted. She skirted rubble from neighboring buildings, keeping her eyes peeled. The soldiers must have transport. Hushed voices drifted to her, and she circled a drunken building to find two male youths attempting to hotwire a flymo several buildings down from the soldiers' base. Excellent.

"You! Hands above your head," she ordered.

"Find yer own," one of the youths said, his red skin and thick dreads marking him as Red Mumber. "This be our vehicle."

His skinny friend nudged him. "She got weapon."

"I'll do a deal," Keira said, focusing on the Red Mumber since he seemed the most dangerous. The other youth was small and wiry, no trouble for her to deal with on her own. "You hotwire this vehicle and take me and my friends to the medical center, and I'll let you both leave with the vehicle and a cash reward."

"Currency?" the Red Mumber asked.

"If you want." Keira said.

"How we know you trustworthy?" The Red Mumber's deep brown eyes glittered with suspicion.

"You don't," Keira said. "All you have is my word."

The youth considered her for a long drawn-out moment. "I know you. Seen you in market. You don't pay, I find."

"Agreed," Keira said. "Would you like me to show you how to hotwire? I have the knack. My mother taught me."

"You know how?" The Red Mumber's red-brown brows rose, broadcasting doubt.

"Yes." Deciding to take a chance, she holstered her weapon and entered the transport. Seconds later the hum of the flymo highlighted her expertise.

"Sweet," the second youth said.

The Red Mumber glanced left then right. "Where your friends?"

"Fly around to the front of the soldiers' base. We might need your help. The injured man is big."

"Cat?" the Red Mumber asked.

"Yes, but he's too injured to shift."

"I come with," the Red Mumber said. "Nasir will bring flymo to the door front."

"Thanks," Keira said and hustled back in the direction she'd come with the Red Mumber youth on her heels. She leaped over a pile of masonry without breaking stride and pushed through the door of the soldiers' base.

"I'm back," Keira called. "I've brought help."

"This be Ellard," the Red Mumber said, turning his accusing gaze on her then sharing his disquiet with Jarlath. "He important."

"He's my friend," Jarlath said. "What's your name?"

"Ollie," the Red Mumber said.

"How is he?" Keira asked.

"He's passed out from the pain. A blessing." Jarlath rubbed his eyes and stood, his posture slumped. "I've stopped the bleeding but the blaster fire has disintegrated the bone. I've done all I can. He needs a healer."

"I help carry to flymo. Nasir out front now. Waiting," Ollie said.

A shout sounded outside.

Keira stiffened. "I'll go and make sure no one steals our transport."

The shouts were closer now, propelling her to speed. She burst from the office, blaster raised to fire.

"It's some of those dudes in red cloaks," Nasir whispered. "This not good. Saw some blow up. They be walkin' bombs."

"Get ready to take off. The others are coming." Keira watched uneasily as the men in red marched closer.

Jarlath and Ollie appeared, the two struggling with Ellard's weight. Keira hurried to help.

A chill wind tugged at her hair, at her cloak and fear rushed to the fore. "Quick. A storm is coming." A rush of rain had swept over earlier, when the last explosions occurred. Coincidence? She didn't think so.

The men in red advanced, their robes blowing back to reveal the uniform of Viros soldiers. Keira gasped. She didn't know how Razvan had managed to turn loyal men to his cause. The rain came closer and the wind whipped her hair and the hem of her cloak. Hard drops of rain stung her cheeks. Sparks started to flash off the men in red.

"Hurry," she shouted.

They managed to half-drag and lift Ellard into the flymo and scrambled after him. Nasir sent the flymo into a vertical lift, rising so fast her stomach remained on the ground. She gulped and Jarlath's arm wrapped around her shoulders.

"We'll make it," he whispered against her ear.

"I feel as if I have bruises on bruises. Every bone in my body is throbbing." She glanced at Ellard's pale, still body and winced. "Sorry. I shouldn't complain when others have it worse than me."

Jarlath kissed her temple, the kiss as soft as his fur. "It's been some day. Most women of my acquaintance would moan about the state of their hair, the ones who didn't faint."

"You don't know the right women."

"I do now," he whispered.

She held the compliment close to her heart, his personal opinion of her raising her flagging spirits. Ellard moaned, but didn't wake.

"Jarlath, the men in red were Viros soldiers. I saw their uniforms when the wind blew up their cloaks. How has this happened?"

Jarlath crouched to check on his friend before rising again. "It tastes of magic. Somehow we need to stop the spell or reflect it back to the source."

"I can't see where I'm going," Nasir shouted. "The rain is too heavy."

"Keep going up," Jarlath ordered.

"Aye," Ollie said, his brown eyes wide and wild. "Plan."

An explosion rocked the ground below them. A ripple of shockwave shook the flymo, and Nasir struggled to keep their vehicle on course, his wiry arms fighting the gravity pull. Finally, the flymo ceased the metallic shudders and leveled.

"Sky is clearing," Nasir said. "Damn, most of the lower city be rubble."

Keira glanced out the clear window and saw he was right. "Might be safer to take Ellard out to the farm."

"We should try the medical center first," Jarlath said. "If they can't save his arm, they'll have a surgeon to remove it. We can't do that."

Keira shuddered and studied the city below. "Someone needs to take control."

"I intend to," Jarlath said. "Just as soon as we get Ellard to a safe place."

"The medical center be in one piece," Ollie said.

"I be doing circle first," Nasir said. "No point landing in the midst of those red frukkers."

"Why did they put a protective barrier around the castle?" Jarlath asked.

Keira tried not to think of the possible scenarios. They popped into her head anyway. "Maybe Razvan wanted to keep the castle intact. Maybe he wants to live there or maybe he's keeping the residents safe to make an example of them at a later time."

"Whatever he's doing, I don't like it," Jarlath said. "By destroying the lower city, he's sliced the legs from the kingdom. Economically, at least. It will take time to rebuild, and the king and the council won't fund the rebuild. It shames me to admit this, but it's the truth."

"What you know of fancy pants at castle?" Ollie demanded.

Keira saw Nasir's attention divided, proving his interest in the answer.

Jarlath hesitated. "Ellard lives at the castle."

"He security for royal prince," Nasir said. "How you know Ellard?"

"He's my best friend," Jarlath said.

"What about her?" Ollie asked, the sharp jerk of his shoulder disturbing his dreads.

"She's my woman," Jarlath said.

"You live at castle?" Nasir asked.

"No," Keira said. "I live on a farm."

Nasir and Ollie glanced at each other. "It be safe?"

"So far," Keira said. "We intend to take Ellard there after we get medical treatment. You could come with us if you want."

The two youths exchanged a look.

"Maybe," Ollie said. "You still owe us currency."

"Yes," Keira said.

"I land over there in park. Only clear space," Nasir said.

It took three of them to haul Ellard to the medical center.

"I go back to flymo. To keep safe," Ollie said. "We wait unless dangerous." With a wave, he ran out the door.

"They didn't recognize me," Jarlath said, and there was something odd in his tone. "They live in the city and they didn't recognize the heir to the throne. What does that say about the royal family? About me? We're so busy living in the castle fortress we've lost touch with our people. We were ripe for attack."

"It's never too late to change," Keira said.

"Maybe. Watch Ellard. I'll find a medical man."

He stalked off, agitation clear in his rigid shoulders. Her gaze slid down his back to settle on his butt, and she sighed. The more she knew of this man, the more she liked him. Jarlath disappeared around a corner and returned a short time later with an impatient man in tow.

"I have patients to attend to," he snapped, his tanned face pulled tight into a glare. "You have no right to drag me from my patients."

Jarlath trailed, his gaze watchful as if he suspected the man might run for freedom. He reminded Keira of a forest wolf stalking dinner.

"Please take a look," Keira said. "We've stopped the bleeding but his arm is bad."

The man crouched beside Ellard. "This is Ellard. Why didn't you say? Go and summon two stretcher boys. Tell them to bring a big cart. Tell them Moses said to shift their butts into haste."

Jarlath strode off to summon stretcher boys.

"What happened?" the medicine man demanded.

Keira crouched beside him. "Blaster at close quarters."

"He's going to lose the arm. Shifting won't help this," the man said.

"Do your best," Keira said.

Jarlath returned and must have overheard. "Please do your best for him, medicine man. Do what you need to do and make him comfortable for travel."

"He'll stay here," the man said. "That's Ellard."

"I'm aware of his identity," Jarlath said. "Ellard is my best friend, and I intend to care for him."

Whatever the man saw in Jarlath's face reassured him. He gave a curt nod. "We're short of staff. I'll need help. You can both scrub and aid me during the amputation."

Keira's stomach roiled and not in a good way. She reached for Jarlath's hand and squeezed in silent comfort while ordering herself to deal. There was no alternative.

CHAPTER ELEVEN

House of Cawdor, Planet Gramite

Razvan paced the confines of his private chamber, a knifelike pain in his side. Frukk. He pressed his fingers to the ache and muttered under his breath.

His personal servant poked his head in the door. "Did you require something?"

"Leave me." Nagging worry stirred Razvan's temper, and his servant retreated, knowing better than to tangle with him in this mood. Something had happened to Marjo or Mareeka, but the surface of his private scrying bowl remained cloudy.

Frukk it! Frustration tasted cold and dangerous on his tongue. He hated not knowing what was happening on Viros. Marjo and Mareeka's lack of contact put him off-balance, made him doubt the next step in his plan.

He stalked to his scrying bowl and peered into the surface in the hope something had changed. "Grata!" he cursed after long moments presented nothing but dull fog.

His women were clever. Tough. They were chameleon shifters and soldiers. He laughed, the sound forced but heartfelt. His lovers could do anything and would come through for him. Of that, he was confident.

They'd introduced the bacteria to the food supply, rendering a large portion of the feline population unable to shift—a fact the House of the Cat had kept quiet but he knew was successful because of Marjo and Mareeka's confirmation. With the help of the wizards, he'd created the magical barrier around the castle, one only penetrable by those of Cawdor blood, and they'd taken control of the lower guard station and turned the soldiers into mobile bombs.

Each of these steps had gone without a hitch, and there was no reason for this next phase to fail. He was worrying overmuch. Yes, Marjo and Mareeka would have matters under control while preparing for his arrival on Viros. Meantime, instead of worrying, he'd focus on the next part of his plan.

He intended to make an example of Keira, but first, he needed to locate the woman. She wasn't lighting fires or using appliances that harnessed flames, which presented a problem.

He needed a storm.

He needed cold weather.

He needed freezing conditions, which would make fire a necessity because Virosians clung to their old ways instead of embracing technology.

A knock on his door signaled a visitor, and his mother hopped into his private quarters.

"How goes the plan, Razvan?" she chirped, her face radiating curiosity. "Tell me. Tell me. Tell me now."

"My plan is moving as predicted," Razvan said, striving for patience. "Where is Carrick? I require his help."

"Com him," his mother said. "Com. Com. Com him."

"It would help if you located him, Mother," Razvan said. "Please do this for me."

Her narrow lips formed a pout, incongruous on her lined face. She studied him for an instant longer then gave a little jump. "I find him. I find. I find."

Razvan held his breath until she hopped from his rooms. Once she'd vanished, he strode to his door and locked it to prevent another interruption. He needed to concentrate in order to make this a big magnitude storm.

He smiled, and this time the action felt more natural.

Keira Cloud would pay for rejecting him.

And her adopted world would pay for giving her shelter.

Of that, he was confident.

Jarlath stared at Ellard, now in a medically induced coma to speed healing. Despite, medical advice, they'd brought him to Keira's farm and now they waited for Ellard to rouse.

Keira tugged his arm. "Jarlath, the medical man said Ellard won't resurface until morn. You need to rest. Hortese said she'd sleep on the other bed and keep watch over him. Please, you can't help Ellard or your people if you don't rest."

His people. A bitter laugh escaped. "None of my people recognize me. They know Ellard, but not me. That tells me I've been a miserable prince. Yes, I attend official functions, but they're for the upper class."

"Feeling sorry for yourself isn't productive," Keira said. "You want the people to recognize you, then take charge and send Razvan off squawking."

Her blunt words made him laugh, the sound emerging with ease this time. "You're right, sweetheart. Sleep now, worry later. In the morn, Ellard will regain consciousness. He's going to be pissed we saved his life."

"The loss of his arm will be a blow. You'll need to distract him. Put him in charge of the battle plan. Ask Cristop, Nasir and Ollie to act as his assistants. Maybe if you chuck orders at him and don't let him think, he'll feel useful. The meds will keep his pain under control. We need to keep his mind busy, and I think this will speed his healing."

"Clever and pretty. When did I get so lucky?" Jarlath reached for her and tipped up her chin in order to steal a kiss. She melted against him, giving and taking in equal measure. His heart swelled as he explored her mouth, took the kiss deeper.

"Right, enough from the pair of you," Hortese said. "Off to bed with you. I will watch Master Ellard. The min he wakes, I'll call you."

Jarlath pulled back but retained Keira's hand. He walked to Hortese and kissed her cheek. "Thank you."

Hortese flushed, her pink skin burning even brighter. "I'm happy to help. Now off to bed."

"You've won her heart," Keira said as she led him up the stairs to the second floor of the manor house. "And she's no pushover. If you can win Hortese, you can win the rest of the population."

"You make it sound easy."

"Nothing worthwhile is simple but you can do this, Jarlath."

He hoped she was right because the last few days had shown him how badly his father was failing the Virosian people and him, by extension.

Keira led him into her chamber. "You will sleep with me."

"Yes." His feline rumbled a soft purr of encouragement.

Keira slid a knife from her boot and placed it on the dresser before she sat to remove her footwear.

"Let me do that for you." Cristo, she was beautiful. His warrior.

He pushed the button to release the snaps on her boots and tugged them off her feet. Next, he removed her tunic and the rest of her garments until she stood before him, naked. "I want you, but I don't want to hurt you. You have bruises on your hip and more on your legs."

"I'm alive. We're both alive. Others weren't so lucky."

"I know. Wait, let me remove the plaster from your face." He peeled the dressing away and traced the crow tattoo with his finger. She shuddered. Jarlath smiled at the reaction and turned his attention to his own apparel. He yanked at his footwear and hopped around like an ungainly bird while removing his boots.

"I haven't thanked you for talking me through the change from crow to humanoid. I...it was terrifying. Actually." Her smile bore a trace of irony. "That's an understatement."

Jarlath paused, his hands at his tunic. "You had no idea you could shift?"

"No, the medical men on Gramite said it was impossible. Only full breeds are able to transform."

"Shifting might come in handy for you," Jarlath said.

"Maybe. I didn't realize the transformation hurt so much. You and Ellard make the process appear effortless."

"We've both been shifting for cycles. It becomes second nature." Jarlath pulled his tunic over his head and rapidly removed the rest of his clothes. Nude, he strode to Keira, his chest tight with emotion. "I'm so glad I decided to take a different path during our cambeest ride. Meeting you is the best thing that has ever happened to me."

She ran her fingers over the stubble on his cheeks. "Come to bed. Make love to me."

He raised her fingers to his lips and kissed the delicate skin of her inner wrist. Their gazes meshed, and he was lost.

Their lips met and he swung her into his arms. He placed her on the large bed and crawled over her body. Softness and hardness pressed together. She sighed and clung, offering her lips again.

He explored her breasts, her waist, ran his fingers over the smooth skin of her belly. He nibbled at her neck and let her feel the sharpness of his canines before soothing the sting with the caress of his tongue.

"You are beautiful and strong. My warrior," he said.

She ran her fingers over his back, let one hand come to rest on his butt. She sighed and made tiny caw-caw sounds at the back of her throat. His feline rejoiced in the encouragement and purred louder than Jarlath had ever heard before.

He urged her legs apart and moved down the bed to taste the heart of her. His tongue curled around her clit and she shivered.

"Good?"

"Yes," she whispered.

Her taste was honey and sweetness, and her quim quivered when he pushed a finger inside her heat. She was hot and ready for him and it made him feel powerful and yet humble. There was no pretense here, no pandering to him because he was a royal prince, and that made their loving even more special.

Jarlath rose up her body and kissed her tenderly, twining their tongues together in a replication of their loving to come.

"Jarlath," she said when he lifted his head.

He smiled and guided his cock to her entrance. With his gaze on hers, he pushed deep in one forceful stroke. The heat of her quim seared his cock as she gloved him perfectly. She lifted her hips, taking him deeper until he wasn't sure where he ended and she began.

He kissed her, unhurried and tender, trying to tell her without words how much she meant to him. They mightn't have known each other for long, but his heart knew, accepted. His feline embraced her too.

Breaking the kiss, he pulled back and set up an easy pace of invade and retreat, invade and retreat.

Keira moved with him, her hips rising with each inward stroke. Pleasure soared through him, starting in his balls and increasing to the point of pain. He gasped as the sensation rose up his cock. His seed exploded from him in hard spurts, the pleasure sweeping to all corners of his body, and he bit her neck, right on the fleshy part where neck and shoulder met. He tasted her blood and shock hit him. Grata, he'd bitten her again. Savage.

Instead of protesting, Keira keened—a reassuring cry of acute pleasure. Her fingernails dug into his shoulders, her gasps loud, frantic. Mindful of last time, he reached between them to give her the extra pressure she required. Her gasps turned to moans, and it was the sweetest music he'd ever heard.

"Keira," he whispered, his finger doing another sweep across her nub while his tongue lapped the wound he'd made on her neck. It had healed last time, and he hoped this would happen again. Biting seemed so savage, yet contrarily, the instinct to mark her felt right and pleased his feline.

Another moan slid from her throat, and he felt the rhythmic surge around his cock. He rubbed her clit again and she screamed. His Keira screamed.

"Pure magic of the good kind."

"Yes." Her mouth cracked open in a yawn. "Sorry. It's been a long day."

"An eventful one," he agreed, some of the joy dispersing from him at the reminder. "Maybe you should soak in your heated pool to help with your aches and pains."

"Go to sleep," she ordered. "Tomorrow we will make a plan to best Razvan, but now we require rest."

"Yes." He parted their bodies, too tired to do anything except draw her into his arms.

Jarlath came awake without warning, his heart hammering in alarm. A masculine voice rose in anger, and he sighed.

He'd recognize the shouts anywhere. Ellard was conscious and bellowing like a bull-steer forced to do something against his will.

"What is it?" Keira asked, her voice laden with sleep.

"Ellard is awake. I need to go to him, explain."

"I'm coming with." Keira slid off the opposite side of the bed. "You might as well sanitize first."

When he opened his mouth to argue, she grabbed his hand and led him into the adjoining room. She turned on her sanitizer unit and pushed him inside.

"I'll get your clothes," she said.

Jarlath sighed and reached for cleanser liquid. She was right. At the very least, it would wake his sluggish mind. He needed to gather fortitude to deal with Ellard.

Keira appeared secs later, his clothes in hand. She set them on a chair and padded over to join him.

Unable to help himself, he kissed her, seeking calm and comfort from her touch before he faced the waiting ordeal. The skin where he'd bitten her was pale with her normal tinge of green. Smooth and unblemished. Unusual, but then he'd never bitten a woman before. She kissed him back then withdrew, reaching behind him to pinch his bottom.

"Off you go," she said. "I will join you shortly. Ellard can shout at you before he takes shots at me."

Jarlath laughed, even though her words weren't funny. Ellard would hate him for this. He knew his friend would rather die than live with one arm. Danion Tetsu would kick him off the security force. He'd reject his son as disabled, and Ellard would blame him. But grata, he'd make the same decision again. Allowing his friend to die wasn't an option.

Once dressed, Jarlath straightened his shoulders and marched toward the loud, furious shouts. He entered the guest bedroom to see Ellard propped up against the pillows, his face red with fury.

"You," he thundered on seeing Jarlath. "You let them do this to me."

Hortese sniffed. "Rude man. Look at this mess you made."

"She tried to feed me like a child."

"That's because he's acting like a youngling," Hortese snapped.

"You must have other work to do," Jarlath said. "I'll clean this up."

Hortese scanned his face, her irritation fading from her expression. "Cleaning materials are in the kitchen. I'll send them with one of the boys."

"Thanks." Jarlath waited until she left before taking another fortifying breath and turning to his friend.

"Why?" Ellard's eyes shone with unshed tears. "It's my weapon arm. I can't do anything without my arm."

"What about all the other men and women who were injured by the bombs. People have died. I need your help to plan our way out of this, Ellard. I know you're angry, but I did what was best for Viros. We need you, one armed or not. You're my friend. I couldn't let you die. You're my friend," he repeated.

"I thought my arm was all right. I thought I'd imagined Mareeka firing at me." His voice caught and his throat worked as he swallowed. "This is my fault. She played me. I recruited her and...and we became close. She played me."

Jarlath sat on the edge of the bed. "It doesn't matter. We learn from our mistakes, and you won't make the same one again."

Ellard snorted, pain clearly written on his plain features. "Father will relieve me of responsibility. I won't have the chance to make the same mistake. Besides, what woman would want me now? I'm not pretty like you, and now I'm missing an arm. What woman would want me?"

"That's fodo crap. Everyone recognizes you. They know who you are and of your position. Not one recognized me. You will help me, Ellard. I don't trust anyone else."

Ellard was quiet for a sec. "Hortese said I'm confined to my bed, that if I attempted to move she'd drug me. She meant it, so what help can I be?"

"If you feel up to it, you need to shift. That will speed your recovery. Then we're going to make a plan. I'll go out with the boys and scout the city."

"I'll go with you," Keira said, appearing in the doorway.

"No, I want you to stay—"

Keira stopped beside him, her scent distracting him. "I'm going with you."

Jarlath didn't argue because her expression told him he'd lose. Besides, he felt easier if she was close. He turned back to Ellard.

"I will be king soon. My father intends to stand aside and let me take charge." With conditions attached. Somehow, he'd get around this obstacle because he wasn't interested in anyone except Keira. "We need to make the kingdom safer and improve conditions for those who live in the lower city, but first we need to get rid of Razvan."

"You trust her?" Bitterness turning Ellard's features hard. "Mareeka strung me along. She was a traitor. Keira wears the mark of the crow on her cheek, and she told Mareeka she was one of Razvan's team."

"I'm no traitor," Keira snapped.

"Enough. I trust her," Jarlath said, and he realized it was true. Every particle of him accepted and believed in her honesty and integrity. She was no traitor.

"First, break the magical spell that is keeping the castle in the bubble," Ellard said.

"How?" Jarlath asked. "Calls aren't getting through any longer." He searched his jacket pocket and pulled out his com. "Nothing," he said. "The com is dead."

"You'll need me to enter the castle," Keira said.

"She's right," Ellard said, his mouth twisting with cynicism as he scrutinized her.

"Does that mean you're going to help us? That you've decided to believe in Keira?" Jarlath asked.

"I'll agree to a ceasefire until we best Razvan," Ellard said with a glower. "But I'll be watching my back because I don't trust her."

"Deal." Jarlath shot Keira a swift glance, registered her pain and stood. "Shift. The medical man said it would aid your recovery."

Ellard jerked his head in Keira's direction. "Not in front of her. And you'd better not tell Hortese. She threatened to drug me."

"I'll go and help Hortese with a meal to break our fast," Keira said, her emotions now gathered and contained behind an impassive expression.

Keira stepped into the kitchen her mind racing in a dozen different directions. She should tell them about Razvan, but if she told Jarlath about Razvan, he mightn't believe her story. Ellard would cast doubt for sure.

Flying stars. No matter what she did, she'd end up in the wrong.

Razvan...he'd do anything to get what he wanted. He wouldn't think twice of telling untruths to fester distrust in Jarlath. No, Razvan must never know of her feelings for Jarlath. She had one of Zarbo's repulsion spells and another to destroy him if she managed to get close enough. Whether the spells would work, Zarbo couldn't guarantee, but it was better than no weapon.

"I'm going into the city again, Hortese. Jarlath needs my help."

Hortese turned away from stirring a pot to scorch her with disapproval. "What's that on your face?" She moved closer, and her eyes widened, bulging to greater prominence. "That's a crow."

"It appeared yesterday."

"You can't go into the city looking like that."

"I can't stay here and do nothing. Somewhere in the city, there's a clue to halt this attack. I have a protection spell, a repulsion spell, and I'll have my weapons." She didn't mention the additional spell to stave off worry in her friend.

"It's madness to get involved, given the way people here treat you. You owe them nothing," Hortese said, waving her spoon in emphasis of her words.

"I want to help Jarlath."

"He's the prince," Hortese said in her blunt way. "He won't marry you. All you'll ever be is his mistress. You'll be repeating history. You told me you didn't want to ape your mother."

Keira shrugged, aiming for careless despite the inner tension tightening her muscles. "The heart wants what the heart wants."

Hortese glanced over her shoulder to ascertain they were alone. Shock still reverberated in her expression when she turned back to Keira. "You love him?"

"We haven't known each other long, but I can't imagine life without him. And that's a problem. He's the prince and will one day rule the House of the Cat."

"Maybe that won't matter."

Keira snorted. "With my reputation? Once Marcus's son and daughter learn of Jarlath's interest in me, rumors will fly like winged cambeests. At best I could take the position of mistress, but after my mother...I won't let myself fall into the same trap."

"You don't speak much of your mother." Hortese's glance held silent questions. "You've told me the circumstances but not who kept her."

"My mother was Xavier Cronan's mistress."

Hortese's face drained of its healthy pink color. "The leader of the House of Cawdor."

"Yes."

"Did Marcus know?"

"Marcus knew. My mother arranged my marriage because I was attracting undesirable attention on Gramite. She wanted me safe off planet."

"Safe from what?" Hortese sent her a shrewd glance. "From whom?"

"The who isn't important."

"You should stay here at the farm." Hortese didn't believe her.

"I can't stay here and do nothing when I can help Jarlath."

"Why can't you let the soldiers do their job?" Hortese asked. "The city is dangerous. I don't want you to get hurt."

"Most of the soldiers are dead and others are trapped in the castle. The advance spies have done a good job of destroying the framework of the House of the Cat." Which was also a worry. Maybe she should try to contact her mother. Now that Razvan had discovered her location, there was no reason to avoid communication. "Are the com units still down?"

"I haven't tried them."

Keira scooped up the nearest com and attempted to call out. "No, nothing. I'll try later."

A peculiar scuffling combined with thumps came from upstairs and moved closer.

"That's it." Jarlath's voice drifted down the stairs. Another thump. A soft curse. A feline growl of anger.

"I think Jarlath and Ellard are coming down to break their fast."

"Ellard shouldn't be out of bed," Hortese snapped. "What are those addlebrains thinking?" She dropped her spoon on the counter and quick-marched to the doorway. "You! Why did you let him shift so soon?"

"It will speed his healing," Jarlath said.

"Come here, kitty-cat," Hortese cooed. "My, you're a handsome one. Let me scratch your ears."

A grumpy snarl vibrated back and Keira bit back a chuckle.

Jarlath appeared first, and her chest tightened, her crow sending a coo reverberating through her chest. They'd slept together, held each other and yet in the short time they'd been apart, she'd missed his presence. He came straight to her side and wrapped his arm around her waist.

Ellard limped up to them, snarled and bit Jarlath on the leg.

"Cut that out." Jarlath slapped at Ellard and guided Keira to the other side of the kitchen out of harm's way.

"Let me get you a saucer of malpack milk," Hortese said to Ellard. "You need to keep up your strength."

Ellard let out a yowl of displeasure, and Keira smothered a giggle. Ellard would bite Hortese too if she didn't stop teasing.

"The coms are still down," Keira said.

"Which makes it imperative for us to enter the city. I'm not sure how to go about recruiting civilians to help in the fight," Jarlath confessed. "Any suggestions?"

"We should take Ollie and Nasir. They know the city and can hand out the protection spells. People will be angry. Some of them will want to help," Keira said.

"You can't go into the city with your face looking like that," Hortese said. "I think I have a face enhancement to cover that mark."

Ellard growled.

"Enough of that," Hortese said. "Take a seat and break your fast while I hunt out the face enhancements."

Keira dug into a berry parfait. There was an extra one on the table, and she shot Jarlath a glance.

"Ellard, you'd better shift if you want to eat," Jarlath said. "This parfait is delicious, and I'd be happy to eat a second."

Keira wasn't sure Jarlath was using the correct approach with his friend, but she remained silent. Maybe using the hard love technique would work best with Ellard. She concentrated on her parfait.

A thump sounded then a big hand grasped the chair beside her. Ellard glowered at her as he sat down. "What are you gawkin' at?"

"Nothing. Anyone want a cup of tay?"

"Please," Jarlath said.

Ellard grunted and she took that as a yes. She poured three mugs of tay and shunted mugs to the men.

"I'm coming with you," Ellard said after a long silence.

"You need to take time to heal," Jarlath said.

"Let me come too. I'll go crazy if I stay here with that woman. I promise I'll remain in the background, but please don't make me into an invalid."

The male had lost his arm. Keira got that Jarlath was trying to treat him as normal, but he wasn't the same. He was missing an important limb.

"We'll get you a sword," Jarlath said. "You can still fight."

"I can." Ellard shoveled a spoon of breakfast parfait into his mouth. "Thank you."

The journey into the city passed filled with tension. Two mature males, three eager youths and her, scanning the ground and air for signs of danger. Each wore a protective charm on their person and carried spares to offer recruit soldiers.

"Everyone clear on the plan?" Jarlath asked.

"Aye," Ollie said, speaking for the other youths.

"Yes," Ellard said.

Jarlath gave Nasir instructions, and he landed the flymo in the castle gardens. Keira exited, and the stench from the dead fish had her holding her nose.

"Hoowee," Ollie said in understatement.

"Let me show you the way out of the garden," Jarlath said. "Get everyone who is willing to help to meet in the square outside the medical center. Meet at midday."

"Aye," Ollie said.

"I don't think the bubble is around the castle any longer." Keira cocked her head, trying to listen for the telltale hum. "I can't hear the hum."

Ellard and Jarlath exchanged a glance.

"One way to find out. Rendezvous at midday," Jarlath reminded the youths.

"We'll do our best," Cristop said.

Jarlath strode to the door and opened it without difficulty. He stepped into the dimly lit corridor. "It's off."

"Why aren't the damn soldiers out restoring order to the city?" Ellard prowled through the doorway. "This isn't good enough."

"Let's go." Jarlath propelled her down the corridor after Ellard.

This time the scent of food wafted from the two kitchens. Jarlath didn't comment but Keira could see his anger. He increased his pace and led them to the ballroom where they found everyone assembled.

The queen spotted them first. "Where have you been?"

The chatter of dozens of conversations ceased and everyone stared at them with varying reactions.

"You weren't in your suite," the king said. "Where have you been?"

Keira glimpsed the fire burning in the hearth and hid behind Jarlath and Ellard. She peeked past Jarlath, almost hyperventilating until she saw the flames remained normal.

"What are you wearing?" the queen screeched in horror. "I told you to dress properly before entering my presence."

"Mother, there are more important things to worry about." Jarlath's tone was hard and uncompromising.

"Yes, the list of names. Have you chosen one?"

"No," Jarlath barked. "Where are the soldiers?"

Ellard's father stalked over to them, his gaze on his son. "They're guarding the perimeter of the castle as I ordered."

"What happened to Ellard's arm?" Someone behind her whispered the question, and Keira wasn't sure if the person was male or female.

Ellard stiffened and a tinge of color collected across his cheekbones.

"What happened to your arm, son?" Danion Tetsu asked.

"Someone shot him." Jarlath's harsh words dropped into the

193

hush. "He's a hero."

"You'll need another bodyguard." Danion tugged on his beard, his brow a map of lines. "Ellard can't do the job with one arm."

That was what caused them concern? Flying stars. "Ellard is capable of carrying out his duties. Jarlath, are we going now?" Keira asked.

"You." The queen's tone held loathing, her jade gaze a visual dagger. "Get out of my sight. You are not welcome here."

Jarlath slipped an arm around her shoulders. The queen hissed in horror and the people present began to whisper amongst themselves.

"I should go," Keira murmured. "The people might think their ordeal is over, but Razvan is determined. He will never give up."

"It sounds as if you know him well," Ellard said, lining himself on her other side. For once his accusation seemed understated.

Keira's stomach twisted in discomfort and she rubbed her belly to ease her distress. She'd have to confess if Razvan made an appearance. "We should go," she repeated.

"Prince Jarlath, we are having a celebration dinner and dance later this evening. Your father and I expect you to make an appearance. Come alone. Your friends are not welcome," Queen Bryna said.

"I won't be staying here tonight, Mother." Jarlath kept his voice low. "There are more important things to worry about."

"The succession is important," his mother said, also in a low voice but hers quivered with anger. She grasped his arm and dragged him away to speak in private, but her passionate words reached Keira and Ellard. "Your father isn't well, and this brouhaha hasn't helped."

"What's wrong with him?" Jarlath asked. "Why didn't you tell me?"

"Instead of playing with their son's emotions," Ellard murmured.

"Oh, I think they're still doing that," Keira said.

"It's important to the House of the Cat to present a solid front. The min things appear wrong bad things happen," the queen said. "I won't let that happen."

"Grata," Ellard cursed. "It's like sticking their heads down a moon-crater."

Keira agreed. Ignoring the truth never solved anything. A reminder to herself because wasn't that what she was doing by attempting to elude Razvan? Her chin lifted as she considered this. It was time to share this information. Past time.

"You will attend this event. We will show our strength, stand tall and thumb our noses at the enemy."

Jarlath snorted, and Keira couldn't help but grin. Ellard bore a similar expression, wiped clean secs later.

"Don't use that attitude with me," the queen snapped. "You will—"

A raucous boom exploded overhead. It repeated, and Keira clapped her hands over her ears. A woman screamed, her terror acting as a prod for the other women. Several shrieked. Rain lashed the skylights and the windows with a sharp rat-a-tat-tat, rat-a-tat-tat, rat-a-tat-tat.

The same type of storm that had rattled the walls and windows of the farmhouse before Razvan appeared. Panic roared through Keira, and she pivoted to stare into the flames of the nearest fire. A shower of embers and sparks exploded from the fireplace at the far side of the room. Another feminine scream rippled through the room.

"Keep calm," a man shouted. "It's only a storm."

This was more and Keira knew it.

Razvan had come to town.

Keira edged behind Ellard yet kept her gaze on the flames. Yes, a face was forming. No one else had noticed yet. As she stared the face grew features, but they were faint and unclear. A tremor rippled through her, and she nudged Ellard with a surreptitious hand.

"What?" he asked in a low, impatient voice. Better than a kick in the head.

"Look at the flames in the fire."

Keira stayed behind Ellard, cowering in truth, and she felt the moment Ellard saw what she'd seen. His large frame tensed and he swore under his breath.

Another thunderous crash reverberated overhead and the illumination flickered, the room going dark before the lighting system righted itself.

She sensed Jarlath moving and stopping beside them even before the lights resumed their normal illumination.

"It's gone," Ellard whispered. "I can't see anything. Can you?"

He was right. The image had faded.

The splatters of rain against the windows reduced, and some of her fear receded.

"Let's go," Jarlath said. "Ellard, are you with us?"

"Hell, yeah. I'm not turning into an invalid because my father thinks I'm defective."

Keira sensed his pain and squeezed his arm in commiseration. To her surprise, he didn't reject her sympathetic overture.

"When your arm is healed enough, we'll find someone to fit you with an artificial one. I've heard they're even better than the real thing these days," she said.

Jarlath laced his fingers with hers and gave her a quick nod of approval.

"And meantime, you can practice your swordsmanship with one hand," she added.

"I'm starting to like you," Ellard said in a gruff voice.

"Good," Jarlath said. "Now that we're in accord let's go kick some Cawdor butt."

CHAPTER TWELVE

House of Cawdor, Planet Gramite

Razvan snarled and tossed the nearest object, a round piece of red-and-black glass, against the wall. It smashed in an explosion of colorful shards and did nothing to appease his frustration.

Something was wrong. He'd known this from the moment his magic men had reported they'd lost control of the barrier around the castle.

But the cause, he didn't know.

Questioning his men had created more questions than answers.

He drew a sharp breath. No, that wasn't quite true. The problem was his triad. The power that normally vibrated through him didn't bear the same piquant sharpness.

Something was definitely wrong.

Time to take the battle to the final stage.

Time to stride forward with confidence.

Time to squash the Virosian bugs.

Razvan strode from his chamber to the room where the wizards were resting, recovering after their efforts. He knocked on the door, giving them the courtesy they deserved for their hard work and loyalty.

"Come."

He stepped inside and scanned their faces. Exhaustion lined their features, the fatigue underlined in their slumped shoulders.

No, he couldn't ask them to transport him now. Despite the urgency humming through him, he'd have to let them rest. Decision made, he sought their spokesman.

"Good job," he said. "Will one night of rest be sufficient before you undertake the spell to open a portal to Viros or will you require two?"

"Two would be best," the man said without hesitation.

He wanted to argue but held his tongue. "Is there anything I can get you? Anything that will aid your rest?"

"We have everything we require," the wizard said.

Razvan gave a clipped nod. "Let me know if this changes."

He withdrew and returned to his chamber. He'd try to contact Mareeka and Marjo again. Although they were working in separate parts of the city, they'd maintain contact with each other.

He tried his com. The call connected but went to recording. Concern increased in him. Marjo always answered her com. He tried Mareeka, and after a long wait, she answered.

"Yes," she barked.

"Darling," Razvan said, some of the tension in him departing on hearing her abrupt welcome. "I miss you."

"Van." Her voice turned softer, more intimate. "We will be together soon."

"In two days. Have you seen Marjo? I can't contact her."

"No." Pain threaded through her abrupt reply. "I feel wrong. Something has happened, but I've been too busy to check on her."

198

"Problems?"

"The soldiers are under my control—the ones who remain. The peasants from the lower city are offering resistance. They're organizing themselves, grouping together to fight back."

"That could be detrimental to our cause."

"I know. I need Marjo at my side. It's time for these idiots to learn there are two of us instead of one person called Mareeka. We're both tired of pretending. Marjo is sick of pretending to be me, and we both hate that idiot Ellard slobbering over us."

"At least she can share the burden."

"Not one of them has a clue we are twin shifters." Disdain coated her voice. Derision.

"I'll be there soon. I've decided to move forward our schedule." Razvan clenched his com harder, trying to act calm and reassuring. Marjo was the steadying one, the one who pulled them into a solid team. "The wizards are exhausted from their work. However, they have assured me after two days' rest, they can teleport me to Viros."

Mareeka's sigh of relief drifted into his ear. "Good, lover. Our objectives will come easier if we're all together on Viros." She sighed again. "I will feel better once I see Marjo."

"Can you travel down to the lower city soon?"

"No." Her strain came through loud and clear. "All of a sudden it takes me every bit of my power to control the castle guards. If I go into the lower levels of the city, the guards come out of their spell and start asking questions."

Worry beaded Razvan's brow and surged to his gut in a bubbling gush. He couldn't rush the wizards, yet every instinct was screaming he'd lose the opportunity to strike if he didn't move. "I'll push the wizards to one day of rest."

"I can't wait to see you, lover. I miss you."

"Miss you too, darling. We'll be reunited soon and will triumph over the House of the Cat together."

Jarlath observed the group of ragtag men and women waiting outside the medical center. More than he expected but were they enough to defeat their enemy?

Didn't matter. They had to try.

Jarlath stepped up onto the plinth of a statue of a huge feline and raised his hand for quiet.

"Silence," Ellard shouted, and the crowd fell silent, faces turned in their direction.

"Thank you for coming," Jarlath began.

"Who be you?" a woman shouted.

Ellard stepped up beside him. "This is Prince Jarlath, heir to the throne."

"Nah, he never leave the castle," someone shouted.

"Aye, he be a toff. Not like Prince Lynx. He a man of the people."

Guilt slapped Jarlath, and his confidence wavered.

"This is Prince Jarlath, and he has been in the city since the bombing occurred. He obtained the protection charms and organized recruiters to gather volunteers. Listen to him," Ellard said.

"He only interested in wellbeing of toffs," a woman spat. "He no gonna help us."

Jarlath gave Ellard a subtle nudge, a signal to remain silent. They had a right to their annoyance, their distrust, because he was a sad excuse for a prince.

He sucked in a deep breath, unaccountably nervous. "I am Prince Jarlath of the House of the Cat. I understand your concerns, but please put them aside while we join to fight our common enemy—the House of Cawdor."

The murmurs rose in a swell of outrage.

"The House of Cawdor is using magic to overturn our city, and we must fight for our freedom. The spells you were given will protect you from magic, but you will still be vulnerable to blaster fire, knife wounds and any other physical weapons."

"What 'bout the red men?" someone shouted.

"The enemy has cursed our soldiers and forced them to wear dangerous robes. When the robes get wet, the water detonates to create a human bomb. Approach those wearing red cloaks with caution. If they're near water or it starts raining, do not engage. We'll divide you into groups, with each group responsible for one level of the city."

"What about the castle?" someone shouted.

"Aye, don't you want us to protect the royal family?"

No matter how Jarlath studied the situation, there was one sole truth. "We need to protect those in the city. I believe there are still soldiers at the castle. They do not require more aid. Free the soldiers from their red robes if possible or escort them to the gates on the east side of the city. Any questions?" Jarlath asked.

"Aye, when do we get paid?"

"Once the trouble is over, present your protection charms to either me or Ellard. We will see you receive the appropriate credits."

"How we know ya keep ya word?" a man shouted.

"You have my solemn promise you will receive the rewards you are due. Once we send the House of the Cawdor running, we will rebuild the lower city. You have my word things will improve in this kingdom."

Every man, woman and youth stared at him, expressions ranging from disbelief to distrust to hope. He understood their doubts, given the past, but he meant every word.

The people who worked hard to make the House of the Cat strong and prosperous deserved the kudos and the rewards rather than those rich and powerful men who balanced on the top of the power triangle.

"Any further questions?" Ellard asked.

Heads shook and murmurs rose.

"Good," Jarlath said. "Split into six groups, and Ellard will assign you a city level to patrol. Keep people from panic and looting, watch for the men in red. Please remember not to approach the red men if they have access to water."

The men and women moved off in groups, determination and confidence etched into their features.

"We haven't addressed the issue of what we're going to do once we've captured the soldiers," Ellard said, after he finished his allocations.

Jarlath shrugged. "We can't plan against magic. All we can do is contain the attack and hope for the best."

"We'll do what we can," Keira said, speaking for the first time. "That's all any of us can do."

"She's right," Ellard said. "We'll check the bottom level and the soldiers' base together, then I'll go to the east gate and organize things there. If we can break the hold the Cawdor have over the soldiers, they should respond to me. They know me, and I think that will help."

"Ellard, how are you? Your arm?"

Ellard met Jarlath's concern with a carefree smile, one Jarlath knew would cost his friend. "My hand is itching like hell. Imaginary cooties."

Jarlath saw through his friend's bravado. His arm was giving him more problems than he admitted. "No matter what your father says, or mine, you are a valuable part of the House of the Cat. Never doubt this. You are more than a friend. You are my brother and we fight side-by-side to the end."

"Thanks," Ellard said. "That means more than you know."

"Enough with the sappy stuff," Keira said.

"You feelin' left out?" Ellard asked.

"We should go," Keira said. "My gut is shrieking danger."

Pain seared through Razvan, even worse than the vibes of unease that had stalked him for the last two days. His mind, his heart, they both told him to get to Viros as fast as he could, yet the physical and mental exhaustion of his wizards hamstringed his urgency.

Fatigue coated his magic men like dew on the plants down on the plains. If he pushed them any harder, his plan would implode and his planning, his scheming would be for naught.

He couldn't fail.

He refused.

Besides, with Carrick snapping at his heels, he didn't have any options except success.

The disquiet bouncing through his bloodstream continued throughout the day, a day of solitude and more planning for him. What to do with the fledgling? How could he make the best example of her?

He wanted to fuck her, had wanted that since he first saw her at the ball many, many cycles ago. Her mother had spirited her away, gifted her to an undeserving Virosian. He'd let her think she was safe...

What to do?

His com shattered his musings.

"Yes," he barked.

"They've killed her, Van. They've murdered my sister."

"Marjo is dead?" he rasped, the unease he'd been feeling making more sense.

"It was her turn to play Mareeka, and she intended to issue the soldiers with red cloaks. The last I heard from her, she'd gained control. I don't know what happened but I'll discover the truth. I'm going to torture them until they wish for death," Mareeka ground out. "I will catch whoever did this and hurt them until they plead for death."

"Mareeka."

A loud keening filled his ears, beat in time with the hard pulses of his heart ventricles. The wailing increased in register until his ears ached.

"Mareeka, listen to me. Please, Mareeka." He made his tone sharp to cut through her anger, her pain. "Darling, please take a breath."

She hiccupped her next sob, and it tore at him, wounded him. "I need to send Marjo's body soaring to the gods. They left her on the ground, Van, her blood pooling around her head." A sob tore at him. "They...they shot off her face, speared her chest."

"We will burn her together, Mareeka. Tomorrow morn, I will come. Together we will avenge your sister, our third."

"I can't wait," Mareeka whispered hoarsely. "I must act with swiftness or her spirit will become lost."

"Tomorrow morn, Mareeka. You have my word."

The com cut off, and Razvan cursed. Without Marjo, Mareeka floated in misery, adrift. She wouldn't wait for his arrival, not given her current mood.

Razvan let out another curse and stomped from his quarters to demand the wizards end their period of rest.

"Look at the smoke," Keira said as she scanned the buildings on this level. Many lay in ruins, but a cobbler's and a butcher's shop had survived intact, against the odds. "That's a big fire."

"It looks as if it's on the lowest level," Ellard said.

The three quickened their pace and sprinted around the last turn before coming to an abrupt halt.

"Someone has set the fire on purpose," Jarlath said.

Keira squinted. "There is a figure on top of the pile of wood."

"Mareeka," Ellard said in a pained voice.

Their steps slowed.

"But who is burning her body?" Jarlath asked.

"No, she's alive. Look." Ellard pointed at a figure who emerged from the soldiers' office. "Mareeka."

Keira gasped. "But we saw her die. She was dead. I don't understand."

Ellard started running. "Mareeka."

"No, wait," Jarlath shouted, but his friend evaded him and raced up to the woman. She was tall and strong and identical to the woman Keira had shot.

"They're twins," Keira said. The only explanation to make sense.

"Mareeka, you're alive," Ellard said and joy suffused his voice as he gathered her against him as best as he could with one arm.

The woman escaped him, her features devoid of emotion.

"Careful," Jarlath said. "Don't trust her. You know what happened last time."

Mareeka whirled on him, hatred blazing on her face. "I'm honored. The prince himself. Not many people see you in person. Razvan will be excited to see his plans have drawn you from hiding."

"Razvan," Ellard said. "What do you know of Razvan?"

"He is my lover, my mate," Mareeka said. "Who killed my sister? Who killed Marjo?"

"I don't know," Keira said. It was obvious her sister's death had unhinged the woman, and she'd snap if they said the wrong thing. "The people of the city panicked after the explosions. There was looting, rioting and many have died from setting foot in the wrong place at the wrong time. I fear we may never find the culprit."

Some of the tension left the highly strung woman. Her

shoulders relaxed but anguish contorted her features.

Ellard stared, dumbfounded. "Sister?"

"You felines are so stupid, so accepting." Mareeka sneered, her contempt bringing an unattractive color to Ellard's cheeks. "Marjo and I had to take turns pretending to be Mareeka and spending hours with you because you made us sick. Bedding you was a chore."

"Don't listen to her poison," Keira whispered. "It's not true."

Ellard shook off her hand and stepped closer to the true Mareeka.

"Ellard." Jarlath placed a restraining hand on his arm.

Behind them, the flames shot higher and fear of a different sort snapped through Keira when a face appeared in the fire.

"Shoot," Keira screamed.

Jarlath fired, but Ellard leaped at Mareeka. The woman avoided him and off-balance, he sprawled face first on the ground.

"My, my," a mocking voice said. "If it isn't the very fledgling I've been searching for."

Keira froze, then to her horror, Razvan's face grew a torso, arms and legs, and he stepped from the flames, a familiar smirk on his swarthy face. He lifted a hand to brush an ember off his night-black hair and smoothed the long tendrils without taking his gaze off her. Next, he stroked his goatee beard. Dressed in form-fitting black, he was a handsome man if one ignored the manic gleam in his button eyes.

"They killed Marjo," Mareeka shrieked. "Kill them all. Smite them with your magic."

"I told you," Keira snapped. "We have no idea who killed your sister." She'd thought she'd knifed Mareeka because Ellard had said it was her. The twins had obviously pulled switches as it suited their needs. Poor Ellard.

Razvan ignored Mareeka's screeches and strutted over to Keira, his amber eyes alight with interest. "I couldn't see you clearly through the flames, but your appearance pleases me. You have grown well, little Keira."

Keira's heart ventricles pumped so fast she started to hyperventilate. Panic tasted dark and rusty against her tongue, helplessness bitter. Fear for Jarlath's life, for Ellard's safety meant she focused on the threat. She straightened her shoulders and glared at her half-brother.

"Not going to give me a proper welcome, pet?" Razvan's eyes shone bright with mischief.

Mareeka tugged at his arm. "What are you doing? We must amend our plan. Without Marjo, we are two. Three is the magical number."

"I don't think that will matter, darling. I have a replacement in mind. The perfect solution." He didn't take his oily gaze off Keira, and her stomach roiled. Her crow pecked and scratched from inside, panicked, agreeing with her fears.

Razvan was unpredictable. Capable of anything.

Keira swallowed as her mind skirted the horrible possibilities. She'd never forgive herself if Razvan hurt Jarlath or Ellard. Never.

She loved him, and it was too late to tell him. Razvan would murder them without blinking unless...

Her crow pecked her extra hard, and she winced. Seemed her crow had fallen for the cat too. Unusual but not impossible, and because of that love, she couldn't let them die.

The House of the Cat needed Jarlath.

He mightn't think he was a good prince, but that wasn't true.

Keira reached up to wipe the enhancements from her cheek. She saw she had Razvan's attention, and the air whistled through his teeth when he saw the crow she revealed. "What kept you, brother? I've been waiting for you to arrive."

Keira forced herself to strut to his side. She pressed a kiss to Razvan's cheek and internalized the impulse to hurl. Her skin crawled and her crow gave an unhappy caw-caw.

Razvan stared at her tattoo in wonder. He ignored Mareeka to brush his finger over her cheek, as if to ascertain it was genuine. "It's real."

Keira inclined her head. "Of course."

"You can shift?"

"Yes."

"But I thought...Father said..." Razvan trailed off, for once at a loss for words.

"It is time to take this planet of fools and shape it into a dynasty. Our dynasty," Keira shot a swift glance at Jarlath, crumpled a bit inside at his expression. Didn't he care about her at all?

Razvan patted her head, as if she were the pet he kept mentioning. "I like the way you think."

"We can't trust her," Mareeka snapped.

"She bears the mark of Cawdor. She is of the Cawdor. She is one of us."

Keira swallowed but didn't make the mistake of glancing at Jarlath again. Maybe Ellard had the right of it, and Jarlath was playing her. Her crow pecked against her breastbone in clear agitation. Keira kept her winces to a minimum and forced away every emotion. She steeled her nerves and prepared to lie.

"Round up the people and force Marjo's murderer to confess," Mareeka said. "Strike now while we have soldiers in place."

"No," Keira said. "The people here are stubborn. They won't confess. Killing them is a waste of manpower, people we will require once we take over the mining operation."

Razvan's laugh rang out in approval.

"Bitch." Ellard picked himself up, his body tense as if he intended to spring at her.

"Silence," Keira snarled and pulled out her blaster to point at Jarlath. "Crawl back to your castle and tell your people to prepare to crown a new king." Please, Jarlath. Please do as I say. "Ellard, you stay right there."

"Traitor," Jarlath said. "All the time you were waiting for him?"

"You don't think a feline would interest me? Nasty, slovenly creatures. You can't even fly." Not that her attempts had been super successful, but Razvan didn't need to know that. Difficult to fly when she didn't have experience. "No, I have been waiting for Razvan's arrival." Jarlath was edging away, putting distance between them while Ellard stood firm like the soldier he was.

"Don't think you can step into Marjo's shoes!" Mareeka's chin lifted, and when Keira met the woman's hauteur with a sneer, Mareeka lost it and flew at Keira. Razvan stepped between the two women, his grin broad enough to reveal his teeth, and drew Mareeka away. He lowered his voice.

Maybe he thought Keira couldn't hear him, but she caught the gist of their conversation. *They needed Keira to gain enough power to master the cats. Mareeka was his true love, the important one. Just play along, and they'd get what they both wanted.*

His confidence set Keira's stomach churning, her survival instincts chirping. So arrogant. So sure of himself. So deluded. Just of thought of him thought of him touching her...

"We'll get rid of her once you're crowned king of Viros," Mareeka whispered.

"Whatever you want, darling," Razvan soothed, but Keira saw his attention shift to her and linger. She pretended she didn't hear, didn't see that his eyes were gloating and full of hot lust.

It appeared he still wanted her and would do anything, remove any obstacle, to have her.

Sick, perverted man. There had been rumors he was Carrick's father, not his brother. She'd asked her mother once about the gossip. Her mother had shifted the conversation and never mentioned the subject again. More than a grain of truth, Keira decided. And that would account for the madness within the ruling family. Interbreeding would do that to a line.

Razvan continued to reassure Mareeka, and Keira took the

opportunity to scan the area. Ellard stood, his watchful gaze telling her he was waiting for an opportunity to act. Jarlath had gone. Some of her tension receded. If she managed one thing today, at least it was to keep Jarlath safe.

Her crow gave an unhappy *caw-caw* and Razvan shot her a sharp look.

"It's true. You can shift. I hear your crow," he said.

Keira stuck her nose in the air. "I do not lie."

"No, my pet. It seems you do not."

"She can't get us into the castle. She's lying about that. Marjo and I couldn't get past the security at the front door. Each of us tried. Didn't have enough experience." She cackled without warning. "Didn't matter. We managed to turn most of the soldiers to our cause."

"You have done well, darling," Razvan said.

Mareeka burrowed against his chest and shot a triumphant glower at Keira. "I am loyal to the cause. We will be successful and mighty as you predicted."

Delusional and scary too. Stay strong. You can do this. "I can get you into the castle."

"How?" Mareeka demanded. "Prove it."

"There is a little known rear entrance. We can go that way if you choose, but wouldn't it be better to walk through the main entrance with our heads held high?"

"Pet, I like your style," Razvan said. "Let's go."

"No, I have a better idea," Keira said. "Tonight the king and queen hold a celebration ball. They think the attack is over. We should wait until the eve and make a grand entrance."

"You let the prince go," Mareeka said. "A mistake."

"Bah," Keira said. "He is a pretend prince. He does nothing. He holds no power. All he does is attend balls and dance with the high society ladies. He is weak. We don't need him. We have Ellard." She gestured at him with her weapon and received a feline snarl in return. "He is the real power at the castle. Once he is dead, their protective structure—the soldiers remaining—will crumple."

"You have a plan." A statement from her half-brother, not a question.

"Of course. We walk into their ball and go straight for the king and queen. They will not expect our bold move, and since you have already decimated their soldiers, it will be easy. We will dress Ellard in one of those red cloaks and threaten to blow him and the entire castle up if our demands are not met." Ellard glared holes through her, and she had to force herself to laugh in his face.

"That is a good plan," Mareeka said, not bothering to hide her surprise. "You are right. She will be useful to us, but we do not require him." She jerked her shoulder in Ellard's direction. "We have others in place at the castle, others we can blow up. We don't need the distraction of a prisoner. Shoot him."

Grata, this wasn't good. "Let me take care of him," Keira said. "You haven't seen each other for a time. Go and rest, mourn and relax as best as you can. We require our wits about us tonight if we are to best these kittens in their own House."

"She might speak sense, but you can't trust her," Mareeka said. "She might talk the right talk but her actions do not match. What's to stop her from letting him go and fleeing herself? Or maybe she's playing a double game and seeks to gain time to warn those who protect the royal family."

Razvan stroked his goatee beard, his amber eyes gleaming as he calculated odds or whatever he did before he came to a decision. "You have a point, my darling." He didn't take his focus off Keira. "Why should we trust you?"

Keira didn't lower her gaze, didn't give into her urge to flee and save herself, didn't so much as blink while her mind considered different angles. "She's right. I could be lying through my beak. Let me prove my loyalty. Let me do this. What's the worst that could happen? Yes, you run the risk of me not following through on my promises, but you have the upper hand here. Playing you would be stupid when you know where I live and can grab me, punish me, kill me soon enough."

"Traitor," Ellard snarled and lunged in her direction.

Keira countered smoothly, stuck out her foot to trip him and kicked him in the arse to propel him to the ground. "So what do you say? Are you willing to give me a chance to prove my loyalty?"

"Oh yes," Razvan drawled and his wide smile made Keira feel soiled. "You're right in that there is no chance of escape. You have this one chance, but make no mistake. Retaliation will come swiftly if you cross me."

"But, Van," Mareeka protested.

"No, I've made my decision, and if she fails us, you have my leave to use your race's traditional methods of punishment."

"Ah." Mareeka brightened. "Torture and decapitation." Her cruel smile pushed a flymo full of horror through Keira but she held her ground. "That might be fun."

"We can't lose either way." Razvan's gaze caressed Mareeka and held an edge of lust. "Keira will be useful to our cause. Very useful indeed. Let us go, darling. We have much to discuss and plan now that we are together again. Keira, take care of him. We will see you later either way."

"No problem. I'll dispose of him and keep guard. Nothing must go wrong before we make our move tonight at their ball," Keira said, her manner decisive. Razvan was more trusting than she'd expected.

"Excellent." Razvan stroked his beard. "Don't disappoint me. This is the only chance you'll get."

Or maybe *she* was the gullible one. She'd need to watch herself every step of the way.

"Don't let him go." Mareeka bared her teeth at Ellard and snarled. "He deserves to die for daring to touch me, touch my sister."

"And he will." Keira didn't know how she managed to hold the woman's hard stare or spout such trash. Ellard was a good man who lived to serve and protect. He would give his life for Jarlath.

"Don't interrupt us," Mareeka said.

"Of course not," Keira agreed. The farther she kept away from them, the happier she'd feel. "You." She jabbed her blaster into Ellard's ribs. "Over here, around the corner and in the middle of the street. I want your body to serve as a warning." She nudged him hard and sent him lurching forward a step.

"You won't get away with this." Ellard straightened and glowered at them all, defiant to the last.

"Oh, I think she will," Razvan said with a chuckle. "My pet has a vicious streak. Why I still have a scar where she bit me many cycles ago. Do you remember, pet?"

"Yes," Keira said, her tone short. "Are you going to supervise or do you trust me to carry out this task on my own?"

"The crow are merciless when they have their sights set on a task," Razvan said with a soft smile. "You have stated your intent and can report back later. Come, darling. Let us rest before our victory parade this eve."

Razvan and Mareeka disappeared into the soldiers' quarters, and Keira saw Mareeka kick the door shut. A statement of ownership. Fine. The other woman was welcome to Razvan, although if she trusted Keira's half-brother, she was foolish. Only one person mattered to Razvan, and that was himself.

"Get moving," Keira snapped at Ellard and dug her blaster into his ribs again.

"Bitch," he snarled.

She ignored his insults and focused on getting him around the corner and out of sight. "Get a move on. I don't have all day."

"I told Jarlath you were trouble. Warned him about you."

"Yeah, yeah," Keira muttered and took pleasure in digging her weapon into his back. His words hurt, and the small mutiny on her part brought a measure of satisfaction. She hope he bruised—the ungrateful lout.

She glanced over her shoulder and saw they were out of sight of the soldiers' quarters. Keira lifted the blaster and fired into the air. Once. Then she stuffed her weapon in her holster. "You can turn around now, Ellard. Give me the cat pendant you wear around your neck."

"No." He clutched at the onyx carving, as if he suspected she might snatch it from him.

"Don't be stupid. Give me the pendant so they believe I shot you. Everyone knows you never take the thing off."

Ellard stared at her and shook his head. "Which side are you on?"

"I thought you were an intelligent man. Hurry, give me the pendant, then go and find Jarlath. You need to come up with a plan to take out Mareeka and Razvan with minimal loss. I have a plan, but I don't know if it will work, which is why you need a strategy too." She held out her hand in silent demand.

Ellard fumbled, clumsy with his one hand.

"Turn around and let me do it."

Silently, Ellard presented his back and she stood on tiptoe to unfasten the cord.

"Use your knife," he ordered. "Cutting it off will make more sense to them."

She did as he said, and pocketed the onyx cat before sliding her knife back into her boot.

"I hope you know what you're doing. I thought Jarlath had seized the opportunity for escape, but you were aware of him the entire time. You let him escape."

She shrugged.

"What are you going to tell them when my body isn't lying in the middle of the street?"

"I'll tell them someone must have shifted your body."

He lifted his hand in a respectful salute—one soldier to

another—and sped away. Keira sucked in a deep breath, watched him disappear while ignoring her unhappy crow. She took two steps toward the soldiers' quarters before coming to a halt.

Blood.

She needed blood on the cobblestones. She pulled out her knife, lifted her sleeve and sliced her arm, letting the drops fall onto the ground in one concentrated area. She scowled. Not enough blood. Where...how...ah! A butcher's shop. She'd seen that one two levels up. A good place to find what she needed.

Ten mins later, she gave a satisfied nod. The patch of fresh blood looked about right, certainly enough to thwart suspicions from Razvan and Mareeka.

Keira made her way to the soldiers' quarters and took a position outside where anyone passing would be unlikely to spot her straightaway.

She had plenty of time to firm up her plan and consider different scenarios. She prayed she managed to pull off the ultimate bluff.

CHAPTER THIRTEEN

J arlath disliked leaving Ellard to the mercies of the lunatic, and even more, he hated leaving Keira. His feline snarled, the fury reverberating through his head for long secs. He ran for safety and slid around a corner, stopping out of sight when he heard Keira speaking.

She was talking of a delay, offering a plan to stall the enemy. Clever and brave. His chest tightened in acknowledgement of the risk she was taking on his behalf, on behalf of the people of Viros when they'd treated her no better than mud on their paws. Keira's gift—precious hours to make plans.

The ball.

He frowned at that. Risky. Ellard in a red cloak. Grata, that didn't sound good. He hoped she knew what she was doing. Time to make his escape. Keira had given him this chance to come up with a plan, was putting her own life at risk to help.

Jarlath set off at a lope and attempted to ignore his feline's unhappiness. His feline hated leaving Keira, and he felt a physical wrench at the parting. Grata, he didn't want to scarper either, but there was more at stake. The people in the city needed help and the House of the Cat required him to forsake his personal requirements. This was for the greater good.

"Shush," Jarlath soothed when sharp claws perforated the tips of his fingers and his canines pierced his gums. "Keira has a plan. We have to trust her to make it work. No point in all of us getting killed." But even as he put his thoughts into words, his heart cried out. Keira was in the hands of that maniac, and the idea sent unease marching down his spine. No matter what Ellard said or thought, Jarlath believed in Keira—her integrity and honesty. She was on their side, remained part of House of the Cat. As he continued to the castle, his thoughts lingered on the scene with Razvan and Mareeka. Despite her bravado, it was obvious Razvan Cronan terrified Keira. He'd caught the thread of nerves in her tight shoulders and her rapid blinking, the gasp of breath before she'd stepped forward to align herself with the Cawdor. And something else occurred to him, facts clicking neatly into place. Her mother had arranged Keira's marriage to Marcus in order to keep her safe.

What to do? How could he help her?

Jarlath thought through their original plan. They'd mass the soldiers, and would attempt to remove their red cloaks to make the soldiers and the city safer. Yes, he'd go to the meeting point and get as many soldiers into position as possible. Perhaps they could find replacement cloaks and leave Razvan with his illusions. Not a bad idea. At least it was a start. Somehow, he'd have to talk his father and Ellard's father into letting him take the lead.

As he ran up to the next level of the city, he noticed things appeared under control. People were outside, clearing the rubble and restoring order. Despite his hurry, he stopped to speak with several, introduced himself to those who didn't recognize him and promised aid.

"Words be worth nothink," a woman said. "We be needin' action."

"I understand, and I won't go against my word. I will prove the House of the Cat cares for its people and not just those with status," Jarlath said and meant every word.

The House of the Cat required change in order to grow.

Other citizens had the same reaction, one Jarlath understood, given the divide in the classes and the current situation. For about the tenth time, he wished Lynx and Shiloh were here. Between him, Lynx, Ellard, and Shiloh, they'd make their parents see reason. If his parents didn't agree to move with the times, he wasn't sure what would happen. Something had to give or the city would implode.

Jarlath made it to the east gate and the open area just outside. Several soldiers, still dressed in red cloaks, stood in a clustered group while their ragtag army of volunteers kept a watchful eye. Their volunteers held an assortment of weapons—bludgeons, knives, a battered black pan made of heavy metal and several had purple tree branches. Having seen the damage the men in red could inflict, Jarlath didn't blame the volunteers in their wariness.

"Good job," Jarlath said when Ollie and Nasir reached his side.

"The soldiers refused to remove their cloaks," Ollie said. "Decided to wait."

Jarlath scrutinized the men, their innocuous red cloaks. A few bore bloody noses and obvious war wounds. They hadn't all surrendered of their free will. "We need to diffuse them somehow. Stay here. I'll speak with them."

"Where be Keira and Ellard?" Cristop asked, coming to join them.

Jarlath saw more of their volunteers arrive with soldiers in red. A dozen soldiers were escorted to join the rest. The volunteers wandered over to their friends and acquaintances. They exchanged greetings, their chatter restrained.

Jarlath studied the soldiers and frowned. Not a good idea to put the red-cloaks together. Amassed like this, they'd cause a huge explosion should it rain.

"There's been a hiccup." Jarlath glanced at the sky, reassured by the brilliant blue and cloudless sky. "I'm going to speak with the soldiers."

Ollie grabbed his shoulder. "You the prince. Need to stay safe. I go."

"No," Jarlath said. "It is up to me to fix this. You stay here in safety."

"No," Ollie said.

"No," Cristop added his objection.

Nasir remained silent, but his expression said he agreed with his friends.

"I have spent my entire life secluded from reality. That changes now." Jarlath strode toward the group of silent soldiers and forced himself to focus on his hastily concocted plan.

"We're coming with you." Ollie matched him stride for stride.

"Fine. You can watch for rain and other sources of water." Jarlath marched up to the soldiers. "Eyes front," he barked. "Attention!"

Conditioned to the abrupt commands, the soldiers formed a line and stood to attention. So far, so good. Although they followed his order, their behavior was off. Some bore sulky expressions—they were the ones who had suffered the bloody noses—while others seemed trancelike with blank eyes and slack features. It was as if someone compelled their actions.

"Why are you out of uniform?" Jarlath barked, channeling Danion Tetsu when he was inspecting the troops for a formal occasion. "Remove those cloaks now."

Not one of the soldiers moved, and Jarlath heard the burst of chatter from their volunteers.

"Drop and give me twenty," Jarlath roared.

To his relief all sixteen soldiers dropped and started doing pushups, counting them off in a staccato fashion.

Cristop tugged on Jarlath's sleeve and whispered urgently, "Don't make them sweaty. Might blow us all up."

Frukk. He hadn't thought of that. "Good point." Jarlath frowned, considered his next move. "Any soldier who wishes to obey my order to remove their cloak may stop doing pushups."

Three froze in the up position. They stood and started to unfasten the toggles on their cloaks. Their hands trembled violently, as if they were acting contrary to another set of orders.

Cristop advanced and unfastened the toggles for the nearest soldier. He helped to pull off the cloak and the soldier blinked, reminding Jarlath of a man awakening from a deep sleep. The soldier regarded his surroundings with wide eyes.

"Attention!" Jarlath roared when he noticed the others had finished their pushups and sagged toward the ground.

All of the soldiers jerked upright then scrambled to their feet, their movements not as sluggish.

"Stand to attention." Jarlath gestured to the youngsters. "Quick. Off with their cloaks."

Cristop and Ollie helped the other two soldiers with their cloaks since their fingers also trembled too much to complete the motor function.

"Excellent," Jarlath said to the three dazed men. "Go and join the men over there. Quick march. Left, right, left, right." To his relief, the three soldiers obeyed without hesitation.

Now for the others. He gestured for Ollie, Cristop and Nasir to join him. "They're hexed. We're going to have to help them remove the cloaks."

"We do one each we finish quick," Ollie said.

Jarlath sucked in a quick breath, awed by their no-nonsense

bravery. "Get ready. You four, step forward." His bark of command galvanized them to action, and they saluted crisply. Well-trained. He could use their conditioned responses. "At ease, men. Guys, let's hurry," he added in an undertone.

With trembling fingers, Jarlath unfastened the toggles on the man's cloak and slid it off his shoulders. His breath eased out when the cloak fluttered to the ground, his heartbeat a loud *boom-boom-boom* inside his head. "Done?"

"Finished," Cristop said.

Ollie scooped up the cloaks and set them on the pile, at the edge of the open ground.

This group of men behaved as if they were awakening from a long sleep. Judging by their expressions, they had no idea of where they were and how they'd arrived in the square.

"Join the men over there," Jarlath said in a gentler voice. He repeated his order for the next four. Three obeyed and one remained planted in the line of cloaked soldiers. "You there. Move."

"The master said I should keep on the cloak," the man said, his face set in stoic lines. "Our job is important, and in the future, others will remember and celebrate our greatness."

"Who is your master?"

"Marjo," the man said without hesitation.

"Marjo is dead," Jarlath said. "I am the new master, and I have changed the plan."

Ollie and Cristop removed the cloaks from the last of the men, and Nasir took the cloaks over to the pile.

"Take off your cloak," Jarlath said.

"No," the man said.

Jarlath's hand snapped out and he grabbed a fistful of cloak. The man jerked from his touch, and before Jarlath could bellow another order, the man sprinted away.

"Don't let him escape," Jarlath shouted.

"He's not going to back down," Ollie said, his tone urgent. "Use your blaster, Prince. Quick."

Damn, he was right. If the man detonated in the middle of the city or hid, they'd have a problem. Jarlath pulled out his blaster and aimed high on his shoulder. The man zigzagged and instead of wounding as he intended, the man staggered. The cloak sparked but didn't explode. Regret suffused him as the man fell and didn't move.

The group of volunteers burst into discussion, heightening Jarlath's guilt at taking a man's life. Still, they kept their distance, and Jarlath understood their reluctance. Apart from the danger, he thought trust was still an issue. They didn't know him, still held reservations about him keeping his word.

"Shot," Cristop said and patted Jarlath on the back. "Had to be done. You couldn't let him run loose through the city."

Jarlath replaced his blaster, the remorse growing as he stared at the pile of red cloaks. Many soldiers had died already, most of them with families. "Any ideas what to do with the cloaks?" He shot a glance upward and was relieved to see the skies remained clear.

"If it don't rain, you could transport the cloaks and use them in the mineral mines during the blasting process," Cristop said.

"Good idea." Jarlath pondered the suggestion, tested the pros and cons. That might be their best hope of safe disposal. "Meantime we'll place them in a waterproof receptacle. Can we find one in the market? I need to speak to our volunteers. Give them instructions." Jarlath strode over to the group of men and women. "Thank you for your help. I'd appreciate it if you watch for any soldiers we've missed, and if you see any looters, send them on their way. Does anyone have any questions?"

"Aye," a buxom woman holding a frying pan said. "When will we get paid?"

Jarlath sighed inwardly. Definitely mistrust. "I'll send word. Do a public announcement as to where you can exchange your magical talismans."

A few mumbles sounded.

"Any more questions?"

When they merely stared at him, he nodded. "Thank you." Jarlath stalked away from the group to join his young aids.

"Where be Keira and Ellard?" Nasir asked. "You never said."

"Captured by Razvan," Jarlath said.

"What? How? Why we no rescue?" Ollie demanded, his dreads dancing with each agitated head jerk.

"Keira has a plan. She pretended she was working on their side and talked them into waiting to take over until this eve at the ball the king and queen are holding."

Ollie's eyes widened. "Ellard be a prisoner?"

"Yes." Grata, he hoped Ellard remained safe and kept quiet instead of mouthing off at Razvan. He wouldn't trust Keira, not since she'd aligned herself with Razvan. Ellard was a black-and-white man, and he wouldn't see the nuances of Keira's plan.

What if Ellard was right? What if Keira had gone over to the dark side?

No! Jarlath dragged a hand through his hair. No second-guessing his actions.

"We need to prepare for this coming eve. I thought we'd dress our soldiers in like red cloaks—make the Cawdor believe they still have their weapons in hand." Jarlath thought through the normal ball routine. "We can set up snipers on the balconies."

"Ballsy to strut into castle with no shooters," Cristop said. "How they know soldiers blow up? Might not blow. And if they do, baddies detonate their arses too."

Jarlath ran through the possibilities and agreed with Cristop. "Magic. It's gotta be something magical. We'll visit Zarbo on the way to the castle. Maybe he can suggest a spell to help our cause."

"I thought you said Ellard be a prisoner," Ollie said, his broad forehead creased in a frown. "There he be."

Ellard trotted up to them.

"Ellard." Jarlath embraced him and felt tears pooling when Ellard held him close for an instant with his one arm. He pushed away, blinked rapidly. "Keira?"

Ellard shook his head and fear swept through Jarlath, his mind darting to the worst scenario.

"Is she dead?"

"She was alive when I last saw her. She told Razvan she intended to shoot me and leave my body in the street as a warning to others. I believed her." Ellard squeezed his eyes shut. "Grata, I believed her, but it was a pretense, and she took my onyx pendant as proof of death."

"You let her take it?" Jarlath asked, shocked. Ellard had worn that pendant since the first moment his grandsire had presented it to him. Shiloh wore a similar one and neither of the brothers ever removed them.

"A small price. She's given us a chance to prepare a trap for the Cawdor. I thought she was going to shoot me," Ellard said. "She had me fooled."

Jarlath embraced Ellard again and hoped they could deal with their parents and fashion a scheme to keep everyone safe.

"I don't like this plan, Jarlath. Too many things can go wrong," Ellard muttered.

Jarlath agreed, but they had to try, no matter the odds. He tugged his cravat and peered up into the galleries surrounding the ballroom. Although he couldn't see them, the snipers were in position. He and Ellard had instructed them to take a shot if the way was clear, but they'd need to take out both Razvan and

Mareeka at the same time. "Yeah, I know. I keep thinking about the things that could go wrong."

"At least we managed to disarm the cloaked men," Ellard said. "Bloody brilliant idea to reissue the soldiers with red cloaks of our own. Cristop, Ollie and Nasir are in place. I placed them as waiters and they have slumber drugs, which they can palm into drinks should it become possible."

Jarlath frowned. "Did you speak with the kitchen staff? Those in charge? They rule the two kitchens like tyrants." Another thing to add to his list of changes. "I don't want them to upset the boys when they're trying to do a job."

Ellard barked out a dry laugh, and Jarlath was pleased to see his friend looking like his old self or at least keeping his pain contained. "The parents were more difficult. Father doesn't believe us."

"I wish Lynx and Shiloh were here to fight at our side," Jarlath said. "I tried to contact them again."

"I did too," Ellard confessed. "Father is treating me like an imbecile and insists I give up my position."

"How is the arm?"

"Still very tender if I bump the stump. I keep forgetting it's not there."

"Keira is right. It won't be quite the same, but an artificial arm will help. Lynx and Shiloh will help with finding the right cybertronics medical man."

"If your father had listened to Lynx, Viros would've had a medical research wing in place at the center."

"I know," Jarlath said. "If Father had listened to half of Lynx's suggestions, we wouldn't be in this position now. Guess I'd better speak with my parents and run through the plan again."

"Hate to say it, Jarlath, but we can't count on them," Ellard said.

His parents irritated him with the way they clung to the past. "I'll do my best."

"I'll give final orders to the soldiers and deal with my father. It will be a case of who can shout loudest."

Jarlath found his parents and their closest friends in the salon having pre-dinner drinks and canapés. Laughter, bright chatter and repartee filled the beautiful room. Every surface glittered, and he fought a sneeze when he passed a huge vase of perfumed white flowers.

"Ah, Prince Jarlath," his mother said. "You're here. Waiter, a drink."

Jarlath scanned the room, taking in faces and looking for anyone who appeared out of place. Just close friends and a surfeit of young women. His lips curled in what he feared was more a sneer of contempt than a smile. His feline grumbled, both of them wanting the same thing, the same woman.

Keira.

Please let her be safe. He had faith in her. She was clever, resourceful, and she'd managed to save both him and Ellard, playing on Razvan's arrogance and his certainty he'd managed to cow the residents of Viros.

"Jarlath."

A familiar voice had him turning, his thoughts returning to the present to see Cristop smirking at him.

Jarlath found himself grinning back as he accepted a drink. The youth had slid into the position with the ease of a chameleon. "How are the others?"

"Good. We be having fun, checking out the palace from the inside. Rad digs."

Jarlath gave a noncommittal grunt. The castle was nothing more than a pretty prison. "What's the feeling in here?"

Cristop gave a contemptuous snort. "They think the attacks are a game and now their troubles are over. Stupid people live in dreamland. Not like you. Not like Ellard."

The compliment sent warmth through Jarlath. In the past, he wouldn't have sought the opinion of a youth. He might have exchanged pleasantries but that was all. He'd changed for the better and felt good about it too. Keira's doing.

"Prince Jarlath!" His mother didn't do anything as common as tapping her foot, but her tone emerged like the rap of a whip.

Jarlath grimaced and took a drink from Cristop. A prop. He couldn't afford to dull his senses in any way.

"Prince, those women over there—the ones standing by the balcony doors. Don't place your drink down when you're near them. They have acquired a love potion, which they hope to use to snare your attention. The one in the green-and-white gown wants to compromise you and force you into marriage."

Jarlath glanced at them and shuddered. "Thanks for the warning. Report if you hear anything else useful. Tell Ollie and Nasir to do the same. Share your information with Ellard if you see him."

"Aye." Cristop moved on, and Jarlath reluctantly joined his mother and father.

"Don't speak with the help. It's common," his mother barked.

Anger burst in him like a red soldier detonating, and it took effort to bite back hasty words. "Did you require something?"

"I washed that nasty stuff off my hands. A queen cannot have greasy hands," his mother said.

"The protective barrier is greasy. It keeps poison from entering through your skin." Jarlath strove for patience and failed. His anger and frustration bled through in his crisp tone. "Father, have you washed your hands too?"

"Not yet, although the queen is correct. My hands feel most odd."

Jarlath frowned. The king looked old and frail, his face gray with fatigue. "Father, are you all right?"

"The king is ill," his mother whispered. "You are making the situation worse because you haven't announced your choice of wife."

"Fine," Jarlath ground out. "The woman over there by the window, the one in the yellow dress. Is she on the list?"

"That is Lady Arabella Lionus-Groves," the queen said. "A wonderful choice." She clapped her hands together. "Just perfect."

"Prince Jarlath, do you mean to choose her as your wife?" the king asked.

"She'll do." Jarlath curled his hands to fists.

"Excellent, we'll make the announcement at dinner," the queen said, her mouth wreathed with a broad smile of triumph.

The king patted his shoulder. "You make me proud, son. You always do the correct and proper thing."

"It would be best to make the announcement during the ball," Jarlath said.

"Of course. Of course," the king said.

"We will announce your betrothal at dinner and later at the ball," the queen said. "Let us share the wonderful news with Lady Arabella and her parents."

His parents started to move away, his mother wearing a pleased smile. Jarlath drained his drink. "Let me get another drink first," he said. "I will join you momentarily."

"Don't take too long," the queen said and placed her hand on the crook of her husband's arm.

With a curt nod, Jarlath skirted a group of young feline shifters dressed in their formal wear. He nodded at an acquaintance and searched for a waiter. Ollie appeared in front of him, flanked by Nasir. They both carried trays of drinks.

"What you be doing?" Ollie demanded. "I hear everything. What 'bout Keira?"

"You diss her," Nasir snapped.

"No," Jarlath said. "I need a distraction at the ball, and this was the best way to place the attention on me when Razvan enters the ballroom."

"You sure?" Cristop barked at him from behind. He carried a

selection of canapés. "Keira be hurt."

"I know," Jarlath said. "I'll make it up to her. Somehow." He glanced up and saw his parents waiting for him. Damn. He grabbed a drink from Ollie's tray and made his way over to the smiling Lady Arabella. He tugged at his cravat. Damn thing was choking him.

Keira's gut churned and roiled in a never-ceasing wave. She refused the food and drink Razvan attempted to foist on her and kept to herself, her mind on her plan of attack. For the special spell to work—the one she'd obtained from Zarbo—she required fire. From memory, there were two large fireplaces in the ballroom. Her plan wouldn't work unless the servants had lit the fires.

"Is there any chance of a surprise attack?" Razvan glanced at both her and Mareeka.

"The soldiers are all under my control and wear red cloaks," Mareeka said.

"Is this true?" he asked.

"Yes," Keira said. "Many of the soldiers are gone. Morale in the lower city is poor. The people resent the king and queen and the ruling classes. They have nothing—no new tech or any hope of obtaining it when only those who are rich have the currency to purchase the necessary technology. Those who live in the lower city must fend for themselves and eke out their existence with few resources. Slavers steal their young. Promise them aid, a job, hope, and not one of them will oppose you."

"She's right," Mareeka said. "They have no weapons, no power. They are ripe for a takeover."

"And the ruling classes?"

Keira sniffed. "They are weak. Those in control hide behind

walls and let their people suffer. Many cling to the old ways and those who do have new tech don't share. This world hasn't modernized like the Cawdor. The people of the Cat have no infrastructure."

"Weapons?" Razvan barked.

"The queen refuses to have weapons in the ballroom. All weapons are left at home or checked at the castle doors." Mareeka chuckled, her sly amusement rubbing Keira's feathers the wrong way. She dug her fingertips into her palms to stall her giveaway reaction.

"What about the prince? He could have warned them," Razvan said.

"He is pathetic, a mere figurehead," Mareeka said with a sneer of contempt.

Keira's heart ventricles picked up in speed and pumped furiously, steering toward panic. She sucked in a quick breath, forced her lips to a mocking smile. "Mareeka is right. The prince will offer no barrier to your plan. He is a mere puppet, his strings jerked by his parents. You do them a favor taking over this planet."

"Perfect," Razvan said. "It appears the oracle was correct since you have both confirmed her words. I am pleased. I am very pleased."

"What about Marjo?" Mareeka demanded. "I want recompense for her death."

"And you will, darling," Razvan said. "I award you the king and queen to do with as you wish."

Mareeka beamed. "I will mount their heads on pikes and place them at the city gates as a warning."

Flying stars and meteors. The pair of them were mad if they thought they could take over without a war. Jarlath and Ellard would fight with everything they had, everything they were. They would never surrender like tame kittens.

CHAPTER FOURTEEN

"W ait! Sir, you must show me your invitation to gain entrance. And, sir! No weapons in the ballroom. The invitation specifically states no weapons of any kind. You must surrender your weapons," a man dressed in navy blue-livery said.

"We've mislaid our invitation. So sorry." Mareeka pulled out her blaster, and when the man put out a hand to accept it, she shot him in the chest. Blood bloomed on his smart tunic. A second blast obliterated his face. He dropped to the floor, dead.

"*Tsk-tsk*. I believe we will keep our weapons," Razvan said to the other servant at the door. "Come, ladies. Let us attend the ball."

Keira stepped over the fallen man and into the ballroom, her left arm linked with Razvan's. Mareeka flanked his other side. Gradually, the animated chatter died and a path cleared. The couples on the dance floor stilled and the musicians faltered, the music giving way to silence.

"Please, carry on with your festivities. Don't let us interrupt you," Razvan said. While his demeanor came across as pleasant, Keira felt the thread of tension in his muscles. "Musicians, play."

After a bumpy and discordant start, the string instruments began mid-song.

"Dancers, dance," Razvan said. "This is a celebration. Pray continue with your normal proceedings."

"I don't believe you have an invitation," a bejeweled woman said, her tone snooty. "There is a dress code."

Keira felt herself gape and hurriedly corrected the deficit. Was the woman stupid? Did she not recognize Razvan? Had Jarlath and Ellard not managed to warn their people?

"It's her," someone else hissed, and Keira wasn't sure of the speaker's sex.

"Keira Cloud, the murderess," a woman said.

Keira turned her head to see her stepdaughter, a sneer marring her pretty face.

Mareeka glanced past Razvan to study Keira with interest. "A murderess. I heard tales of a woman who murdered her husband. This was you?"

"Yes," Keira said.

The whispers rose and swelled with excitement, Keira's reply passing like a magical wave from person to person. Foolish felines. Let them gossip. Let them treat her like a pariah.

They were the stupid ones.

The enemy walked amongst them and they worried about propriety.

"Why don't you and Mareeka join the dancers?" Keira suggested. "Let me scout a good spot for our announcement. Do you have any suggestions?"

"By the fire," Razvan ordered. "We might require it for a quick exit."

"I will arrange it," Keira said.

"We shall dance after we greet the king and queen," Razvan said. "Can you see them?"

"They will be over the other side of the ballroom," Keira answered. "I'll show you the way."

The people in front of them stood aside and let the three walk the length of the ballroom. Jarlath stood with his parents, a woman dressed in yellow clinging to his arm as if she were afraid he would escape. Jealousy struck Keira like a slap to the cheek, and she had to rip her gaze from him to focus on the king and queen.

"I have met them before," Keira murmured to Razvan. "Would you like me to make formal introductions?"

"I believe I would. All these cycles I have missed you, pet, but I see you haven't wasted your time here on Viros. Your contacts are invaluable."

Keira didn't reply. Instead, as they approached the royal family, she watched Jarlath. He ignored her presence to whisper to the young woman. Pleasure flushed the woman's cheeks. He was flirting with her!

The queen noticed their presence first. She looked them up and down and frowned. "Who are you?" Keira saw the instant the woman recognized her. "You," she spat at Keira. "My son announced his betrothal tonight. You can't have him now."

Keira lifted her brows. She didn't understand these people, their entitlement and arrogance. They were delusional. "I would like to introduce Razvan Cronan, ruler of the House of Cawdor and his consort, Mareeka. Please make a line and take your bows."

The king and queen gaped. They shot swift glances at Jarlath, their faces turning pale. He'd failed to convince them of the danger. It was up to her to succeed unless Jarlath had other plans. She glanced at him and caught him fondling the woman's breast. No, not fondling, but his actions—his finger teasing along the skin of the woman's décolletage—skirted proper in a public venue. Her crow let out a furious squawk, one she couldn't suppress, one colored with pique and jealousy.

"They are slow to respond," Razvan drawled.

"Line up now to pay your respects," Keira ordered.

Jarlath removed his hand and straightened. "Best do as she says. We don't want our eve spoiled by formalities. Let us greet the man, drink to his health then return to dancing."

He strode over to Razvan and offered his hand. Razvan stared before accepting the handshake.

"Your hand is sweaty," Razvan said with distaste. "In one sense this pleases me, although it doesn't feel pleasant."

"Forgive me," Jarlath said with a smooth bow. "Welcome to Viros, my lord." He straightened and moved into the background.

"Next," Keira said, her tone sharp when everyone hesitated. "You, Lady. Greet Razvan, the new leader of Viros.

The woman—Keira couldn't recall her name—gasped and lifted her nose. "I will not. I refuse."

Keira opened her mouth to prompt the woman with a sharp directive, but Mareeka pulled out her blaster. The woman dropped and hit the floor before Keira had a chance to blink. Blood spread from the hole in the woman's chest and turned the delicate green dress a brilliant red.

A woman screamed. Another fainted. A man cried out, his distress nearing hysteria.

Mareeka waved her weapon. "Remove the body. Now."

Keira focused her gaze on the men and women waiting in the makeshift line. Their expressions ranged from horror to shock. "Remove the body."

Jarlath pushed through the crowd and lifted the woman into his arms. He stalked from the ballroom, and Keira watched him the entire time, her heart crying out for the man she loved. What they had was impossible. She'd known from the start. Funny how it hurt so much more now that she was presented with the evidence of him with another woman.

"Next to shake hands with the new leader," Keira said in a verbal prod.

The elderly man nearest to them sprang forward, his hand extended, his puffy face wreathed with hearty cheer. "Welcome."

"I approve of your bossy nature," Razvan whispered in her ear. "You are even better than I remember. You please me."

She had to work hard to contain her shudder of distaste. His scent was wrong—strong and overpowering, and her crow pushed and clawed, communicating her dislike of this usurper touching her other self.

"Thank you. Where are the king and the queen? They are not exempt."

"I see them at the end of the line," a buxom woman stammered.

"Ah, yes," Keira said. "Thank you."

The receiving line moved at a fast clip with none of the reluctance shown by the first woman.

The young lady who'd hung off Jarlath's arm earlier preceded the king and queen.

"I'm pleased to meet you," she said, a faint tremor throbbing through her words as she rose from her curtsey.

"Your name?" Razvan asked.

"L-lady Arabella," she whispered.

"I'm sure we will see more of each other," Razvan said.

Lady Arabella cast him an uncertain glance before she joined Jarlath. The woman seemed perfect for the prince—young and beautiful and without an unsavory reputation. No doubt she was a virgin too, and the clear cat tattoo on her cheek proved her feline status.

Razvan turned to the next in line—the queen. "How delightful to meet you."

The queen glared at Keira then offered her hand, her manner stiff and grudging.

To her relief, Mareeka laughed. "You will become used to your new lower status. Give me your tiara. I want it."

"No, this is an heirloom. I—"

Jarlath appeared beside his mother. "Give Mareeka the tiara, Mother."

When the queen was slow to move, Jarlath removed the jeweled circlet and handed the glittering headpiece to Mareeka. "I hope you enjoy wearing this tiara. It has passed down through many generations of our family."

"But, Jarlath—" the queen said.

Jarlath cut her off and led her away. "Let Father bid our new leader welcome."

"Make us space near the fire," Keira ordered. "Your new leader is feeling the cool temperatures on this planet." True because he was shivering even though she, herself, felt overly warm. Still, his chill worked in her favor. "This is the king."

The king stuck out his hand, taking Razvan's smaller hand in his grasp.

Razvan pulled his hand free and wiped it on his trews. "Your hand is as damp as your son's. Sweaty palms must run in your family."

"I do apologize," the king said with suitable gravity. He coughed and pounded his fist against his heart. "I'm sorry. I haven't felt well...my age."

Razvan sneezed and rubbed his chest ventricles, a frown on his swarthy face. "It must be the Virosian climate."

Yes. Exactly what she desired in order to use the repulsion spell, although if she had the opportunity, she'd prefer to knife the dirty cur in the heart. "Come and sit by the fire," Keira said. "Mareeka, would you like a seat by the fire too?"

"Yes," Mareeka said, and the woman seemed pleased at Keira's willingness to serve her.

"I'll be back in a min. Meantime, why don't you have a drink? Razvan, there are hot mulled liquor drinks or I can order cool drinks for you if you prefer." She gestured to a tray of steaming drinks, held by Cristop. Not by a flicker of an eyelid did she betray she knew the youth. Others were accepting drinks off the tray, not hesitating as they watched the unfolding drama, although she noticed they kept a wary distance. "These drinks are a specialty of Viros. Perfect for when the weather turns cold."

"I'll have a hot drink," Razvan said. "Inhospitable place. 'Tis either unbearably hot or very chilly."

"With sweetener?"

"Yes," Razvan said.

Cristop palmed the drug so expertly she almost missed the action, then the youth added bee-honey and handed the drink to Razvan.

"What would you like to drink, ma'am?" Cristop asked with absolute deference. Once Mareeka chose her drink, Cristop added something to her drink too.

Relief flooded Keira. She wasn't working alone. They had a plan after all. She might not have a future with Jarlath but at least they had a present. With that, she'd have to be content. Making good on her word, she pulled up two velvet-hair stools and placed them close to the fire. She also arranged for a small float table for the couple.

Once she led Razvan and Mareeka over to the fire, she clapped her hands. "Start the music. Go back to your dancing."

Gradually the nervous chatter became more natural, and Keira wondered where Ellard was hiding. She glanced at Jarlath and found his dark head close to Lady Arabella's. Pain kicked her hard in the chest, and she dragged in a calming breath in an attempt to ease the ache. It didn't help.

Instead of letting her jealousy gain traction, she studied Razvan. The drug was taking effect since his eyelids were at half-mast. Mareeka, however, seemed more alert.

"Would you like some canapés?" Ollie asked, proffering a tray at

Keira.

"No, thank you," Keira said.

Ollie stood on her foot, and Keira winced.

"On second thought, maybe I will. Is that space-crab?"

"It is, but I recommend the malpack pies," Ollie advised. "The chef has a way with pies."

"I'll go with your recommendation," Keira said, and she was relieved when Ollie gave her an approving nod and removed his hefty weight off her foot.

"And you, miss?" Ollie asked.

"I want space-crab," Mareeka said. "Two."

"Of course. Let me give you a napkin," Ollie said.

"I like this." Mareeka waved a languid hand. "People waiting on me. Sparkly jewels. If only Marjo were here to enjoy this party." Her hand went to the butt of her blaster, and for one awful moment, Keira thought she might shoot Ollie simply because he stood closest.

"Would you like the waiter to leave the tray?" Keira asked, subtly sliding between the pair.

"He should get more," Mareeka ordered.

"Of course." Ollie bowed, playing his part to perfection.

"Would you like something to eat, Razvan?" Keira asked.

"No. Don't feel well," he snapped and slapped his hand against his stomach. He attempted to stand and failed.

Mareeka jumped to her feet, brandishing her blaster. "Poison! They've poisoned you. Cast the spell. Detonate the place," she screamed.

"Caw-caw-caw." He made a series of rapid rattles and clicks and interspersed them with rhythmic caws, none of which Keira could decipher. A thundering sound rattled the very ceiling of the ballroom. Dark clouds formed, and Keira found herself gaping in stunned surprise.

The ladies started to shriek and wail.

"It's raining," a woman shouted.

"How is this possible?" a man demanded, his gaze on the clouds studding the ceiling.

She shot a glance at Razvan and saw the triumph on his face as rain started to fall in earnest. Anxiety crashed through her. The soldiers stationed around the ballroom wore red cloaks. They all going to explode if it kept raining.

"Why is it raining?" she demanded.

"I don't like to lose," Razvan said.

"You!" Mareeka wavered on her feet, her face turning pale and sweaty. "You're part of this. I knew we shouldn't have trusted you."

"I have nothing to do with this," Keira denied.

Mareeka fired and only Ollie's quick reaction saved Keira.

Cristop and Nasir pulled out blasters of their own and returned fire at Mareeka.

Around them several ladies screamed, the harsh sounds of panic creating a stampede for the door. A lady fell, clumsy in her gown and short train. A gentleman tripped over her and went down on his knees, sliding along the damp floor.

"Poison," Razvan muttered and tried to stand. He wavered like an old man with worn-out legs.

Mareeka was down and unmoving.

Keira kept her attention on Razvan, on his face in an attempt to gauge his next move. Their gazes connected and held.

"You drank." Razvan's tone was accusing, and she saw the sec he realized she wasn't on his side. He went for his weapon, but she was ready for him, her knife arcing through the air. She struck his chest, at his heart ventricles. He let out an eerie scream and fought like a demented Jambian ogre, flinging his arms and trying to head butt Keira.

Keira gasped and struggled to yank her knife free. One strike wasn't enough. Her knife pulled from his flesh with a horrid sucking noise, and she struck.

Again.

Again.

Again.

Using every bit of her strength, she yanked the knife from his flesh. Razvan groaned and frustration had her echoing the sound. The frukker was still alive. She stabbed the knife at his chest, farther to the right this time, and he went down to his knees.

"Could have been great together," Razvan rasped. "You warrior. Knew that. Wanted you. Fool."

Keira kicked him in the chest, and he went down, the life flooding from him in a pool of black-tinged blood. She stared at the man who had made her life on Gramite dangerous. His arrogance and the assumption he'd cowed the people of Viros had been his downfall.

She tugged her knife free and cleaned the blade with Razvan's robe. Then she checked his pulse, searching for the telltale kah-boom, kah-boom from his heart ventricles. There was nothing.

The darkness lifted. The clouds vanished and with them, the rain.

Keira stood, aware of the silence in the big ballroom. She turned to see those remaining staring at her in stunned shock.

"What are you staring at?" she snapped. Everyone was blurry, as if she were staring through a window from the outside, looking in.

Someone tapped her on the shoulder and she whirled, her knife positioned ready to strike.

"Whoa," Ellard said raising his hand in front of him. "It's me."

Keira blinked and the red rage shrouding her sight cleared.

"Murderer," a voice whispered from the rear.

The whispers picked up in velocity until they resembled a litany. Murderer. Murderer. Murderer.

"Don't listen to them," Ollie said, coming to stand at her side.

"You need to go," Ellard said. "Jarlath told me to arrange

transport for you."

Keira stared at him, tried to read him and failed. At a loss, she shoved her knife into her boot. She walked over to Mareeka and crouched to check for signs of life. The woman was also dead. Keira removed the tiara from her head and stood.

"She's got my tiara," the queen shouted. "Don't let her take it. Thief!"

Keira stared at the woman in stunned surprise then bitterness took over. "Why would I want a stupid tiara? I'm a farmer." She thrust the sparkly headpiece at Ellard. "Where is my transport?"

"They're kicking you out of the palace?" Ollie said in disbelief. "I don't be gettin' these people."

"Head up their butts," Cristop said, his top lip curling in disdain.

Nasir spat on the polished ballroom floor. "Ungrateful frukkers."

"The transport is outside the castle, in the square," Ellard said. "This way."

He led them past the whispering, gaping upper classes. Keira stalked with her head held high and ignored the rude comments. Ollie and Nasir flanked her and Cristop walked behind. Disbelief was a heavy cloak, weighting her down. She had helped to save them, killing their nemesis and they were kicking her out of the castle, banishment her payment.

CHAPTER FIFTEEN

J arlath sent his parents to their suite and called for a medical man to look at the king. Neither of his parents argued, which told Jarlath how bad the events of the night had affected them. His father appeared years older when Jarlath had bid them good night.

He turned his attention to the mess and the debate in the ballroom.

"Arrest her," Danion Tetsu ordered "And those guttersnipes who pulled weapons in the presence of the king and queen."

"Father," Ellard said, but his father ignored him to issue more orders to a different group of soldiers.

"Make sure Keira gets back to her farm," Jarlath said to Ellard. "I'll try to keep everything under control here."

"Done," Ellard said and disappeared into the throng of angry and fuming men.

A pity none of them had managed to take a stand while Razvan and Mareeka were alive. Over to his right a woman was carrying on as if Keira had planned the entire attack instead of saving them from Razvan.

Irritated with their empty-headed posturing, he climbed on top of a chair and roared for attention. "Quiet!"

The screeches and hysterics faded away, leaving blissful peace.

"Everyone return to your homes," Jarlath said.

"No," Danion Tetsu said. "We must gather statements while the attempted coup is fresh in our minds. We must arrest the woman and make an example of her so no one else thinks to destroy our mighty house."

Jarlath bit back his instinctive insult since Danion was a respected military leader. Once he got the foolish man alone, he intended to let rip and tell him what he really thought.

Starting tonight, there would be changes at the House of the Cat.

Jarlath strove to keep his voice level. "Keira Cloud is a hero. Thanks to her, we were able to concoct a plan to rid ourselves of Razvan and stop him grabbing our valuable resources."

"She walked into the ballroom arm-in-arm with the leader of the House of Cawdor. She wears a crow tattoo on her cheek," a senior minister shouted.

"Aye, if that isn't an admission of guilt, I don't know what is," someone else yelled.

"Arrest her," a female suggested.

Jarlath recognized the voice. Keira's stepdaughter would, of course, benefit from Keira's arrest.

"Enough!" Jarlath shouted.

When the remaining men and women continued to ignore him, he slipped his hand into his jacket pocket and pulled out his blaster. He fired it into the air and managed to hit a chandelier. Jarlath winced when the glittering crystals struck the floor and shattered. Not exactly what he'd intended, but since it missed the crowd and created noise, he'd own his misfire.

"Everyone return to your homes now. Soldiers will patrol the streets and anyone found outside their homes will be arrested," Jarlath said in a crisp voice.

"You can't do that," Danion spluttered.

When no one moved, Jarlath lifted his blaster and fired at a woman's bobbing headdress. This time his aim was true.

"Desist," he ordered. "The next person who argues will lose an arm."

There was a rush for the door and the ballroom emptied with dispatch.

"You can't do this," Danion blustered. "You have no right. I am head of security."

Ellard entered the ballroom and sent a quick nod in Jarlath's direction. Relief filled him. Good, at least Keira should be safe at her farm with her people and the three boys' protection.

"I have every right," Jarlath snapped. "I am heir to the king. My father is not well, which puts me in charge. If you refuse my orders, I will relieve you of your duties."

The older man stared in disbelief. "You can't do that. The king is the only one who can sack me."

"Fine," Jarlath said. "Ellard, make sure he doesn't leave until I return."

Jarlath strode to his parents' suite and pounded on the door. A servant answered and Jarlath pushed through. "Where are my parents?"

"In their chambers, Prince," she whispered.

Jarlath stormed into his parents' bedchamber and found his father abed. "Give me the power to rule the House," he demanded. "You have promised me the power and I want it now."

"You're not officially betrothed," his mother said.

"'Tis done," Jarlath said. "The announcement was made at the ball. With the way gossip spreads in this city, most people will know by now. We do not require a formal announcement." He turned his attention to his father. "Give me the power now, Father, so I can start fixing things."

"Everything will right itself once that woman is arrested," the queen snapped. "The kingdom was running without a hitch until Marcus Cloud took her to wife."

Jarlath focused on his father. "Transfer the badge of power to me, Father. I will do what is best for the House of the Cat." He silently willed him to hand over control.

His father blinked and focused on his hands. His thin chest rose and fell in shallow breaths.

Jarlath wanted to rant and argue and had to force himself to wait for his father's response. This was a time for patience.

Finally, finally, his father nodded. "You are right, son." He reached for Jarlath's hand and squeezed then tugged him to sit on the bed. "I, King Hazan Leandros of Viros, cede to my heir, Prince Jarlath Leandros of Viros. I give you my position, my responsibilities and the office of leader of the House of the Cat." He released Jarlath's hand and fumbled with the golden chain around his neck. "I give you the kingship. May the House of the Cat prosper under your guardianship." He placed the familiar golden cat pendant into Jarlath's hand and curled his fingers around it. "Place the pendant around your neck and it will be official."

"That's it?" Jarlath asked in surprise.

"The proper ceremony should take place," his mother said. "I don't approve of this unseemly haste."

Jarlath ignored his mother and fastened the pendant around his neck. Power shimmered through him once the golden cat rested against his breastbone. The weight of the sovereignty settled over his shoulders and slid through his veins.

"It is done," his father said. "Long live the king."

"Thank you, Father."

"Jarlath, since you are now king, you will need to take care of the announcements tomorrow. You can announce your betrothal and make it official."

"No, Mother. I will be taking care of business tomorrow and making sure the enemy won't return. There is much to do." He stood and headed for the door of their suite. If his mother thought to rule the House via him, she should think again. He did not intend to marry Lady Arabella.

"But, Jarlath—"

"No, Mother. I am the king and I will rule in the manner I see fit."

Jarlath returned to the ballroom.

"This is ridiculous," Danion Tetsu thundered.

Jarlath ignored him. "Ellard, can we arrange transport to visit Keira?"

"But it's—" Ellard broke off to stare. "You're wearing the king's pendant."

Jarlath bowed from the waist. "King Jarlath, if you please. Danion Tetsu, I relive you of your duties and appoint your son Ellard as head of security."

"You can't do that. He's useless with one arm."

Jarlath witnessed the pain on Ellard's face and whirled on Danion. "Get out," he snarled. "Don't show your face here until you apologize to Ellard."

"You'll regret this," Danion said and clomped from the ballroom.

Ellard bowed. "Congratulations, King Jarlath."

"You're my best friend, Ellard. Please call me Jarlath if we're alone. I'm going to Keira's place. I'll stay the night if she'll let me."

"Do you think that's a good idea?" Ellard asked. "What about Lady Arabella?"

The knock on the kitchen door came late, hours after they'd returned to the farm. Too wired to sleep, Keira stood at a counter, her fingers busily sorting nuts for roasting. A scowl formed when the tap-tap-tap repeated more insistently.

"Damn fool will wake the entire household." She stomped to the door and yanked it open. "Jarlath. What are you doing here?" She suspected she knew.

Now that they'd routed the enemy, the House of the Cat would need to shore its defenses and move on into the future—a future without her. He was coming to say goodbye.

"Keira." He stomped inside and yanked her into his embrace. Secs later, his mouth covered hers in a hard kiss, a passionate kiss. She melted into him, her heart ventricles bursting into a choppy pace and her crow's happy caw-caw echoing through her mind.

This—Jarlath—it felt so right, yet she was wrong allowing him to do this. Jarlath was betrothed to another.

She pulled back to survey his handsome face. "We shouldn't do this. You're betrothed to Lady Arabella." He hadn't even changed his clothes after the ball, and he stood before her, resplendent in his black jacket and trews with a snowy-white shirt. Stubble shaded his jaw, giving him a more dangerous look, one she'd become smitten with. This was how she'd remember him in the future.

"I had to come, Keira. I couldn't let you think I believed you were part of Razvan's plot to take over the House of the Cat. I know you risked much to help save our House. You're brave and courageous—I've never met a woman like you before. Tell me about Razvan, about your life before you came to Viros."

Her heart ventricles soared then plummeted with disappointment. They were not words of love, and why should they be? She stared down at the pile of nuts in front of her. They owned an auto-sort, which she could have used and managed the job in half the time, but she'd wanted to keep busy. Now her hands trembled, and she forced her shaky digits to comb through the yellow nuts and check for signs of rot. "There's not much to tell."

"But you're related to the men who lead the House of Cawdor."

Keira squelched her inclination to flee and rubbed the back of her neck instead. "It's not something to brag about, especially when I crave a peaceful life." A burst of sound—not quite a laugh—escaped her. A little irony wrapped up in black humor. "I didn't get my peace, but I tried."

"When did your mother meet Xavier?"

"They met at a party when she was eighteen cycles. She told me it was love at first sight for her, and I believe he felt the same way about her. Her family tried to break them up, told her there could be no future between them, but they started to meet in secret, and even though he married a crow of high breeding, they have continued to see each other on a regular basis."

"They didn't plan to have offspring?"

That laugh burst from her again, and she pulled a face. "I am a medical miracle. No one thought a Cawdor and Greenmont could produce a child together. It was one of the reasons Xavier's family gave against the match. Some thought I was an abomination. Others thought I should be sequestered and subjected to experiments. My mother loved me and kept me, despite the opposition from her family. Xavier set her up in her own house and visited her there. My mother raised me as a Greenmont since those were the characteristics I displayed. My crow didn't make itself known until I met you, so as far as I knew I took after my mother." She risked a glance at Jarlath and found him watching her steadily. There was no distaste, and she took heart from this, her breathing becoming less strained.

"And Razvan? What about him?"

"I met him at a ball. His reputation preceded him, and I didn't need my mother's warning to stay away from the arrogant crow. I intrigued him and he wanted my innocence. He was persistent, used to taking whatever he wanted, and when I refused his advances, he..."

Jarlath growled, the protest rattling up his throat. "Did he—"

"No! No." She swallowed. "He tried but I escaped. My mother realized the danger and arranged my marriage to Marcus. There was talk of my marriage to one of the Cawdor casino bosses. My father favored this. I-I suspect he decided it would be better to send me off planet because Razvan was determined in his pursuit. He made my life very difficult."

Jarlath growled again, a low sound of fury. "If the man wasn't already dead, I'd take pleasure in wringing his neck. Why Marcus? He was much older. His children are a similar age to you."

"Marcus was dying—a wasting sickness. He didn't want anyone to know, and he wanted a woman who was knowledgeable of herbs and medicines." She lifted her chin and met Jarlath's gaze with a trace of defiance.

Jarlath's eyes widened.

"I didn't kill him. He wanted me to when the time came. He made me promise to speed him on his way when the pain became too much. I treated him with herbs and eased his symptoms. His heart gave out one day, so I didn't need to keep my pledge. I was a good wife to him. I respected him, but there was only friendship between us."

He nodded. "Did you see your father often?"

"He never acknowledged me in public, and my mother sent me to my room during his visits. I didn't see him much."

"But you were close to your mother."

"Yes." She still missed her, although she tamped down the sentiment.

"You could com your mother now. There is nothing to stop her from visiting you here, if that is what you wish."

"I...yes." She brightened at this thought then her shoulders sagged when she recalled the dilemma she faced with Jarlath.

"Hey." Jarlath rubbed his fingers over her crow tattoo and kissed her again. Sweet and enticing, she had no defenses and relaxed into his embrace. His slow, drugging kisses pulled her to a magical place where passion ruled. Her knees weakened until they felt like noodle-food and she clung to him, a small cry of objection issuing from her when he parted their lips.

"Can I stay for the rest of the night? And so we're clear, there won't be much sleeping."

One final night together before reality intruded. A woman made of sterner stuff would find the fortitude to send him on his way. She wasn't that woman.

Taking his hand, she led him to her bedroom. Jarlath closed the door and prowled to her, his bright green gaze on her. He peeled off his black evening jacket and let it fall to the floor, his white shirt following in the same manner to reveal his chest. New was the golden pendant hanging around his neck.

Keira licked her lips and stared, unable to glance away. Her pulse raced, her breasts prickled with the need for his touch. He stepped nearer, his expression intent and full of sensual promise.

"I want you more than I have ever wanted another woman," he whispered while his busy hands unfastened her plain black tunic top and pushed the garment down her arms, trapping her hands at her sides. He nibbled across her collarbone, gently biting and tasting her. The rough, sensual play of his teeth shot pleasurable sensations darting across her skin.

She gasped as his lips moved to her breasts, confined in plain black synstretch. He unfastened the front opening and her breasts spilled free. He glanced up, his eyes heavy with desire.

"So frukkin' beautiful." His hoarse words kicked desire to the depths of her sex, and her heart ventricles thundered.

She struggled to free her hands, desperate to touch in return.

"Please, let me touch you."

"Anytime." He pulled back and freed her from the rest of her clothes. He lifted her off her feet and set her on the sleep-bed. His hard body pushed her into the mattress, a welcome weight and she wrapped her arms around his shoulders and offered her lips for another kiss.

His fingers lightly circled one nipple, bringing a shudder of delight to the surface. She breathed in his masculine scent and groaned when he lowered his head to suckle at her breast. The hard draw of his mouth sent ribbons of sensation unfurling and tightening deep in her womb. She kissed him in return, pressing kisses everywhere she could reach and writhing beneath his bigger body.

He laughed, his chuckle husky and full of satisfaction. "You are the most amazing woman." One of his kisses landed on the swell of her breast, the next on her flat belly, right in the middle of her stomach. He moved lower, parting her legs and settling his body into the gap between.

She moistened her lips, breathless and waited for his next move.

A puff of warm air burst against the heart of her sex, then he bent his head to lick along the seam of her folds. The rasp of his tongue was an additional stimulant, abrasive and decadent. He glanced up to catch her reaction, and she smiled at the flare of desire in him. Jarlath made her feel beautiful. He made her feel like a desirable woman instead of an outcast.

"Touch me," she demanded.

"My pleasure." He followed the same path again with his lips—a firm lick—but he didn't stop short of her clitoris. He traced around the nub, teasing it, teasing her until she let out a soft sound of protest.

"Jarlath, I want to touch in return."

"Soon," he promised. "You taste good." He pushed a finger inside her and secs later licked his digit clean of her juices.

"Delicious."

He stroked her slick folds and pinched her clit, the jolt of sensation making her jump and cry out. "Jarlath, please. I want you inside me."

"Soon," he promised, and he pushed two fingers inside her heat. He curled them and hit the spot that made her gasp.

"Jarlath." His name was a protest, but he laughed and continued stroking her internally and used his mouth externally. With deliberate probing strokes, he pushed her arousal higher and higher until she came with a violent spasm of pleasure.

Gradually, he eased up on the contact. He grinned and caressed her cheek, his expression one of tenderness. "You look beautiful with the flush of green in your cheeks." He kissed her, and she tasted herself on his lips. They kissed for a long time, slow and languorous exchanges that had them both breathing fast.

Jarlath stood to remove the last of his clothes and footwear, his gaze predatory as he stared at her. Her gaze drifted down his body to his cock, and a shudder went through her. He settled on the sleep-bed again and rose over her, tangling their legs. He sucked in a breath and let it out in a hiss when she rocked their lower bodies together.

When she did it again, a rough growl vibrated in his chest. He plundered her mouth and forced her legs apart with his thigh. He lined up his cock and pushed inside her with one hard thrust.

"Damn, that feels good. Hot and wet and tight around my shaft." He pulled out and slid home again, burying himself in her heat. His fingers branded her flesh, and his tongue thrust into her mouth. He increased the pace of his thrusts, changed the angle and the familiar low pressure swelled within her.

Ecstasy swept over her with the speed of a meteor. She convulsed around his cock with a rhythmic pressure that had Jarlath cursing.

His nostrils flared and he slowed his pace, as if he wanted this to last. Each time he pulled out was very slow while his inward strokes were done at pace. Incredibly, she felt the rise of passion again, the sensations growing and increasing until she thought she might explode.

Their lips met while the clawing tension grew. Jarlath pulled back and slid into her, pulling a hushed moan from Keira. Her muscles clenched with each impalement and her breathing became harsh, her muscles locking as she strove for completion.

"Keira," he said, his forehead pressing against hers. A humming note of pleasure followed his next stroke. He increased the speed again and she felt the sharp staccato beat of his heart against her breasts. His teeth grazed her shoulder, bit down on the fleshy spot where he liked to lick and bite. Pain poured through her, instantly eclipsed by pleasure so overwhelming she wondered if she'd survive. He thrust into her again, rocking his pelvis to increase the friction. He hit the right spot and another explosive orgasm raced through her, secs before Jarlath pushed into her with a hard stroke. He halted fully embedded, and she felt the convulsive heave of his muscles as his climax thundered through him, heard his groan of pleasure.

For long moments they lay panting, their bodies as one. Keira felt and heard the contented coos of her crow but couldn't find the energy to smile. Jarlath had worn her out. She skimmed her fingers over his face and trailed them down his neck.

"Jarlath." She strummed a shaky hand over one shoulder, her fingers encountering the pendant she'd noticed earlier. "Isn't this the king's pendant?"

"Yes." The corners of his eyes crinkled in echo of his smile. His gaze stroked across her breasts to linger at her neck then his gaze met hers, full of male satisfaction. "My father passed leadership to me after everyone left the ball."

"Congratulations." She had to force out the words because this was the death knell. It was as she'd thought when he'd first turned up at her door.

This was goodbye.

"I love you, Keira." Jarlath smiled his expression tender. "The day I met you was the best day of my life."

Keira forced a return smile while inside she died a little. They had no future. How could they when he was the king, and she would always be the usurper from the enemy planet, a woman regarded with suspicion.

"Can I come back tomorrow? I have much to do at the castle, but I can spend the night here."

"I don't want to be a mistress, Jarlath. I've told you before. I refuse to stride in the footsteps of my mother."

Jarlath's brow creased and he stared. "No, that's not what I—"

"You're betrothed to Lady Arabella. I'm not mistress material, and I don't want to get in the middle of your betrothal." Keira scowled. "It's bad enough with my stepchildren badmouthing me. After tonight, you can bet they'll start spreading rumors of my perfidy with the enemy." She sighed, thinking about the emotional turmoil to come. "You should leave."

"No, that's—"

Keira scrambled off the sleep-bed and scooped up her clothes. She pulled on her tunic. Her fingers trembled as she fastened the placket, but at least she wasn't naked now.

Jarlath sat up on the bed, seemingly uncaring about his nakedness. Puzzlement carved into his face as he studied her expression. "I—"

"No!" Keira grabbed her trews and focused on pulling them up her legs. Nothing he said could change the facts. He was king, and she was a widow from the House of Cawdor.

The enemy.

As much as she loved him, there was no future for them.

"Jarlath, please leave. I don't want...I can't do this anymore. Just go." She took one final look at his handsome face and forced herself to walk away from the man she'd come to love.

Chapter Sixteen

"What the frukk?" Jarlath stared at the empty doorway, and a chill rippled over his skin. He leaped off the bed and grabbed his clothes, dressing while his feline grumbled in disapproval.

Mine. Mine. Mine.

He'd marked her, and even though the mark wasn't visible at her throat, he knew it was there. His feline had embraced both her and her inner crow.

Keira belonged to him, and he belonged wholly to her, not Lady Arabella nor any other woman. He loved her, and this was how she treated him? By throwing his love back in his face?

His com buzzed, and he answered with a bad-tempered, "What?"

"It's me," Ellard said, sounding harried. "Just a moment," he roared. "The king will attend the meeting in two hours. He's exhausted after the events of yesterday and requires his rest. Tell the council two hours."

Jarlath checked the hour and his brows rose. These council types started work early.

"I'm sorry," Ellard said, speaking to him again. "I've stalled as long as I can. Everyone is concerned and close to panic. They require your reassurance." He paused to take a heavy breath. "Also, Lady Arabella's father has contacted the palace. He wishes to discuss settlements."

Jarlath yanked on the pendant of office. The golden chain wasn't tight around his neck but right now, it felt as if someone were pulling on the pendant and choking the life from him.

"Did you hear me?"

"Yes. I'll head back now and enter the castle via our rear entrance. I might make a surprise visit to the kitchens to order a meal to break our fast. Anything special you'd like?"

"A new arm would come in handy," Ellard said, his tone a hairsbreadth from tetchy.

Jarlath sobered, his hand tightening around his com. "I can imagine it's frustrating, but I'm glad we were able to save your life. Call me selfish, but I don't think I'd manage to get through this without you."

"I've been telling you that for years."

"I know. Any luck contacting Shiloh?"

"No, the com goes through to the message box. Lynx and Shiloh could be anywhere."

Jarlath pulled on one boot then shifted the com to his other hand and eased on his second boot. "I hope they turn up soon. We could do with their help." He stood. "I'm leaving now. It seems quiet, or at least it was when I flew over the city. The soldiers have stopped the looting and most people have hunkered down. See you soon."

After checking the hour again, Jarlath walked downstairs. He found Keira in the kitchen. "I have to go."

"I think that's best."

"Keira, I don't know what happened. I—"

"We had sex," she said. "That's all. It's been nice knowing you, King Jarlath. I doubt our paths will cross in the future."

Cristop ambled into the kitchen. "Thought I heard voices." His gaze went from Keira's stony face to Jarlath and back. "What's wrong?"

"Nothing," Keira snapped. "The king is just leaving."

"King?" Cristop asked. "Should I bow?"

Jarlath ignored the youth's smirk. "This isn't over, Keira. I'm coming back tonight."

"You're not welcome," Keira said in a hard voice. "Return at your peril."

Anger built in Jarlath. "I will be back." He strode from Keira's house before she had a chance to lay down an ultimatum, one they might both regret. What was wrong with the woman? He'd claimed her, and he wasn't letting go this easily.

Back at the castle, Jarlath headed to the rear entrance after leaving the flymo at the royal garage.

"Who goes there?" A soldier challenged him. Better, Jarlath thought, even though his presence was inconvenient.

"King Jarlath," Jarlath said, pulling back the hood of his cloak.

The soldier snapped to attention and saluted.

Jarlath returned the gesture with a crisp return acknowledgment. "Good morn."

Surprise sprinted across the man's face before his expression blanked again.

Jarlath strode through the gardens and almost sighed when another soldier stopped his progress.

"Who goes t-there?" This one was younger and less experienced.

Jarlath went through the same procedure again. He entered the castle and broke into a trot. At the first kitchen, he stuck his head inside.

"Prince Jarlath," a young girl said, her words drawing the attention of the other staff. He recognized her as the girl he'd met and escorted to the kitchen.

"It's King Jarlath now," he said. "Ellard and I would like to break our fast. Can you send a tray to my quarters with enough food for both of us please?"

"Yes, King Jarlath," she said when everyone else just gaped at him. "I will arrange a tray."

"Thank you, Gertrude." Jarlath left, long strides taking him to his suite.

"King Jarlath. You're here," Ellard said with obvious relief.

"More problems?"

"Your parents wish to see you after the council meeting."

"Call me Jarlath, please, Ellard. At least in private. The food will arrive soon." Jarlath stalked to the window and stared down at the square, his mind going to Keira.

"I thought you'd be looking more rested or at least happier after spending the night with Keira."

Jarlath turned to study his friend. Ellard's face appeared drawn, lines bracketing his mouth and dark shadows displaying his lack of sleep.

"Keira kicked me out," Jarlath said. "The minute she saw the king's pendant something changed. Told me she didn't wish to be a mistress and I should return to the castle. I tried to tell her I had no intention of going anywhere, but she wouldn't let me speak."

Ellard's brows drew together. "She's right, Jarlath. Unless she consents to act as your mistress, there is no future for the two of you. You're betrothed to Lady Arabella. Soon you'll marry."

The very idea filled Jarlath with repugnance, and he growled to show his displeasure.

"I thought this was what you wanted. You're the king now. You can change things, make life better for the people."

Jarlath gave a tired nod. The people deserved a break. They deserved to have improved conditions and a better standard of living. "Do you know what the council want to discuss?"

"They mentioned the formal announcement to the people," Ellard said.

Someone tapped at the door.

"That will be breakfast," Jarlath said. "I wouldn't mind a quick wash and change of clothes. Won't be long." Jarlath didn't wait for an answer but headed for his sanitizer room. He stripped, his nostrils flaring when he caught the scent of Keira on his skin.

His mate.

He stepped into the sanitizer and pushed the control buttons for wash, rinse and dry. The process was quick and efficient—a practical and modern addition to the castle. Most of the wealthy had a few modern appliances, but the public who resided in the lower city still used bathhouses. Change, he thought. Their minerals were a finite resource. They needed a new shipping port with larger berths to support more visitors. They needed to attract further investment and to open to more trade. They needed income from tourists and perhaps businessmen.

And then there was the disease creeping through the shifter part of the population. Somehow, he'd beaten the blight, and the scientists needed to discover how he'd done this.

All things to discuss with the council.

When Jarlath returned to his reception room, the scent of fried meat and tay filled the air.

"You will attend the meeting with me," Jarlath said.

"Me? They won't allow me entrance."

"We'll see about that," Jarlath said.

The council meeting commenced half an hour later than scheduled. The ten men who aided the king in the governing of the city sat in stupefied silence, regarding Jarlath in the same manner a space mouse regarded a cat who was about to pounce.

They stared at each other, glanced at him and stirred uneasily in their seats. One coughed as Jarlath laid out the first part of his plan to improve life for the occupants of the lower city.

When their expressions became increasingly incredulous, Jarlath waited for them to begin their rebuttal. He'd already fought the battle for Ellard to attend the meeting and won. He was confident he'd win his other skirmishes too. These men were stuck in the past and he intended to shake things up and kick the House of the Cat into the future. Willingly or kicking and screaming—it didn't matter to Jarlath.

Progress would happen.

"We must arrange the formal announcement later today," one of the men said in the pause.

"And discuss the coronation," another added.

"A week of feasting and celebration," a third said.

"No," Jarlath said. "We'll hold the formal ceremony in the square, but there will be no celebration. The funds should be applied to rebuilding the city."

Appalled silence fell, and Jarlath decided to lay out the rest of his plan now. He began slowly, detailing his ideas to bring the city into the future, and when he finished everyone regarded him with expressions akin to horror.

"We can't cut the palace budget, your majesty," one said. "We must keep up appearances."

"Taxes on wealth aren't the answer," another cried.

Jarlath massaged the bridge of his nose and strove for patience. "It is wrong for a few to live in luxury while the rest lives in poverty and hardship. We will budget. Who is the treasurer?"

"Me, your majesty." A thin male with a pallid complexion lifted his right hand. "I am the treasurer."

"The budgets require trimming. Report to my suite with the palace and the city books once the meeting ends. Now, security.

We need to recruit more men. I expect some of the city men will report to the castle today, expecting payment for services rendered. Treasurer, please arrange a clerk to handle this."

"How will we know which men to pay, your majesty?" the treasurer asked, his manner timid.

"They'll hand in protection spells and receive their wages in return. Ellard will aid you with this. Ellard, offer any who are interested a position in our army. Standard rates."

"Yes, King Jarlath," Ellard said.

Jarlath almost grinned at the honest humor he saw in his friend's face. He was enjoying this meeting much more than the councilors.

"Your majesty," a councilman protested. "Our soldiers have always come from the upper class. The people should not receive the same wage."

"If they put their lives in danger to protect those in the city, they will receive the same wage. See to it. Who is in charge of buildings?"

"Me, your majesty." This councilman was rotund and red-faced, his eyes a dark green, signifying the loss of his feline.

"I want you to tour the city and draw up plans for the rebuilding. Take some soldiers with you and several assistants. Talk to the people and ask for their opinions. Tell them to send written submissions to the castle. I will consider every submission. We want modern, practical buildings. I want another team to plan a spaceport large enough to receive ships from distant planets. Decide on the best area to build the port."

"Yes, your majesty," the rotund man said, scribbling notes furiously.

"Is there anything else that requires our immediate attention?" Jarlath asked.

"The coronation," one said.

Jarlath frowned, his thoughts drifting to Keira. Mate. "Tomorrow at noon. Make the announcement today—you don't require my presence for that—and tell everyone the coronation will occur in the square. I will make the explanation as to why we are diverting from tradition during the formal ceremony."

"Yes, King Jarlath," one of the men said.

"There is much to do," Jarlath said. "I suggest we meet at the same time every day for the foreseeable future. That way we can make rapid decisions. Any questions?" Jarlath scanned their faces and decided they appeared suitably shattered. "Right. I want each of you to look at your areas of responsibility and report back to me at our meeting on the morrow. Look at your budgets and trim the fat." Jarlath stood. "Ellard, with me." He strode from the council room, paused. "I think I've rattled them enough at present. My parents next."

"I'll wait in your suite."

"No, you're my shadow. I want you to witness everything that happens today."

Jarlath knocked on the door to his parents' suite. A servant opened the door and he stalked inside. "Mother, you wished to see me."

She set her cup of kafe down. "Ellard, wait outside."

"No, Mother. I have much to do today. Ellard is discreet. You can say what you wish in front of him."

His mother glared daggers at him. "You have changed, Jarlath, and not for the better. Don't tell me you attended the council meeting dressed as you are?"

There was nothing wrong with his clothes. They helped him to blend—maybe not when he was in the castle but when he was out on the street. "Mother."

"Very well." She peered down her nose at Ellard until his friend broke their visual dual to stare at his feet. Mollified, she turned to her son. "You must set a date for your wedding."

Jarlath sighed, sad his relationship with his parents had come to this. There was no way to make this palatable. "Mother, I won't be marrying Lady Arabella."

"What?" The word came out at a near shriek.

His father entered the reception room, still dressed in a robe. "What is the matter?"

"Jarlath has just informed me he doesn't intend to marry Lady Arabella."

"But—" his father began.

"I have a mate already. It would be wrong of me to wed another."

"You can't—"

"I am not discussing this with you. I am telling you what will happen. I cannot continue with the betrothal. I intend to explain the situation to Lady Arabella and her father, but I will not change my mind."

"It's that woman," his mother spat.

"That woman has a name, and she is my mate," Jarlath said. "Now, if that is all, I have an appointment with Lady Arabella."

Leaving his mother spluttering, Jarlath wheeled away and departed his parents' suite at a fast clip.

Ellard trotted to catch up. "I hope you know what you're doing."

For the first time this morn, Jarlath's heart rate settled instead of keeping up the agitated pulsations. His feline calmed instead of bucking beneath his skin. This was the right thing to do, following his instincts. To grata with anything else.

The meeting with Lady Arabella and her father was just as difficult as he imagined it would be. Lady Arabella burst into tears and ran from the room. Her mother shrieked long and loud until Jarlath's head started to ache.

"Enough," Jarlath barked. "Ellard, please take Lady Dawn for a walk in the garden until she recovers. I need to speak with Lord Innes in private."

Ellard shot him a dirty look but ushered Lady Dawn from the

room.

"Lord Innes, I realize I've handled this situation badly, and I apologize for my behaviour. I needed my parents to cooperate in order to best Razvan and a betrothal was the quickest way for this to happen."

The older man surveyed him with shrewd intelligence. "You're not sorry enough to go through with a marriage to my daughter."

"I have a mate. If I married your daughter, it would make for three unhappy people."

"My daughter is unhappy now."

"I know, and I'm sorry. I'd like to try to make amends," Jarlath said. "I have big plans for the House of the Cat, some of which I've put in motion. I require honest men who are willing to work for the good of the House. This is an active position. You won't be a figurehead. I will expect you to perform to the best of your abilities."

Lord Innes cocked his head. "This apology of yours is a double-edge weapon."

"Yes." Jarlath appreciated the bluntness of the man and also his astuteness. "But in the future, those who prove honest and reliable, the men whom the king surrounds himself with will receive prestige and position in return for their hard work. If you're expecting kickbacks or riches, don't bother. I will apologize with a financial boon and leave it at that. If you choose to take up my offer, you'll receive the respect of the people, and I believe that will garner additional benefits for you and your family."

"I accept," Lord Innes said. "Do you have a specific position in mind?"

"Yes, that of foreign trade and investment. I have set in motion plans for a new space port large enough to handle the bigger ships. It is up to you to find ways to attract those ships to Viros. How does that sound?"

"An exciting opportunity. I would be a type of ambassador."

"Yes. At first I'd like you to discuss your plans with me and the council, but once we have our improvements set in motion, you'd have greater authority and autonomy."

"I'll get started right away."

"Excellent," Jarlath said. "The council is meeting each morn for the foreseeable future. I would like you to attend the meetings and report your findings. Is that acceptable?"

"Yes, your majesty."

"Excellent. Please pass my apologies on to your wife and daughter. I am very sorry they became involved in this mess."

"I will, your majesty."

"Good. I appreciate your understanding," Jarlath said. "I will see you in the council meeting room in the morn."

They shook hands, and Jarlath went to release Ellard from his duties. Two items to check off his mental list. So far, so good. Unfortunately he didn't believe he'd manage the third and final item with the same ease.

His parents wouldn't be quite as understanding.

Keira moped all day, despite the large number of tasks awaiting her attention. Luckily Cristop, Nasir and Ollie were eager to work and set to with cheerful chatter.

"It's good to hear the place alive with youngsters," Hortese said.

"Yes."

"Will we go to the market tonight?"

"No, I think it's best to miss the market this week. The people in the city are jumpy at present."

"And the prince?"

"It's King Jarlath now," Keira said and silently cursed. She didn't want to think about the man. Thinking about him and acting on her attraction had placed her in this situation, made her miserable. "He won't be coming here again. It's time to make more berry wine. I think I'll go and pick berries."

"Want company?" Hortese asked.

"No, you stay here to supervise our new crew and maybe start on drying some more herbs. Those packets of herbs we made for repelling cooties have sold very well. We're almost out."

"Right you are. When will you return?"

"When I've filled six containers, or sooner if the birds have beat me to the berries. I'll be back for dinner."

She wheeled her trolley to the berry bushes nearest the house and started picking the fat fruit. The task allowed her mind to wander, and it skipped right to Jarlath. Oops, that would be King Jarlath. She had to remember. He was a betrothed king and galaxy-miles out of her social sphere.

Keira forced her mind to her future, which was much safer than dwelling on Jarlath.

A crashing sound jerked her from her task. She whirled to see a shaggy black cambeest galloping in her direction. The creature skidded to a stop and sniffed at her face and chest. A contented rumble came from the beest.

"Black, what are you doing here?"

He rumbled again, a low deep sound, and Keira laughed in delight. She scratched behind his ears, and when she stopped, he gave her a nudge—an order to continue with the petting.

"He must have scented you." Jarlath limped toward her, rubbing his backside. A pink leaf adorned his wind-blown hair along with a purple twig. Mud splattered his boots and his black tunic bore a rip where it had caught on a branch. "At least no one saw me tumble off this time."

"Not very dignified for a king," Keira said, and she told her foolish heart ventricles to stop racing. Predictably, her crow started to flap and scratch beneath her skin, as she always did when Jarlath came near. She gestured at her face. "You have dirt."

He gave a rueful smile and rubbed his cheek vigorously. "If you tell, I'll deny everything."

They stared at each other for a long moment, and Keira had to fight his magnetic pull. Who was she trying to fool? She wanted him. Her crow squawked, and she took half a step before her brain kicked into gear. She clenched her hands at her sides and stared at him wordlessly. Black seemed to realize he was surplus to requirements and wandered off to graze.

"I told you I'd return." Jarlath broke the taut silence.

"And I told you not to. I can't do this anymore, Jarlath. I care for you, and I can't keep seeing you without wanting to spend time with you."

"That's what I want to hear," Jarlath said. "I love you, and I want to marry you."

When she started to protest, he placed his fingers over her mouth.

"Wait. Let me finish. Today I went to visit Lady Arabella and her family and told them that I didn't want to marry her because I was mated to someone else—you."

Keira gasped and gazed at him, shock kicking her in the chest, stealing her breath. "But...but..."

Jarlath closed the remaining distance between them and drew her into his arms. "No buts about it. I am no longer betrothed to anyone, but I intend to remedy that very soon."

"But what about your parents? They don't like me. Your head of security wants to arrest me."

"We reached a compromise," Jarlath said.

"What sort of compromise?"

"I intend to relinquish the crown."

"What?"

"I am going to step aside in favor of my brother Lynx."

"No. No, I can't let you do that," Keira said. "You're the heir.

You were born to be king."

"I'm miserable when I'm not with you. My feline is cranky, and you're all we think of, every spare min." He ran his hand down her back, and a shiver rolled across her skin. Everything he said was how she felt. Her crow was plain despondent and wasn't shy about letting her know.

"I...I can't let you give up everything for me. Later you'll come to regret this gesture. You'll resent me."

Jarlath cupped her face in his hands and stared. Something brightened and sharpened in his eyes, and she realized she was seeing his other self. Her crow gave a victorious caw and it resounded in her head.

"What if you change your mind?" she whispered.

"No chance of that," Jarlath said, and his confidence went some way to persuading her. His brow furrowed then cleared. "As far as I'm concerned I won't change my mind, but it's understandable you're skeptical. I'm still handing the crown to my brother, once we can locate him, but you and I can take our relationship at our pace."

Keira felt herself gaping and snapped her mouth shut. Jarlath grinned, and something in her heart ventricles shifted, tightened.

"We can take things as slow as you want until you're certain of me."

"But...but..." Her mind was working at half-pace, not giving her the answers she sought. "I can't bear your children. We're different species. You should have children."

He smiled tenderly and brushed a strand of hair off her cheek. "Silly woman. We have children already. Together we've collected Cristop, Ollie and Nasir. They might not be of our blood, but without even discussing the matter, we've decided to look after them, make sure they stay out of trouble, give them a home. That's family, Keira. We've already formed a family. My feline has claimed you. We can wait for you to catch up."

"You sound so certain."

"I am." There was a trace of male arrogance now, and it pulled a grin from her.

"I need to finish picking berries."

"I'll help." Jarlath took a container off her trolley and started to pick fruit. His fingers plucked the red berries efficiently and he'd soon filled his container. He started on the last, his focus pushing Keira back to her harvesting.

Jarlath truly intended to give up the crown for her. The idea was overwhelming. Accepting his plan...

"All done?" Jarlath asked.

She glanced down at her half-filled container. "Yes."

"Good. It's a gorgeous day. Why don't we both shift and play together?"

"P-play?"

Jarlath gave one of his wondrous grins, and her insides knotted in appreciation. He was so handsome, and he was offering himself to her, giving up everything. For her.

"You haven't had a chance to shift at will. I'll talk you through the change."

"I-I don't..." She trailed off, realizing the words forming on her lips were a lie. She would like to shift, the excited caw-caw of her crow confirming her thoughts. "What do I do?"

"From memory, you shifted with your clothes in place." He glanced her up and down, his lips quirking into a grin. "More's the pity. Black should be safe enough here and your berries, if you cover them. I'll take care of that once you've shifted. Do you remember what to do?" At her frown, he continued. "Close your eyes. Picture your crow in your mind and focus on nothing else. Imagine flying, the wind beneath your wings, teasing me by fluttering out of reach. Are you doing that?"

"Yes." She followed his instructions and soon the prickle of magic fizzed through her veins. Once the magic commenced, her shift proceeded rapidly and her heart ventricles soared, pumping extra fast. Her skin absorbed her clothes then feathers sprouted along her limbs and chest. Her bones reshaped, her arms transforming to wings.

A caw-caw forged up her throat and when she glanced down her sight was sharper. A small animal crept through the undergrowth, cautious and wary. She could hear the soft pants it made, the stirrings of panic as it froze.

"You're beautiful in bird form too." Jarlath smoothed a finger over her feathers, then moved away to take off his jacket and shirt. "Your black plumage has a faint green tinge."

She watched him with awe. This beautiful man wanted her. Although she'd thought it before the notion bore repeating. Maybe then she'd come to believe.

His change was quicker than hers and an instant later, he stood in front of her, his sharp white teeth visible through his gaping maw. He was happy, she realized, and the emotion bounced straight to her. She flapped her wings and instinct took over, lifting her off the ground.

Jarlath barked and sped along a forest path. At a corner, he paused to wait for her and she beat her wings harder, the physical exertion leaving her breathless yet exhilarated. She shrieked a caw of triumph, her next caw-caw-caw sounding like a chuckle.

Jarlath flicked his tail and shot in the opposite direction. Keira tried to stop and forgot to flap her wings. She let out a panicked squawk and attempted to slow her fall to the ground by flapping extra fast. Jarlath got there first and broke her fall. Her claws dug into his flanks as she struggled for balance. When her heart ventricles ceased their choppy beat, she hopped off him then sidled closer to him, giving a soft coo. Jarlath rumbled in return.

Keira took off again, reveling in the freedom and the shared experience with Jarlath. They played until her wings ached, and fatigue reduced her to hopping.

Back at the clearing, Jarlath shifted. "Remember how to transform back?"

She caw-cawed and started the process of transforming back to humanoid.

"How was that?" Jarlath asked.

"Exhausting but fun. So much fun. It's as if I was only half alive before."

"It's better when the experience is shared," Jarlath whispered, and he drew her into his arms. Their lips met, and she was lost, lost in Jarlath. Her arms curled around his neck and she offered herself without reservation.

Busy hands removed her clothing, pushed her tunic top aside. He flicked his tongue over her nipple and took it into his mouth. The rest of their clothes ended up discarded on the ground.

"I love you so much, Keira. I don't want to imagine my life without you in it." He kissed her, parting her lips with his tongue and explored the soft recesses of her mouth.

"But you're giving up so much," she said when she was able to speak again.

"And gaining much more in return. Come, don't you love me a little?" He lifted her off her feet and set her on top of a patch of pink grass.

She grinned up at him, brushed her hand over his cheek when he dropped down beside her. In this man she saw all the strength and character any woman wished for in a lover and partner. "Yes." She felt her lips curl upward, the smile digging into her cheeks. "Yes, I love you, you impossible man. I'm happy when I'm with you and when we're not together, my mind is with you."

He rolled on top of her. "It's the same for me." Satisfaction glittered in his features and he kissed her again, unhurried and deep, as if he wanted to brand her with his touch. His hands skimmed her curves, tweaked a nipple, and she clung to him, rocking her hips in invitation. Already pleasure and desire roared through her and she needed him filling the emptiness inside her. Craved him. "Put your cock inside me."

"My pleasure." The corners of his eyes crinkled as he aligned their bodies and pushed inside her, the gradual stretch feeling perfect.

The surge and retreat created a decadent friction, and he caught her groan of approval with his mouth. He dragged out every sensation until she thought she might explode. When he lifted his head, his smile was one of love and caring and an underlying hunger that had velvet tension coiling in her lower body.

She licked along his jawline, took tiny nibbles from his throat. When she paused at the fleshy part where neck and shoulder met, he groaned, his entire body shuddering.

"Bite me, Keira. Please." He cupped her head, as if he was afraid she'd retreat.

She licked the spot, kissed it, and another shudder sped through him. He'd stopped stroking into her, instead remaining fully embedded while she kissed and nipped and teased him.

Finally, he voiced a protest. "Keira, please."

"I don't want to hurt you."

"You won't, sweetheart. Please, I need this."

The love in his eyes decided her. She lowered her head and licked the spot, pulling a needy groan from him. Emboldened, she gave him a hint of teeth. His cock pulsed inside her while his ridged abs rippled. She licked once and sank her teeth into his flesh until the coppery taste of blood filled her mouth. A moan escaped her while Jarlath cried out. She froze, thinking she was hurting him, but the jerk of his hips and the pulse of his cock said otherwise.

"Ah, Keira. Keira." He groaned and shuddered.

The warm wash of his semen filled her quim, and she wriggled, her tongue flicking over the place where she'd bitten. His entire body jerked again, his groan one of enjoyment and satisfaction. He withdrew and pushed inside her again while his finger slid between them. The sensations built and built and a hungry little moan squeezed past her lips. Then, he bit her in the same spot he'd bitten her before.

It was delectable agony, and the bite felt so, so good a scream built in her throat. The sensual tension snapped, a spasm of white-hot pleasure searing through her lower belly and streaking to her toes.

"Yes, Jarlath. Yes."

She was vaguely aware of him licking the spot and with each lave another spasm of delight shot through her. She writhed beneath him, each breath coming fast and choppy.

Jarlath lifted his head and pressed his forehead against hers. "I love you, Keira. Say you'll marry me."

"Yes," she breathed, her mind still floating and full of ecstasy. "Wait, where will we live? I'll smother if I have to live in the castle."

"I thought I'd move in with you here at the farm, although we'll need to spend the odd night at the castle, at least until we track down my brother. Can you cope with one or two nights a week at the castle?"

Keira sucked in a deep breath and idly scratched her cheek. "I can try."

"Thank you. I know my mother won't be easy, but the castle is a big place." He kissed her cheek and pulled from her body.

"Are you sure about this?"

"Yes." Jarlath climbed to his feet and offered her a hand. "Let's dress and get those berries home, so we can tell everyone the news."

CHAPTER SEVENTEEN

Waking up with Keira wrapped in his arms was the best feeling ever. Jarlath brushed her hair back from her face and bent to kiss her. He froze midway there and stared. Her cheek was a smooth and healthy color with her normal green tinge. The crow tattoo had disappeared overnight.

"Keira."

She stirred, yawned. "Is it morn?"

"She's complaining about me keeping her awake already."

Keira rolled toward him, giving Jarlath a glimpse of her back. Interesting.

He caressed her cheek, right where the tattoo used to sit on her skin. "You know your tattoo?"

"Is the skin irritated? It was very itchy last night."

"It's gone," Jarlath said.

"No! Let me see." She jumped off the sleep-bed and peered into her looking glass. "It's vanished. How strange."

"Not exactly." Jarlath's gaze ran down Keira's bare back and the large crow tattoo now gracing her back.

Keira turned back to him, her gaze shooting to his biceps. "Wait. Where's your tattoo? It's not on your arm."

Surprise hit Jarlath. He stared at his tattoo-free arm. "Check my back."

"There is a big black leopard covering most of your back. How did you know?" The wonder in her voice brought a smile, and the feel of her fingers running over his skin pushed a tremor through his body.

"Your tattoo is on your back too. You're sporting a big black crow."

"No!" She turned back to the mirror and attempted to study her back, giving Jarlath a great view of her front.

"I like it when you flash me," he said, his grin wicked and a little predatory.

"What does this mean?" Keira asked, a cute wrinkle marring her brow.

"According to the House of the Cat written history, when a couple mate in their human forms and their felines accept each other, the tattoos are a symbol of their bond. Of course, I've read of variations to this. There was one instance of a feline shifter mating with a non-shifter and the mating bonds formed and turned the non-shifter into a feline. I think we're another anomaly—two different shifter races mating. Your crow and my feline accept each other. We love each other, and the tattoos make our match official. No one can argue with this."

"You think?"

"I know," Jarlath said firmly.

A tap on the chamber door had them both turning in that direction.

"Yes?" Keira called.

"Hortese said it's time for you to get up. She said we have an important day before us and need to break our fast together." Ollie sounded as if he was repeating Hortese word for word.

"We'll be there in a few mins," Jarlath said.

"Hortese said to tell you not to make her climb the stairs," Ollie said.

Keira laughed, humor lighting up her face. "We'd better move. We don't want Hortese marching up here."

Jarlath climbed off the sleep-bed and prowled toward her. He twined his fingers with hers and led her to the sanitizer.

When they made it downstairs, Hortese said, "About time." Her shrewd face took on a pleased grin. "Pleased to see you both so happy. Will you all be home for dinner this eve?"

"Yes," Jarlath said.

"Ellard too, if he'd like to come and stay," Keira suggested.

"Perfect," Hortese said.

"I'll sneak some bottles of Joyous wine from the castle cellar," Jarlath said. "We'll make it a celebration for our mating." He reached for Keira's hand, his happiness finding an outlet in a broad smile. He'd never felt like this before, and despite the cost of his love for Keira, he wouldn't change a thing. He could still serve his House and support his brother, the new king. People in the House would accept Lynx as their king while they'd never truly accept him, not if he stayed with Keira.

The fact didn't bother him one bit.

Jarlath tied his cravat and surveyed his image in the mirror of his suit at the castle. He turned to Keira. "How do I look?"

"Handsome."

He closed the distance between them and brushed his lips over hers. "Thank you for being here to support me. And I apologize for my mother's rudeness."

"She doesn't like me. It's all right," Keira said. "I thought I'd com my mother now that Razvan is dead. It would be a good idea to learn who takes over as ruler of the House of Cawdor."

"True." Jarlath checked the time.

"You're nervous."

He laughed, the sound carrying an edge of wryness and self-derision. "Until now my life has been very different. I've attended balls and public functions for the upper class. I've trained in self-defense with Ellard and his father and learned how to ride. Public speaking hasn't been on my agenda." Another sardonic laugh burst from him. "I don't know what I'm worried about. I doubt anyone will come to listen to my speech."

"Oh, Jarlath." Keira wrapped her arms around his waist and pressed her cheek against his chest. "You're a good man. A natural leader. Of course people will want to listen to you." She glanced up and the love he saw made him caught his breath.

"I love you."

"I love you too. It was never like this with Marcus."

A tap on the door announced Ellard's arrival. He stepped inside, his chin held high with pride, despite the empty sleeve of his ceremonial jacket.

"Enough of the mushy stuff." Then he grinned. "I can't believe the old myths about each of us having a mate is true."

"You believe us," Keira said.

"Jarlath showed me his tattoo earlier and said you had a matching one of a crow on your back. I offered to check your tattoo, but Jarlath didn't like that idea," Ellard said, offering his friend a smirk.

"What? He tells a joke," Keira said.

Ellard sobered. "I was wrong about you, Keira. I don't care what other people say—you're good for Jarlath, and for what's it's worth, you both have my full support."

"Thank you." Keira stood on tiptoes and pressed a kiss against his cheek. "You're coming to the farm with us tonight? We're having a celebration dinner."

Ellard patted her hand. "I'll be there. King Jarlath, you ready?"

"Just Jarlath, please. Lead the way." An annoying jump of nerves had him pressing his hand to his stomach.

Keira seemed to sense his anxiety and curled her fingers around his. Her touch soothed both him and his beast, and when he stepped into the balcony room of the castle, he had his nerves under control.

"What is she doing here?" his mother demanded.

"Keira is my mate," Jarlath said.

"Leave the boy alone, and let us get this ordeal done," his father said in a tired voice.

"She is of our enemy. I will not have her here. She helped you trick your father into making you king. Now you intend to throw this gift away." His mother was winding up into another of her tirades.

"I will wait here out of sight with Ellard," Keira said, offering a silent message of acceptance by squeezing his fingers.

Jarlath sent his mother a stern look, an order to silence her viperous tongue. The firming of her lips told him message received. Jarlath stepped onto the balcony, flanked by his parents.

The castle crier waited on the balcony and straightened when he saw them.

"Hear ye! Hear ye!" His voice boomed through the auto-amplifier. "All stand for King Jarlath."

Jarlath stared down at the square, packed with the people. He didn't think he'd ever seen so many Virosian massed together before.

"All hail King Jarlath!"

Their words rippled through the square, taking Jarlath by

surprise. He stared at the many faces—those of the upper class seated in a roped-off area and the other citizens crammed in the remaining space.

"Please start, Jarlath. The sooner we end this travesty the better," his mother said.

"Bryna, cease your torment of the boy. He is doing what he believes is right," his father snapped. "I don't want to hear another word."

Jarlath acknowledged his father with a nod, took a deep breath and waved at the people in the square.

"Thank you for taking the time to listen to me today. The House of the Cat has come through a period of turmoil, and I want to salute you, the people, who stood strong and helped us to repel the enemy. We have already set plans in action to help rebuild the city and intend to introduce many such improvements to make all our lives easier and to encourage visitors and investors to the planet of Viros.

"As your lives have gone through upheaval, so has mine. My father has decided to resign his position of king and has passed the pendant of power to me. The constitution of the House of the Cat states the king must be betrothed or married to a woman of suitable birth. Unfortunately, I am unable to discharge this part of my responsibility because I am not willing to undertake my duties without the help of the woman I love.

"Therefore, it is with regret that I must pass the pendant of power to my brother, Prince Lynx. My parents and the members of the council have agreed I may continue as interim ruler until Prince Lynx returns to Viros.

"I intend to carry out my interim duties to the best of my abilities until Prince Lynx is able to accept his role as king. My brother is eminently suited to this role, and he will have my full support during the transition and once he wears pendant of power.

"I wish him and you, the people of Viros, a prosperous and happy existence. May the House of the Cat flourish with success."

Jarlath bowed and retreated, leaving his parents on the balcony to receive the cheers of the people.

"Good speech," Ellard said.

Jarlath walked straight to Keira, only relaxing when he touched his mate. He tugged her against his side, tossing a wicked grin at his friend. "Thanks. You know, I can't wait to see Lynx's face when he learns he'll be king."

Ellard guffawed. "It'll be a moment of history."

"He won't want to be king?" Keira asked.

"Once Lynx gets over the shock he'll make an excellent ruler," Jarlath said. "We won't worry about my brother. He'll come home soon. Meantime, we have work to do and a mating to celebrate."

He grinned at the woman who'd grabbed his attention and pulled him from his narrow world, the woman who pushed him to be the best he could, the woman he loved with all his heart. Sometimes taking a different path yielded the greatest riches. He gave her a quick squeeze and stole a kiss.

Ellard rolled his eyes. "Take the rest of the day off. Go home and do whatever new mates do."

"I like the way he thinks," Keira said.

Jarlath felt his grin widen. "Me too. You're in charge, Ellard." He tugged Keira down the corridor. "We'll start the celebration in my suite."

Keira's joyous laugh echoed with happiness. "An excellent plan. See you later, Ellard."

Left alone, Ellard snorted softly and shook his head as he ambled in the opposite direction. Interesting times ahead. Of that, he was certain, and in truth, he was looking forward to the challenge.

Long live the king.

They just had to find Prince—ah—King Lynx first.

Where is King Lynx? Read *Seized & Seduced* to learn more! (https://shelleymunro.com/books/seized-seduced/). Turn the page for a glimpse of *Merry & Seduced*, the next story in my **House of the Cat** series.

EXCERPT - MERRY & SEDUCED

"Do my ears look pointy in this?" Kaya asked, cocking her head so her blue hair swung away to reveal a jeweled ear cuff.

"Very funny." Camryn O'Sullivan plucked at her hair in telltale irritation. "Tell them, Ry. None of them are taking this seriously. Earth isn't ready for aliens. It's gonna be bad enough facing my brother and his wife again after all these months. I don't want to worry about the population of New Zealand panicking because they think it's an alien invasion."

Amme Vanak stood in the background, leaning against a wall of the flight deck of the *Indefatigable*, a smirk tugging her lips. This argument had been ongoing ever since Ry announced they'd visit Earth for Christmas. A summer Christmas since they were going to the southern hemisphere, and she couldn't wait. The conversation never failed to entertain her, and she suspected the crew enjoyed teasing Camryn.

"What do you say, Amme?" Nanu, the ship's engineer and pilot, drew her into the discussion. The beads on the ends of his braids clacked as his attention shifted from her back to Camryn. "Do you want to do some sightseeing on Earth?"

Of course she did. "As long as I can regulate my skin tone."

Her cyborg nature allowed her to change her skin tone to blend. Her other characteristics were less noticeable. When she was a child, the categorization committee on her home planet of Sheng had determined she would profit their society most by entering the profession of childcare. Then, like all children on Sheng, she'd undergone enhancements to complement her natural inclinations.

Her enhancements included increased empathy for children, the ability to think and learn quickly, extra physical strength and stamina to keep up with the young and fend off attacks on her charges if necessary. Perfect eyesight. Excellent hearing. Perfect health and antibodies added to guard against most known diseases. On Earth, she'd appear humanoid. She was luckier in that respect than Kaya with her pointed ears and bright blue hair or Gweneth with the cat tattoo on her cheek and Mogens who flashed from black to white depending on his mood.

"I have the solution for those of us who don't appear humanoid." Mogens violet eyes sparkled in his white face—an indication of happiness and contentment. "Never fear. We shall all visit Camryn's family. We shall have fun. I have read this in the clouds."

A spurt of excitement fizzled through Amme, and she grinned at Mogens. Camryn had told them so much about Earth, and they were eager to explore and experience a New Zealand Christmas. The southern hemisphere. Hot weather. Beaches. Barbecues.

"What sort of solution? Have you trialed it?" Camryn asked, suspicion coloring her tone while her gaze sliced and diced, forging a path to the truth.

"On myself." Mogens' long broad nose lifted in a show of dignity. "My appearance represents the biggest challenge since it fluctuates from black to white and in between. The cream I've developed turns my skin a golden brown. If I change my robes for those things you called jeans and a T-shirt, I'll pass as a human." He winked at Amme.

Amme felt her mouth drop open. Well! Mogens was very pleased with himself.

"Fine, that's one problem solved, but where are you going to hide the *Indefatigable*?" Camryn asked, spearing each of them with a glower in turn. "You can't just park it in the middle of a paddock and leave it there. My brother is going to notice. His employees and neighbors are sure to remark on a hulking big spaceship parked on the lawn."

"Nanu and I have a plan," Mogens said.

"Of course you do," Camryn said drily.

Ry placed his hands on Camryn's shoulders and pulled her against his chest. His handsome features held a wealth of tenderness as he stroked his mate's shoulder and arm. "Stop worrying. We have the *Indy* covered. No one will come upon our ship. I've told you this. Your brother will be pleased to see you."

"I hope so."

Amme moved forward to stand beside the woman who'd become a close friend. They'd spent a lot of the voyage together, discussing their lives and sharing personal experiences. "Of course he will. Once he gets over his shock, I'm sure he'll be excited to see you. Are you going to tell him about becoming a feline shifter? That you're no longer fully human like him because you mated with Ry?"

"Maybe." Camryn's brow creased then she pulled away from Ry to pace back and forth in front of the view screen. Her boots beat a tattoo on the bridge floor, the sound becoming increasingly rapid as her mind wrestled with her fear. "I guess. He's not going to believe a human can turn into a black leopard without a demonstration."

Amme exchanged a glance with Ry.

"Let's go and workout," Ry said. "It will rid you of some of your nerves."

"If workout is code for sex, then I'm staying here to help Nanu," Jannike, Ry's second-in-command said. Built like an assassin warrior, the tall blonde woman maintained a serious mien. Most thought she lacked humor. Amme knew better. The woman hid her humor bone and soft heart. She often acted the champion for those who were weaker and unable to stand up for themselves.

Camryn's troubled gaze swept them, and she let out a huge sigh. "This visit is going to be a disaster. I just know it."

Grab your copy today
https://shelleymunro.com/books/merry-seduced/

ABOUT SHELLEY

USA Today bestselling author Shelley Munro lives in Auckland, the City of Sails, with her husband and a cheeky Jack Russell/mystery breed dog.

Typical New Zealanders, Shelley and her husband left home for their big OE soon after they married (translation of New Zealand speak - big overseas experience). A twelve-month-long adventure lengthened to six years of roaming the world. Enduring memories include being almost sat on by a mountain gorilla in Rwanda, lazing on white sandy beaches in India, whale watching in Alaska, searching for leprechauns in Ireland, and dealing with ghosts in an English pub.

While travel is still a big attraction, these days Shelley is most likely found in front of her computer following another love - that of writing stories of contemporary and paranormal romance and adventure. Other interests include watching rugby (strictly for research purposes), cycling, playing croquet and the ukelele, and curling up with an enjoyable book.

Visit Shelley at her Website
https://shelleymunro.com

Join Shelley's Newsletter
https://shelleymunro.com/newsletter

ALSO BY SHELLEY

Middlemarch Shifters
My Scarlet Woman
My Younger Lover
My Peeping Tom
My Assassin
My Estranged Lover
My Feline Protector
My Determined Suitor
My Cat Burglar
My Stray Cat
My Second Chance
My Plan B
My Cat Nap
My Romantic Tangle
My Blue Lady
My Twin Trouble
My Precious Gift
My Grumpy Wolf

Middlemarch Gathering
My Highland Mate
My Highland Fling
My Elusive Mate
My Valiant Princess
My Highland Wedding
My Highland Billionaire

House of the Cat
Captured & Seduced
Claimed & Seduced
Merry & Seduced
Stranded & Seduced
Seized & Seduced
Hunted & Seduced
Festive & Seduced
Betrayed & Seduced
Enticed & Seduced

Dragon Investigators
Blue Moon Dragon
Blood Moon Dragon
Black Moon Dragon
Snow Moon Dragon

Dragon Isles
Liza
Cherry
Rena
Sasha